A PROPER
facade

OTHER BOOKS AND AUDIOBOOKS

BY ESTHER HATCH

Roses of Feldstone

A Proper Scandal

A Proper Charade

A Proper Facade

All Hearts Come Home for Christmas (contributor)

The Holly and the Ivy (contributor)

A PROPER *facade*

a novel

by award-winning author

Esther Hatch

Covenant Communications, Inc.

Cover image: *Man Standing in front of Mansion* © Abigail Miles / Arcangel

Cover design copyright © 2024 by Covenant Communications, Inc.

Published by Covenant Communications, Inc.
American Fork, Utah

Library of Congress Cataloging-in-Publication Data

Name: Esther Hatch
Title: A Proper Facade / Esther Hatch
Description: American Fork, UT : Covenant Communications, Inc. [2024]
Identifiers: Library of Congress Control Number 2023951560 | ISBN 978-1-52442-647-7
LC record available at https://lccn.loc.gov/2023951560

Printed in the United States of America
First Printing: August 2024

30 29 28 27 26 25 24   10 9 8 7 6 5 4 3 2 1

For the 2022 USTA Nationals 3.0 Women's fourth-place tennis team
Look us up. We are kind of a big deal.

Affection is a coal that must be cool'd;
Else, suffer'd, it will set the heart on fire.
—William Shakespeare

CHAPTER 1

DESPITE HIS TIME SERVING IN the army, Nicholas Kendrick, Duke of Harrington, had never fought in battle, nor had he ever killed a man.

That statistic was about to change—in the halls of Parliament. Nicholas had spent weeks preparing his speech on increasing the amount of funds sent to Ireland but had only managed to make it through half of it before Lord Rayleigh's bored and nasally voice interrupted him.

"We are funding an unprecedented amount of soup kitchens as it is," Lord Rayleigh said with a sigh, as if the topic of Ireland had run its course years ago, no matter the fact that people were still starving there. "There are work houses for those who cannot afford food. Besides, we all know the words of Sir Charles Trevelyan, 'God has sent this calamity to teach the Irish a lesson.' You may be too young to understand this, but people don't learn lessons if they aren't allowed to fail. And how can they fail with all the money we are pouring into relief for them?"

Fail? Nicholas hadn't been talking about failing. Children were starving, and the whole country was riddled with grief. "Perhaps, Lord Rayleigh, *we* are the ones who need to learn a lesson. A lesson on compassion and charity."

Immediately the room erupted—men muttering about the government not operating a charity house, others claiming Britain had no need for lessons. Nicholas tried several times to bring the discussion back to his speech, but the time to connect with anyone was over. If he had any eternal power, he would condemn to the devil every single one of the men defending their right to sit idly by while others died. But seeing as he hadn't been able to put the earthly power he held as a duke to any good, he doubted anyone would listen to his useless curses.

So he shouted just one, telling Lord Rayleigh where he could go, and then bit his tongue on the rest of the curses and stormed out.

He strode through the empty corridor. Nicholas was a blasted duke, but he might as well be a currier when he stepped into Parliament. Peoplei tossed his ideas into the bin like they were the daydreams of a child. And every time he failed to convince Parliament to fund relief aid more fully in Ireland, he felt like he was reading about Donald's death all over again.

Donald had been his only friend in the army. They had both been outcasts, Nicholas because he was the sole heir to the Harrington title and Donald because of his Irish heritage. Nicholas hadn't been allowed to stand beside him on the battlefield. General Woodsworth had tried to treat Nicholas like any other soldier, but even he couldn't take the risk of sending a future duke into battle.

Donald had died alone, fighting for a country that would turn its back on his people. But battling for Donald's extended family and homeland in Parliament *should be* something Nicholas could do.

Footsteps sounded behind him, and he wanted nothing more than to ignore them, burst out of the door, and jump into his carriage.

"Harrington." Nicholas's feet stopped immediately. Two years of listening to General Woodsworth's commands had made him obedient to that voice. Nicholas turned to see General Woodsworth, now Lord Woodbury, striding toward him, his large frame practically filling the corridor. "Lord Rayleigh shouldn't dare talk to you like that."

Nicholas couldn't keep the frustration out of his voice. "He is probably trying to make me fail so I can learn some noble lesson."

"That is utter bullocks, and most of the room knows it. If this were the army, he'd be demoted or dishonorably discharged by now. I'm not sure why you made me join this circus when I could've been enjoying retirement instead."

"Yes, well, this isn't the army, my vote doesn't outweigh anyone else's, and whatever influence the title of Harrington had died with my father."

Woodbury's weathered face showed no emotion. "Many more people respect you than you think."

"If that is true, I wish they would speak up now and again."

"They will. Leadership is earned. You need to give it time. Establish yourself as someone who is steady and reliable, and they will come around."

Woodbury didn't have to say out loud what he meant by that. Nicholas hadn't always been reliable or steady, and many of members of Parliament still saw him as the hotheaded and brash young man he'd been in his youth. He was no replacement for his father, and all of London knew that. But despite the folly of his youth, Nicholas was a better man than his grandfather had been. He wished the rest of the world could have seen how hard he had tried in the army. How much he'd changed. "Thank you, Woodbury."

"I'm going to go back in there and give them all a piece of my mind. I watched too many Irishmen die for this country to sit by while their children starve. Want to join me?"

Nicholas smirked. He'd seen Woodbury make grown men grovel. He might not be ranked as high as Nicholas, but Woodbury had the respect of the nation. No one, not even Lord Rayleigh, would interrupt him.

Nicholas swallowed hard. The only thing he wanted to do was escape the madhouse behind him, but running away wouldn't help. He nodded, and the two of them walked back in silence.

Parliament was silent while Woodbury addressed them, and his tales of Irish bravery had seemed to move a few of the people who had ignored Nicholas. But at the end of the day, no one wanted to put up anything for a vote. The Irish problem had lasted so long, not enough members of Parliament cared anymore. But the length of a famine only increased its horrors, and Nicholas didn't understand how so many men could look their own children in the eyes when they got home, knowing they hadn't done anything to help other men's children who were emaciated from a lack of food.

Nicholas barely registered the carriage ride home. When he opened the door to his house, the sharp, bouncing notes of *Good King Wenceslas* invaded Nicholas's ears. He clenched his jaw. Hadn't Mother sung that song enough the day before? Christmas had come and gone a month ago, but that didn't stop Mother from singing, not only out of season, but out of tune. It had been two years since Patience had married, and he and mother had managed—more than managed. They even sang together at times, but he couldn't concentrate with all this constant signing.

Especially not after the fiasco that had just happened in Parliament. If Father were still alive, that speech would have gone very differently. Nobody would have dared interrupt Father. He'd single-handedly brought honor back to the Harrington name, rejecting the lasciviousness and debauchery of his own father and making the Duke of Harrington stand for solid conviction instead of weak resolutions.

Nicholas ignored the missed high note and grabbed his letters from the hall table, then strode into his study. He sat at his desk, pushed aside the estate papers he had been working on the day before and opened the first of his letters.

The moment he saw the surname at the bottom, his fingers tightened, crumpling the corner of the letter. Why was Lady Plymton's uncle corresponding with him? He skimmed past the opening pleasantries, and then his eyes froze over a single line.

Lady Plymton would be returning to London from Spain. A new widow, she had deemed four months an adequate time to morn her husband's death and was going to be reentering Society.

Four months.

How could a woman only mourn a husband for four months?

He'd stayed in mourning for two years after Father died.

And why the deuce had Lady Plymton's uncle thought he needed to be warned? Lady Plymton was nothing to Nicholas. Not anymore. She'd destroyed his life once already. The lack of deference in Parliament hurt, but it didn't hold a candle to losing his father's respect. He crumpled the letter and threw it into the bin. Why was he even in London? If Lady Plymton was coming, perhaps he should return to Brushbend. The thought of running into her made his stomach twist like he'd eaten spoiled potatoes. He'd spent most of the past four years here, trying to live up to his father's name, but the situation in Parliament only showcased how far he still had to go. The last thing the House of Lords needed was a reminder of Nicholas's past.

A knock sounded at the front door, and Mother's voice hitched to a blessed stop. The silence that followed was a balm to his soul. He rubbed a hand down his face. Praise the heavens that Patience had scheduled a visit every Thursday morning. His sister could keep Mother talking for at least an hour.

If Patience was here, that meant her husband, Ottersby, would be alone. It was time Nicholas accepted the fact that he wasn't making progress with Parliament on his own. Woodbury was right. Nicholas needed to establish himself as a respectable leader like his father. He needed a plan, and no one was better at formulating a plan than Woodbury's own son and Nicholas's brother-in-law. It was time to pay Ottersby a visit.

CHAPTER 2

"Harrington. To what do I owe the pleasure?" Ottersby strode decisively into his sitting room. His jacket was, as always, impeccably pressed across his broad shoulders and his cravat in perfect order. No one could see him and not know he was Lord Woodbury's son. He walked like a soldier even though he'd never been one. "I hope Patience hasn't caused you any trouble."

"Patience?" Nicholas shook his head. "No."

Ottersby gestured toward a sofa in front of the fireplace, and Nicholas marched forward and sat down. In front of him was a small table, upon which rested a few books and a wooden duck. This one looked as though it came from India, a contrast to the matching pair on the mantel. Ottersby waited for him to sit before taking his own seat on the opposite corner of the table.

What exactly had Nicholas come here to say? Ottersby's father had told him to give his problem time, that people would eventually come to respect him. But Nicholas had been the Duke of Harrington for three years already without much headway, and the people in Ireland didn't have time. Ottersby cleared his throat, but what could Nicholas say? *I am a joke. A duke who no one feels they need to listen to. And on top of that, the constant singing in my own home is going to send me into an early grave.* Nicholas smoothed his lapel even though it was clean and starched to perfection. His valet knew how important making a good impression was. Maybe he should start with the less pressing of his issues. "I'm thinking of moving Mother into the dower house."

Ottersby's eyebrows rose, though he didn't say anything. He was a good man, but he was only talkative when Patience was around. Or perhaps Patience was talkative enough for the both of them.

Nicholas swallowed. "I need one place where I have some control, and since it is looking like Parliament isn't an option, I'd like at least to be able to feel like my home environment is governed by me."

Ottersby nodded. "And so, you plan to marry? I'm not certain that is the best way to have *more* control over your household. Mine was set on its head the moment Patience placed a foot in it. And she was a maid at the time."

"No, I don't plan to marry. What makes you think that?"

Ottersby raised an eyebrow. "That is typically the cause for moving a mother into a dower house, is it not?"

"You don't think she would agree to it otherwise?"

"I don't think you would ask her. The two of you aren't exactly stellar at conversing."

Nicholas tapped his fingers on the arm of the sofa. Ottersby was right, of course. If he was better at speaking to Mother, he could simply ask her to stop singing so much. Or keep her singing to times when he was out of the house. But he couldn't do that. She was still hurting for Father, just as much as he and Patience were, even if he hadn't realized it when she'd gone to Paris four years ago and left her two children alone to mourn him.

Ottersby tugged on his sleeves and then matched Nicholas's rhythmic tapping on the arm of his own chair. After four taps, Ottersby looked up. "Unless you *were* to marry."

Nicholas waved his hand in Ottersby's direction. "Controlling Mother's singing is hardly a reason to marry."

Ottersby tipped his head to one side. "Have you no other reasons, no desire to marry?"

Nicholas gritted his teeth. He should have led with his Parliament issues. This conversation was spiraling out of control. Over the past few years, he'd been overwhelmed with the task of keeping all of his estates running and making certain the *ton* knew he was his father's son and nothing like the Dukes of Harrington before Father. He wasn't certain how long it would be until he felt settled enough with *that* title to take on the title of husband as well. Not to mention, he would have to court a woman in order to marry. His fingers stopped tapping, and he clenched the fabric of the sofa in his hand. Courting was a prospect he didn't allow himself to think about. It was more uncomfortable than Mother's singing would ever be. "I'm certain someday I will need to fulfill that duty, but I hardly think this is the time."

Ottersby cleared his throat. "Patience would disagree. She has been worried about you."

Worried? Why would Patience be worried about him? Did she think him not capable of managing his own affairs? "She and I don't have a long history of agreeing about things."

Ottersby chuckled. "Why don't you think you should marry?"

"I think I *should* marry . . . someday. But now is not the time." How often had he overheard whisperings when people didn't realize he was nearby? *"Nicholas Kendrick? A duke? Can he even grow a full beard?"* He could. He simply preferred to be clean-shaven. His influence in Parliament and, blast, even Lady Plymton returning to London weighed heavier on his mind than Mother's singing. "I've only been the Duke of Harrington for four years. I'm still adjusting to that. I'm not ready for more change."

"My marriage came only three months after receiving my title. Having a wife has proven to be a wonderful benefit. She handles all of our social functions, and she speaks to the other lords' wives and even to the lords. Patience has done a better job of establishing my position than I ever could have done on my own."

That was simple for Ottersby to say. He had married Patience—a lady of extreme influence, the sister of a duke. And Ottersby had *wanted* to get married.

Nicholas didn't have time for women. When he'd been younger, his interest in women had done him no favors. The letter in his wastebasket was a testament to that. He'd mostly avoided them since his time serving under Lord Woodbury.

But Ottersby did have a point. Nicholas had been attending all the social events of the Season with the intent of solidifying friendships among the *ton*. He had spent his time speaking to men and avoiding women. Four years into his dukedom, and he was still seen as an untested upstart.

If he married, Mother would move into the dower house, *and* he would gain an ally in his work. At twenty-five, most lords considered him too young and inexperienced to truly wield the power of dukedom. But if he had a wife . . . Not just any wife, but the right wife . . . Perhaps more of the peerage would listen and respect his ideas.

He rubbed the back of his neck. Was he actually considering this? Would a wife somehow help him get the aid he had been fighting for? "Ottersby, before you met Patience, didn't you have a list of women you were considering marrying?"

Ottersby's face was suddenly flat, emotionless and bland. His eyes darted to the door as if Patience would suddenly walk in. "That was a long time ago."

"But you still have it?"

"Do you think Patience would allow me to keep a list of women I considered marrying?"

Nicholas smiled. It was hard to know what Patience would allow. "I think she would enjoy looking over that list and telling you how fortunate you are that you ended up with her instead of any of them."

Ottersby's face softened into a smile. "We may have done that a few times. But I don't have it anymore. It was a ridiculous thing to have in the first place."

No, it wasn't ridiculous; it was logical. Extremely logical. If Nicholas did decide to pursue marriage, he wouldn't leave the selection of a wife to chance. And instincts? His were bullocks. If he were to marry, he would do it as his father had—with purpose and clarity. Above all, marriage was a contract between two people. He simply needed to find a woman who would fulfill her end of the contract in a way that would be satisfying to both of them. "Do you remember who was on it?"

"Are you asking me to name the women on that list for you to consider as marriage partners?"

Nicholas didn't answer. Ottersby was a smart man. He knew exactly what Nicholas was asking.

Ottersby grimaced. "You do understand that I was very painstaking in detail to *my* position in Society when making that list? No one who would've made a good match for me would make an advantageous match for you."

"What were your criteria, then? Perhaps we can reproduce a similar list, specific to me."

Ottersby pulled at the cuff of his sleeve again. "That list almost had me married to Miss Morgan. It was a terrible idea."

"Miss Morgan wouldn't have been so terrible. She has a solid standing in Society." Miss Morgan was one of the few women in London Nicholas had regular interactions with. He had to. She and her family knew about Patience having lived in Ottersby's home as a maid before they'd married. "Perhaps I should consider her. It would at least ensure her silence about certain matters. And I have no doubt she would agree to marry me."

Ottersby paled. "She tried to force me to marry her after my father received his title. And her influence is nothing in comparison. She would be a bad choice, Nicholas, in every regard. I was extremely fortunate to escape her grasp. She doesn't even compare to Patience."

"No one compares to my sister, which is fortunate for everyone."

"I won't agree to help you if Miss Morgan's name ends up on your list."

"Don't put her on the list, then. You're right. I need someone with a title, at least."

Ottersby shook his head, but he stood and walked to the writing desk. Before pulling out a sheet of paper, he looked back at Nicholas. "Patience won't like this."

Nicholas waved his hand in the air. "You said she was interested in me getting married."

Ottersby tipped his head and sat. "Yes, but not like this."

"I'm comfortable with this method, and that is what matters." Nicholas stood and positioned himself over Ottersby's shoulder. "I don't need a love match. I need someone to help me solidify my place here in London." And he needed to keep his head, especially with Lady Plymton returning. Finding someone to court before she even arrived would be ideal. Ottersby's idea was sounding more and more fortuitous. Why shouldn't he get married? Especially if he courted and married properly and didn't allow his emotions to rule his actions.

Ottersby lifted the end of his pen to his nose and cleared his throat. "And someone whose company you enjoy?"

"Of course. But most ladies make for enjoyable company, don't they?" Nicholas patted Ottersby's shoulder. "That part should be simple enough." Ottersby made a strange coughing sound in the back of his throat. "The tricky part will be finding just the right woman to exert her influence on Society."

Ottersby sighed and grabbed the paper and lifted it into the air. "Let's make the list in my study. I have my rulers there, and I think we may need them in order to properly categorize the women."

Nicholas wouldn't argue with that. The idea of an almost mathematical formula calculated to choose the perfect woman for him to marry felt . . . miraculous. Armed with such a thing, choosing a wife could be done without tempting his weakness for a beautiful face and soft skin. He followed behind Ottersby, but the man had suddenly taken to walking very slowly. How did one go about hurrying someone from behind? Couldn't he sense Nicholas's urgency? This was no ordinary day.

This was the day Nicholas Kendrick, Duke of Harrington, would find himself a wife.

CHAPTER 3

"MAMA, DO YOU REALLY THINK the necklace is necessary?" Mercy sat on her bed, resting her feet before an evening that would be filled with dancing. Kate had finished Mercy's hair but was only halfway through one of her Irish tales when Mama had asked her to leave the two of them alone in Mercy's bedroom. Luckily, it was one of Kate's stories Mercy had heard before. Her toes tapped to a silent rhythm against her footboard. She wasn't great at resting them, not when she knew she had hours of enjoyment ahead of her. "Certainly, the earrings and jewels in my hair will be enough." Mercy pulled at the large emeralds around her neck. As much as she loved them for their history, waltzing in them all evening was certain to give her a headache. If it were up to her, the only jewelry she would ever wear would be the thin silver bracelet Kate had given her. It was lightweight, unobtrusive, and a reminder of her maid's friendship.

Mama paced in front of Mercy's bed. "Unless royalty arrives at the Stafford ball, this necklace should be the most stunning in the room. No one has better emeralds in their family than we do."

Mercy was well aware of the source of pride Mama's emeralds were to her. She had heard the story many times of how her grandfather, the fifth earl of Driarwood, had gifted them to her grandmother after he built himself a grand hunting lodge.

Mercy had never thought the tradeoff quite worth it. She would much rather have a hunting lodge than a cumbersome strand of emeralds. But the story held an even deeper meaning to their family of four. Papa had gifted them to Mama *before* they were engaged. It was scandalous, but it was also the turning point in Papa's parents finally accepting the fact that he was determined to marry Mama, despite her lack of title or family connections. "Why today, Mama? I've never worn the emeralds before. I'm not certain I should."

Mama pulled her up from the bed and pushed her toward the mirror. Standing behind Mercy, she squeezed both of her shoulders and looked at the two of them together in the reflection. "Your father and I have been talking, and we think it is time for you start to look at balls as opportunities not only to dance, but to make a match. We have been indulgent thus far. You've already had two Seasons, and I believe you've enjoyed them, but there are reasons a woman of your age attends balls, and it isn't only for the dancing."

Mercy's eyes widened, and she craned her neck to look back at Mama. "You've always told me I could take my time finding a husband."

"I did." Mama smiled, but her lips were tight. "And you have. I am only saying it is time to start looking a little more intently. What about Mr. Beauford? I have seen you dance with him at most of the balls."

Mr. Beauford? She had been dancing with him for ages, and Mama had never mentioned him before. "That is because he's an excellent dancer."

"Perhaps that could make him an excellent husband." Mama's eyebrow rose along with her shoulders, like she was making an offhand remark. But nothing about Mr. Beauford had appealed to Mama last week. What had changed?

"Mama, first the emeralds and now Mr. Beauford? Is something wrong?"

Mama laughed and daintily patted the tendrils of Mercy's expertly styled hair. "Of course not. Your father is interested in taking a tour of the Continent, and we would like you settled before then. We are happy to wait, of course, but a little prodding never hurt. We simply would like to see you happy."

"With Mr. Beauford?" She tried to picture herself spending a quiet evening at home with him, conversing with him, or . . . his lips on hers. She shook her head. Mr. Beauford was an excellent dancer, but there had never been a spark of interest in his dark-brown eyes, no hands lingering longer than necessary. The time was long past for theirs to be a relationship of passion. Her parents were desperate for each other during their courtship, and they'd been thrilled when Rosalind had fallen madly in love with Richard. Mercy had cut her teeth on two of the greatest love stories of all time, and now Mama thought she might settle for Mr. Beauford? There was only one reason he sought her out at any ball they both attended.

They both loved to dance.

And that had to be the absolute worst reason to marry a person. Marriage would mean they would dance together less often, not more.

Mama waved her hand in the air. "Your father and I thought perhaps you and Mr. Beauford were forming an attachment."

Mercy frowned. "I hadn't thought so."

Mama shrugged. "If not Mr. Beauford, then perhaps there is someone else. Has no one caught your eye in the past two years?"

Plenty of men had caught her eye. She wasn't blind, and London had an excessive number of well-dressed bachelors. But she hadn't found anyone she wanted to settle down with. She hadn't even found anyone she hoped would come calling—some still did, but not by any encouragement on her part. Her main concern had been food, conversation, and dancing. One couldn't plan on finding the love of her life. That person would come in like a bolt of lightning when she least expected it. She would feel a pull to him . . . their eyes would meet across the room, and they would know . . . "No," she answered Mama. "There are many kind and good-looking men. I simply don't really know any of them. And none of them excite me."

She ran her fingertips over Mama's emeralds. They were no hunting lodge, but every time Mama's eyes rested on them, she softened and looked almost as young as she did in her marriage portrait. Perhaps Mercy should start trying harder to find the man who would keep her feeling young no matter how old they grew together. Rosalind had been ready to fall in love during her first Season, and certainly enough, Richard Young had swept her off her feet. Even still, couldn't Mercy do that without the emeralds? As much as she loved what they symbolized, they were gaudy and unlike her.

At least her dress was simple. They had ordered it months ago, because the lavender silk had made Mama sigh in satisfaction and reminisce about some of her old ball gowns. Thankfully Mercy had been able to order it in her usual style, one that was simple and comfortable for a night of dancing. If she were ordering the gown now, would Mama have asked for a wider and deeper neckline or more ornamentation? Mama had never expected her to dress to please others. So why now? Why the emeralds?

"Well," Mama said. "You can't really get excited by someone you don't know. Show a bit more interest in them. You will be surprised at how far a few questions can go." Mama spun her around so they were face-to-face. She grasped both of Mercy's shoulders in her hands—softly, so she wouldn't damage the soft puffs of her lavender sleeves, though Mercy could tell she wanted to grip her tighter. "Lady Yolten is still in Paris with Lord Yolten, so you won't have a friend to distract you. Tonight, I would like you to find three men and encourage them. Make them aware of the fact that you wouldn't mind it if they came calling."

Mama had never considered Penelope—Lady Yolten—a distraction before. Mercy was fortunate that many of the *ton* had snubbed Penelope simply because she'd been the daughter of a manufacturer before marrying Lord Yolten. It paved an easy path for the two of them to become the best of friends. Why would Mama be happy she wasn't at the ball? "But shouldn't I—"

Mama placed a finger to Mercy's lips. "Please, do this. You are an extremely pleasant young lady. It shouldn't be much trouble to find yourself a husband."

With Mama's finger on her lips, she couldn't have responded, even if she had known how. Ever since Rosalind married six years ago, it was simply Mercy, Mama, and Papa against the world. They'd always felt like a team. They loved their time together, reading at home or walking through Town. Mercy had come out and started attending balls, but she had always assumed it was more because Mama and Papa had tired of leaving her home alone and wanted her to join them for social functions. Rosalind had flirted and danced her way through her first Season before Richard captivated her on their first meeting. The two of them had been nearly scandalous in their affection for each other before their marriage. Mercy was determined to take as many Seasons as she needed until she could find a man to love her as Richard loved Rosalind.

Mercy would never settle for less.

Mama pulled her finger away from Mercy's mouth and grasped her by both shoulders again. "Three men. Each time you go to a ball, I want you to look for three men who interest you. They can be the same men each time, or if you get to know one of them and he doesn't please you, find another one to take his place. It would make your father and me very happy to see you settled with a good man."

Mercy opened her mouth to protest, but something in Mama's eyes made her pause. An edge of worry, the inability to meet her eye. Papa had been acting similarly for a few weeks, but this was the first time Mama had seemed out of sorts. Something must have happened.

Mercy sighed. "All right. I'll wear the emeralds. And I shall put forth more of an effort with at least three men tonight. With Penelope still at her country estate, it isn't as though I'll have anyone else to speak to." Mercy was friendly with many women, but Penelope was the only person in London who made speaking as entertaining as dancing.

"Even if Lady Yolten *were* in Town, she wouldn't begrudge you some extra time with a few gentlemen." The lines at the corners of Mama's eyes changed from worry to the smile lines Mercy was used to. "Something tells me we will be receiving an abundance of flowers tomorrow."

Mercy couldn't find it in herself to smile back. Something was different, and it wasn't a small thing. She needed to find out exactly what that something was, and she needed to find it soon, before her parents became like so many other parents, only finding joy in her if she was acting correctly and looking for a husband.

But how did one go about discovering parents' secrets? A ball seemed to be the perfect place to answer that question.

CHAPTER 4

NICHOLAS STOOD WITH PATIENCE AND Ottersby by the punch table. Patience sipped her punch as the three of them inspected the attendees of the Stafford ball. Nicholas had tried to bring the list of women to the Stafford's ball, and Ottersby hadn't seen a problem with the idea, but Patience had forbidden them to do so. That problem could have been solved by Ottersby not mentioning the list at all, but the two of them had an unhealthy habit of sharing everything.

Although, perhaps she was right on this score. If he or Ottersby dropped the list, or if someone had looked over their shoulders while they were perusing the young women listed there, that would've been very unfortunate, indeed. Perhaps Patience was right. At least in this one instance.

Nicholas slid closer to Patience. "Who is the young lady standing by the window in the rust-colored gown?" She was pleasant-looking and well-dressed, with not a stitch out of place.

She tipped her head up toward him. "I don't know."

"Ottersby?"

Ottersby shrugged as well.

Nicholas noticed a few members of Parliament with young ladies nearby. They could be daughters and, therefore, eligible matches for him, but they could also simply be friends. He had spent hours rehearsing and memorizing the most powerful men in London, but Nicholas hadn't thought to catalog or seek introductions to their daughters. And now that he had a list of them, he couldn't even put a face to more than one or two names.

Lord Nimbly was one of the few men who had treated Nicholas with camaraderie, and he was a well-respected viscount. Next to him stood a blonde woman in a blue gown. "What about the woman standing next to Lord Nimbly? Do either of you know her?"

They both leaned forward and almost simultaneously shook their heads. "Do you know anyone here?"

Ottersby shrugged. "I know a few of the men, but for the most part, this ball is a bit too rich for my blood. The old me wouldn't have had an opportunity to come to something so well footed."

Patience stepped closer to Nicholas. "I attended almost no balls before marrying Anthony, and we honestly haven't been very social since the wedding. I'm afraid we aren't going to be much help."

Nicholas groaned. "I should have brought Mother. At least she likes to talk to people."

Patience gave a surprised laugh. "And let Mama know what you are planning? Impossible. She would choose a bride for you if you didn't find one quickly on your own. Are you prepared for that?"

"No, and it won't come to that. I'm perfectly capable of finding my own bride." He looked down his nose at Patience as if he were the stuffiest of men. "You may not know this since you haven't been very active in Town, but I am quite a catch."

Patience didn't seem to notice his haughty glance. His humor was usually lost on most people. But he wasn't going to dwell on the implications of that. Patience simply raised her brows. "The only eligible duke under fifty? I am certain you are, Nicholas, but choosing a wife should also be about who you want to spend time with, and that might take a bit more effort."

Nicholas waved Patience's comment aside. "I'm not worried. I generally seem to get on with most people without problem." Anyone would be preferable to Mama and her nearly constant singing. "Although, if pressed, I would prefer that she didn't sing."

Patience laughed. "Be careful what you wish for. You may end up with someone who cannot sing but manages to try every day."

"Very amusing, Patience," Nicholas said, low and slow. "I won't. Not with Ottersby's list to guide me."

Patience clicked her tongue. "Yes, because *Anthony's* list did such an amazing job for him."

Nicholas smiled. "It did. Look how happy the two of you are."

She raised an eyebrow at him. "I wasn't on his list, Nicholas. You know that. Plus, I'm not certain you should be putting so much weight in your ability to get along with anyone. You do remember that I lived with you and ended up running away."

Nicholas scoffed. That was her fault. Patience and her blasted pride. He was about to tell her as much when a woman coming into the ballroom caught his eye. She was clothed in a gown of pure white, cut and fitted by a master and simple in its elegance. There were no embellishments, and the sleeves were smaller than every other gown in the room. Her dress was a study of tastefulness that he rarely found at such gatherings. At balls, women typically strove to stand out with extra embellishments. Flowers, jewels, and even birds, at times, were used to make a dress more elaborate than those of the women around her.

This woman had done the opposite, and yet, the effect was what those other women had strived for. In the gown's simplicity, the woman wearing it shone. He tore his eyes away from her and cleared his throat. "Do either of you know the woman in white?"

He had pointed at the other young ladies or explained who they were with, but he didn't need to elaborate this time. Both Patience and Ottersby knew exactly of whom he was speaking.

Patience bounced. "I know her a little. Lady Marion Miles, daughter of Viscount Redding." She tipped her head so her mouth was near Ottersby's ear. "Anthony, based on the way my brother is ogling her, I hope you have her on the list."

Nicholas straightened his back. "I never ogle women." He made certain of it.

Patience patted his arm. "That is the truth. I think the only woman I've ever seen you take notice of was Miss Morgan, and that was for my sake. But, Nicholas, you are looking for a wife. It is probably time to start ogling—a little, at any case."

Nicholas scoffed. The woman, Lady Marion, was beautiful. He could appreciate that, in a calm and calculated way. He was not ogling. He was not being inappropriate. But Patience's words had him doubting his choice. Perhaps it was better to select someone who did not intrigue him. Someone he could court rationally without any sort of physical impediments. But now that he had mentioned her, he might as well follow through. Patience wouldn't rest until he did. "I suppose I should ask Lord Stafford for an introduction."

"That would be the next step," Ottersby agreed with a nod.

One step at a time. The thought of finding one person to share the rest of his life with made the couples around him fade. Every move of the woman in white was augmented. She might be the woman he was looking for. He ignored the slightly ill feeling in his stomach. If he did everything properly, what could go wrong? He had a plan: introduction, courtship, marriage. It was a system that had worked for countless other humans. There was no reason it shouldn't work for him.

He strode across the room to find Lord Stafford. It was time to take the first step.

CHAPTER 5

Lady Marion hummed.

Constantly.

She had managed a few words at the beginning of their dance, but then she'd grown nervous and the humming had set in. She found her voice once again after the dance finished, but only enough for a barely perceptible thank-you. Perhaps Patience had been correct, and finding a wife may take a bit more time than he thought. It was a pity. And it was also regretful that Lady Marion's mother had noticed his interest. Nicholas bowed with a smile and put his arm out to escort her back to her mother. Lady Redding's face was split into an almost aggressive grin. Whatever her family had paid for that dress, they were obviously now hopeful it had been an investment well spent, as it had caught the notice of a duke.

Whispers followed them across the ballroom, the typically low murmur of the ballroom transforming into a continuous rumble of voices. He should have known that asking for his first introduction to a young lady would cause a stir. It was as if all of London had awoken to the fact that he was unattached and finally ready to wed.

After trying not to meet Lady Marion's mother's eye more than absolutely necessary, he extracted himself from her family's presence and strode away from the ballroom. His first attempt at finding a wife, and he had already failed. His usual pastime would be to play a few cards, but he knew exactly what would happen the moment he set foot in the room. Every man with an eligible daughter would be attached to him like a . . . well, like a calculating parent with an eligible duke in the room.

Perhaps he should have found himself a less public place to start implementing his plan to marry. Gone about it quietly somehow. But it was too late now.

He reached the doorway of the cardroom and stopped. The muffled voices of the men floated out from the room, and he caught a few snippets of conversation. His name was on almost everyone's lips . . .

What had he done? Why hadn't Ottersby foreseen this? For all of their planning and list making, how had neither of them realized the stir Nicholas would make once the slightest inkling of his intentions were known?

"What are they saying in there?" A soft voice behind him made him jump backward and spin around. A young lady in a lavender gown with impressive amounts of jewelry stood behind him. Her eyes flashed toward the cardroom. "Business?"

Nicholas glanced left and right down the corridor. What was she doing here alone, without any sort of a companion? Her dress was well cut and showed off her slender waist. The neckline of her gown was not low to the point of using her decolletage to attract attention, but low enough to allow the double-layered emerald necklace to lie on her chest without cluttering her gown. A few whisps of her hair had escaped, and she seemed slightly out of breath, as if she had come from a vigorous dance. What was she doing here? Had she been pushed by her mother to follow him?

But the spark of interest in her eye was directed at the cardroom. It didn't seem to have anything to do with him or being alone. She leaned forward, an ear toward the door. Nicholas seemed forgotten as she concentrated on the men's voices. "No, not business," he replied. If it were business the men spoke of, he wouldn't have stopped outside the door; he would have joined them. "Gossip," he said.

"Is there much of a difference?"

Nicholas tipped his head to one side. Something about her was familiar. Where had he seen her before? "Certainly. Business is . . . well . . . business. It is important workings of Society. Gossip, on the other hand, is complete—" He shook his head. "Drivel."

She stepped closer, but not to him or, rather, not for the purpose of getting closer to him. She was trying to get closer to the door. He slid aside. "And what kind of drivel are the men spewing out tonight?"

He tried to control a growl that threatened to escape, but he was only half successful. "Some nonsense about a duke."

She stepped next to the wall and placed her ear upon it. "A duke?" She paused to listen. Now that she had usurped his position by the door, he could only see the back of her head. Her hair was as ornate as her necklace, filled with medium brown or, rather, dark blonde—blast, he wasn't certain what to call that particular color of hair—curls that had been expertly tucked with jewel-studded hair pins. She must be the daughter of someone significant. Which of the wealthy ladies on Ottersby's list did he not know? Basically, all of them. She could be anyone. But he must know her a little. She had spoken to him as if they had been introduced, and he had seen her face somewhere before. Sometime long ago.

She pushed away from the wall, turned around, and caught his eye. Hers were a vibrant green. No wonder she wore emeralds. Beneath her eyes, a smattering of freckles increased her look of playful camaraderie. They were close enough that even in the dim lighting, he could also see an abundance of freckles against the pale skin of her chest, though they were mostly covered by her necklace. He leaned forward, trying to make out the patterns there more clearly. Some of the spots were light, barely discernible, while others were like a splash of spice smattered on cream.

One of her graceful hands went to the emeralds around her throat, and he froze.

What the devil was he doing? Memorizing the location and saturation of the woman's freckles? What was he planning to do with that information? Draw a map? He shouldn't have even noticed them. His eyes should have remained on hers like a gentleman. He raised his gaze, but the glint in hers didn't make him feel any more gentlemanly. He swallowed hard, stepped backward, and tucked his hands behind his back. Meeting a woman in a corridor was *not* part of his plan. And for good reason. He was not to be trusted. He should not be alone with a woman. Or, more to the point, *she* should not be alone with *him*.

"You shouldn't be here. Not alone. Where is your chaperone?"

A disarming pout rose to her lips, and she raised her eyes to the ceiling, obviously unconcerned about his admonition. "I can barely hear them," she said, ignoring him. "They weren't speaking about rushed marriages or getting rid of children or anything of that sort?"

He blinked at her, then muffled a surprised laugh, grateful to have her say something that got his mind off her skin. Getting rid of children and rushed marriages? Is that what she thought men spoke of? "No. Do you know someone looking to get rid of children?"

She tipped her head to one side. "I don't know, perhaps," she said, and then pursed her pert rose-colored lips together, turned back around and brought her ear to the wall again.

He stood behind her, not certain what to do. He shifted from one foot to the other. Her hand shot out, and she turned around again, waving him forward. What did she expect him to do? Listen at the wall like she was doing?

If he wanted to hear what the men were talking about, he would simply walk into the room. The Duke of Harrington didn't listen at walls.

Her eyebrows raised, and she leaned toward him. "They are speaking of your duke."

He cursed softly under his breath, stepped to the wall, and leaned his head down just as she had. But he didn't touch his ear to the wall. Not quite. He did have some restraint.

A voice rang out clear, as if the man behind the wall was hoping everyone in the room would hear him. "I've got three daughters ranging from fifteen to twenty-one. Should I ask him to take his pick of them?" Laughter erupted in the room, and Nicholas pushed his head away from the wall in disgust. He knew that voice. It was Lord Rayleigh. He wasn't interested in Nicholas's ideas, but he would be happy to have any of his three daughters become his wife? He clenched his teeth together. "It sounds as though they are speaking of getting rid of children, after all."

"Well, of course they are. Apparently there is an eligible duke running around London. Harrington—I've heard of him. He is young *and* a duke. Who wouldn't want that for their daughters?"

So, she didn't know him. Or she was a very good actress. How did he know her? "But what of those daughters? How would their parents know he is what *they* would want?"

She laughed. "Everyone wants a duke."

"Even if the duke is an ingrate?"

"If he were young, rich, *and* an ingrate, I suppose only three-quarters of the *ton* would be lining up to marry him."

Nicholas clenched his jaw. This was the kind of reasoning that had gotten him in trouble when he was younger. Being a duke should not negate his need for a moral compass. It should increase it. He should be an example, not someone who took advantage of others.

Unfortunately the talk in the cardroom only supported this woman's claims. Anyone. He could marry practically anyone. Even this young lady. At least she could talk to him; that was an improvement on Lady Marion.

Of course, she didn't know who he was, and that most likely made conversation easier. But a woman who spoke so freely to a man in an empty corridor would likely also speak freely to a duke. Patience's reminder that he should find a woman he liked rang in his ears. Perhaps Ottersby's list wasn't the best idea.

There was a beautiful, intriguing woman right in front of him. Her eyes, skin, and smile were like magnets, drawing him. He could step closer, lean in, and see how she responded. Father wasn't here anymore to judge him.

He swayed forward, only slightly. The woman didn't even seem to notice, but the infinitesimal loss of space between them sent a wave of panic through him. His chest tightened. His right hand fisted and he had to bite his lip to stop himself from slamming it into the wall. This is why he had avoided searching for a wife. It had been only one measly day, one evening of opening himself up to the idea of a relationship with a woman, and already his devotion to his father was wavering. Had he truly learned nothing in the army? Was the only reason he'd managed to stay respectable where women were concerned because he'd avoided them altogether? Had it actually made him a better man than he had been with Lady Plymton?

He needed to find a wife, and it couldn't happen soon enough. Some men had the self-control to manage long courtships, but Nicholas was not one of them. He cleared his throat, determined to stay calm. "Surely not three-quarters."

"Do you think more? Being a duchess would be a lot of work, and if the duke was also an ingrate . . ." She turned, and her eyes were bright, even in the dimly lit corridor. "I think at least a quarter of the women would rather settle for a well-mannered earl." She raised her eyebrows in a cheerful way he had never seen anyone do before—first one and then the other, as if they were dancers following each other's steps. "Or even a baron."

"Ah, settling for a baron. Every young woman's dream."

Her face fell slightly. "It wasn't my dream when I was a girl. I was much more interested in soldiers."

Her eyes dipped low, and her face turned, and suddenly he knew exactly who she was.

CHAPTER 6

A HOLLOW STILLNESS ENVELOPED HIM. He closed his eyes a moment to catch his breath.

Memories of Donald pounded through him. He had been the best of men, and Nicholas should have been on the battlefield with him. Not sitting at home reading crop reports.

She was older now than on the day she had come to collect her father after Donald's funeral. She had been crying almost inconsolably. He had asked Donald's father about her, thinking perhaps she had been a sweetheart Donald had never mentioned.

But she wasn't. Mr. Young had been just as confused as he had been. Her older sister was married to Donald's younger brother, Richard, but as far as Mr. Young knew, Donald had never met the girl. Donald certainly hadn't ever mentioned her.

That young girl, inconsolable and unembarrassed by her grief, was the first person Nicholas had thought of when his mother hadn't mustered up tears for her own husband.

But who was she? Donald wasn't ranked, so it wouldn't follow that his younger brother had married someone with a title. Yet those emeralds around her neck flaunted wealth. Perhaps her family had recently come into money. What was the name of Donald's brother's wife?

"Being the wife of a soldier would not be an easy task."

"Oh," she nodded, "I know." Her eyes clouded over, and he wondered if she was thinking back to that gloomy day five years ago. But then she blinked hard, and her smile returned. "But it wouldn't be as demanding as being the wife of a duke. Can you imagine the parties and the elegance a woman would have to have? I would hardly qualify."

"Qualify? Is there some list of requirements in order to become the wife of a duke?" He violently ignored the fact that he'd argued just that with

Ottersby. The whole idea seemed preposterous to him now. For all their plotting, he hadn't listed "capable of strong feeling" as an asset, and suddenly that asset had jumped to the top of his list. Freckles might make the top five. What else had he missed?

The sound of her laughter filled the corridor. He had seen her cry and now laugh. Both were equally fascinating to him. "Do you honestly think there isn't?"

"Perhaps this particular duke would not expect his wife to do anything she didn't want to do," Nicholas said. "Perhaps he could throw his own parties, and he wouldn't care if she weren't accomplished in all of the art forms ladies are taught." Especially if one of those artforms was singing.

The woman's shoulders bounced, and she bit her index finger, most likely to stifle another laugh. "Oh no, I guarantee you social planning skills would be at the top of any self-respectable duke's list."

He stepped away from the wall. That was *not* at the top of his list. Rank had been. "I suppose this means you aren't one of the ladies who would be interested in marrying a duke?"

She turned around and blinked. "The thought hadn't crossed my mind. I can't imagine a duke being interested in me."

He took a step back and surveyed her. Critically. First of all, she *had* made an impression on him the first time he saw her. She'd been young then, but she was certainly not the youngest woman out in Society now. Her laughter was pleasant, and unlike Lady Marion, she wasn't afraid to speak. But she was standing outside the cardroom with a complete stranger, eavesdropping on the men inside. It was a definite mark against her. But seeing as he was doing the same thing, perhaps not an insurmountable one. There were worse things. And those blasted freckles. Something told him he would be counting them in his sleep after the ball. He blinked hard. Freckles shouldn't make the list, and they definitely shouldn't make the top five. Nothing physical needed to be anywhere near the top of that list. He needed to forget them.

"Do you sing?"

Her eyebrows furrowed as if his question made no sense. "Do I sing?"

"Around the house, as you write letters, or look over menus? Would you sing in those types of situations?"

"In those types of situations? No."

"Then perhaps the duke would be interested in you."

Her gloved hand went to her mouth, this time covering it completely. She was as bad as Patience—always ready for a laugh. Once she was calm, she raised those dancing eyebrows, dropped her hand, and leaned forward. "I hardly think that would be the most important characteristic of a future duchess."

He raised his eyebrows back at her. Two could play at that game. "The Duke of Harrington doesn't have a perfected list of characteristics he is looking for, but when he does, *that* will be at the top of it."

She pulled her head back and tipped her head to one side. "How could you possibly know what—" She paused. Her eyes slowly slid from the top of his head to his chest and waist. She took in the fine cut of his clothing, then continued her perusal down to the shine of his shoes. He had never been so thoroughly examined before in his life. It was all he could do to hold still, instead of pulling back his shoulders or turning his head slightly to one side to make his profile more favorable. After what seemed like ages, but was likely only a few seconds, her eyes widened. "You *know* him. Is he a friend of yours?"

This was his chance to introduce himself. He *should* introduce himself. More accurately, he should have someone introduce them to each other, but he was a little late for that. However, the memory of Lady Marion's lack of conversation still irked him. Would every woman stop speaking the moment they found out his title? The woman in front of him waited for his answer, her brilliant eyes practically shining in the dark. He couldn't do it.

"I might."

Her eyes sparked again. "And is he looking to marry? As everyone is talking about?"

"He is thinking seriously about it."

"Well." She tipped her head with a grin, and a curl slipped out of her coiffure. He had the sudden urge to touch it and tuck it back into place with one of those pins of hers. "It is a serious matter."

He didn't reach for her, but he didn't step away or ball his fists either. He simply stood his ground. "Definitely."

The corridor was silent. Even the men in the cardroom seemed to have settled down. Not even a low murmur came from the room. His eyes were locked with hers, and the air around them crackled with energy. Energy he hadn't felt in a long time.

He could simply ask this woman to marry him and be done with the whole blasted ordeal.

He could marry her, count those freckles, and fall asleep every night with his last sight being her thick lashes closing over her gemstone eyes. She'd said the majority of women would marry a duke without considering his person at all. What side of the majority would she fall on? He could chance it. He leaned forward, his body acting almost of its own accord, wanting to be closer to this woman who had intrigued him more than anyone ever had, not just once but on two separate occasions.

His foot edged forward before he caught himself. He blinked hard and took a deep breath. He should not be here—not in a corridor and most definitely not alone. The woman in front of him was an innocent, bright young lady. She should have nothing to do with him. At least not like this. Not improperly. He caught one last glance at the specks across her nose and cheeks, then tipped his head in a very short farewell. He turned on his heel and strode away.

He was being ridiculous. And he was *never* ridiculous. Not anymore. The farther he got from the woman, the sicker he felt to his stomach. What was it about her laugh, her skin, and her complete lack of respect for societal rules that had made him revert to a man who was so uncalculating?

Was it the fact that he had seen her before? Or was it simply that for the first time since his father had passed away, he was allowing himself the possibility of connecting with another human being? He didn't know. Whatever had just happened was incalculable to him. An unsolvable mathematics problem that would never add up.

When the world no longer made sense, it was time to retreat. There was no pressing forward when plans made no sense, and his brash idea to simply propose to the woman was the most irrational thing to run through his head since he had been seventeen years old.

He made it back to the ballroom before realizing his abrupt departure must have been terribly rude to . . . to . . . Blast. He didn't even know her name.

That woman.

He made his way distractedly through the crowd, nodding briefly to the men and women who tried to start a conversation as he passed. He finally reached Ottersby and greeted him with a distracted nod as well, before looking around the room. He couldn't see her. She hadn't returned. She must still be eavesdropping on the men playing cards. Alone. Where was the woman's chaperone? Should he send Patience to stand with her? Patience would have no qualms about listening in on men's gossip.

"Where's Patience?"

Ottersby tipped his head in the direction of a large group of women. Patience was in the midst of them, laughing about something.

Interrupting a group like that would be a resounding mistake. The woman in the corridor would be all right. Her chaperone would have to go looking for her at some point.

But as the minutes ticked on, he debated the wisdom of counting on a chaperone who had lost track of her responsibility in the first place.

Just as he was about to leave Ottersby to extract Patience from the women— a task that would lead to much more blushing and flirting and simpering than he felt he could stomach—the woman in emeralds returned to the ballroom. She stood out even more than the woman in white had. Not because of her clothing or even the jewelry and ornate design of her hair. Light seemed to focus on her, leaving everyone else around her dim in comparison. He waited until she joined a small group of people to turn to Ottersby.

"Who is that?" Nicholas asked. He had asked about so many women this evening, one more shouldn't make Ottersby suspicious.

"Who?"

"The woman in emeralds, speaking to Mr. Beauford."

Ottersby narrowed his eyes. "Hmm. I recognize her. I don't believe she was on *my* list though. Which means she is either titled and therefore not someone I would have thought I could convince to marry me, or she is . . . not."

Ottersby had the grace not to say what else he meant by that statement. If she wasn't titled, and she wasn't on his list, then she was not well-positioned enough to merit being on Ottersby's list.

"I think Patience may have been right about the list being a bad idea."

Mr. Beauford led the woman in the emeralds to the center of the dancers. The strains of a lively Viennese waltz jumped off the quartet's strings.

She was an excellent dancer. Mr. Beauford was also an excellent dancer, and he must be an excellent conversationalist as well, because her laughter managed to drift all the way to where he and Ottersby stood watching them.

"Should I ask Patience to discover who she is?" Ottersby asked.

Nicholas shook his head. "No." The woman was too carefree, too free with her smiles and laughter and much too ready to speak with a stranger in a corridor. He had been attracted to the depth of her feeling, but if a person could feel deeply enough to cry at a stranger's funeral or laugh in the middle of a waltz, was that truly a depth of feeling? Or was she simply mercurial? A woman who could easily love any man and move from one to the next was not at all the type of woman he was looking for. He'd seen enough of that from Lady Plymton. Still, those freckles mocked him. Even from across the room, he wished she would remove the heavily adorned necklace and show off the tiny spots that splashed across her chest. God had given her adornment enough. She needn't try to compete with Him.

He shook his head. Men didn't marry women based on the flecks of color on her otherwise pale skin. He joined Ottersby in surveying the room once again. Every once in a while Ottersby would discreetly point out a woman from the list they had made together, but he barely noticed them. He certainly wouldn't recognize them the next time he came in contact with them. Despite an inordinate number of candles, the ballroom seemed to dim. With both Lady Marion and the woman in emeralds, he had felt a jolt of excitement at the prospect of marriage, but with both of them now eliminated, he was left with a room full of women who had never interested him in the first place.

Patience extracted herself from the group of women and made her way to Ottersby's side. She smiled toward the room, but under her breath she whispered to Nicholas, "If you aren't planning on proposing to Lady Marion, you had better ask a few more women to dance this evening. Everyone is talking about your special attention to her."

Nicholas sighed. The business of finding a wife was already growing tedious. "Anyone in particular you would like to suggest?" he asked.

"Lady Bryant is here. I find her fascinating." She turned toward Ottersby. "We really need to invite them to join us for supper again soon."

"I can hardly squash rumors by dancing with Lord Bryant's wife. There must be some other lady who has caught your attention."

Patience joined them in casting her eyes about the room. "Oh, what about the honey-haired woman with all those emeralds? She looks interesting."

Nicholas clenched his jaw, and Ottersby shot him a calculating look. She did look interesting. She was even more interesting alone in a corridor, but interesting wasn't exactly what Nicholas was looking for. He needed a woman with a solid place in Society and connections he could count on. And blast Patience for being much better at describing hair color than he was. Honey. It was the perfect name for those gold-and-brown locks. "Do you know who she is?"

"No, but I can find out. In the meantime, please find someone else to dance with. I should have guessed what a sensation your interest in Lady Marion would have caused, but I didn't, and now I'm quite tired of being asked about your intentions. I thought that was a brother's duty, not a sister's."

Nicholas arched an eyebrow. "You never gave me much of an opportunity to fulfill that duty, seeing as you were in love with Ottersby before you were even presented to Society."

Patience shrugged and wove her way through the crowds, presumably to find the name of the woman in emeralds. Ottersby nodded toward a few of the women on the list, and Nicholas strode over to the closest to ask her to dance. He didn't need to sway and weave through the crush like Patience had. Men and women alike stepped to the side to make a path for him. It was one of the perks of being the highest-ranked individual at almost any function he was involved in. If only Parliament would give him such deference.

Nicholas quickly roamed the ballroom and asked three more ladies to dance. All were titled, and every one of them beautiful in her own way, but none of them excited him. And that was not a problem. He didn't need to be excited about marrying. He simply needed to find someone compatible. He didn't need to allow emotion or longing to overshadow logic. The last thing the Harrington title needed was another marriage like Patience and Ottersby's. The amount of work that mess had caused him was preposterous. He'd had to get Ottersby his title, for heaven's sake.

Not that he regretted it. Ottersby's father should have been titled long ago. His only qualm now was that he told the Queen that Ottersby would make a fine courtesy title for General Woodsworth's son. He should have thought through how often he would need to call his brother-in-law by the undignified-sounding name.

Laughter from the honey-haired girl had floated near him multiple times throughout the evening. Frankly, it was distracting. Dancing should be controlled, calculated, and measured. There was no need to laugh and lean in toward each other like all of her partners seemed to do.

After Nicholas finished dancing with the three women he had asked, he was ready to permanently retire to the cardroom. No one could say that he paid any special attention to Lady Marion now that he had danced with three other young eligible women as well. He said as much to Ottersby as they strode side by side down the red-carpeted corridor.

"That is unfortunate."

"Why?"

"Patience found out your lady's name." His lady? What the devil did Ottersby mean by that?

"I don't have a lady." But his steps quickened at Ottersby's use of the word *lady*. If she were titled . . . if she were a lady in her own right . . . He could manage a bit of levity if she were titled. The *ton* and, more importantly, the lords of Parliament whom he was trying to influence, would forgive her that. Encourage it, even. Nicholas could be broody and quiet enough for the both of them at social functions. It could be an advantage to have a captivating wife.

Ottersby brushed aside Nicholas's protest. "The woman with the emeralds. Her name is Lady Mercy Rothschild, the second daughter of Lord and Lady Driarwood."

She was titled.

Driarwood. He knew that name. Donald had mentioned it when his brother had married, and Nicholas had simply forgotten. Lord Driarwood had a positive outlook on the people of Ireland, but Nicholas hadn't gotten around to speaking with him. He'd been too concerned with trying to turn the opinions of those who disagreed with him. He forced himself not to smile, even though he was walking fast enough now, they were only a pace away from running. Her father was an earl, and while not the highest-ranked man at a ball like this, *she* outranked all but three or four of the unattached women in the room.

"How did you miss her on your list?"

Ottersby's habit of pulling on his sleeves reared its head; he tugged on each one making certain his appearance was impeccable. Nicholas had insulted his list-making capacities . . . a grave offense. "Driarwood . . ." Ottersby rubbed a hand down his face. "I remember the family, but she hadn't been presented to Society when I made my list. I would have liked to add her because her family hadn't seemed particular about titles and positions. Her parents are the product of a very well-known love match, and her older sister married an untitled gentleman—"

"Richard Young," Nicholas finished for him.

Ottersby blinked. "Yes, actually. How did you . . . ?" Ottersby waved a hand. "It doesn't matter." He glanced back toward the ballroom, and even though it was most certainly Nicholas's imagination, he could make out the sound of Lady Mercy's laughter over all the other noises coming from the room. Ottersby smiled and turned back to Nicholas. "Shall I find her address?"

Nicholas didn't bother answering. They both knew if Ottersby didn't, Patience would.

And on the slight chance that Patience didn't?

Nicholas would do it himself.

CHAPTER 7

THE SUN WAS HIGH IN the sky before it managed to sneak between the drapes and wake Mercy. She stretched, her legs stiff from a night of dancing. Mama had asked her to be pleasant, and pleasant she was. The three men she had paid special consideration to had seemed delighted by her more marked attention. Even Mr. Beauford had seemed loathe to leave her side, a strange departure from their typical interactions.

It was rare that Mama asked anything of her, and despite the niggling worry that she could be entering into relationships without knowing whether she wanted them, at least she would be able to give Mama a good report at breakfast. She flung the bedcovers off, sat up, and rang the bell for Kate. She wouldn't worry about those men. Not at the moment. At the next ball, if given the same assignment, she would find three different men to charm. It might get her a reputation as a flirt, but better that than an unwanted and passionless marriage proposal.

When she entered the breakfast room, Mama and Papa were sitting at the table, their plates used, but empty. They stopped talking. Neither of them was smiling, and until two weeks ago, smiling at breakfast was typical. Mercy sat down and reached for some of the bread and cheese. "You didn't need to wait for me."

"We were anxious to hear more of your thoughts from the ball," Papa said with a smile that looked forced.

Mercy gave him a brilliant smile back. "The supper was excellent, and the quartet superb."

Mama shook her head, not even attempting a smile. "You know what your father means. The dancing and your partners—did you enjoy them as well?"

Mercy eyed Papa. Mama always shared everything with him, so he most likely knew about Mama's challenge. It was one of the things Mercy loved about their marriage. Still, it felt strange to speak of giving special attention to men with her father in the room. He had never been one to push her into marriage like the fathers she had overheard talking in the cardroom. He would never be a man to barter with his daughter's life for a better position in Society. He hadn't done so for himself, and he'd never regretted marrying Mama. "I always enjoy dancing."

Mama tapped a finger next to her plate. "You know what I mean. Which men did you enjoy dancing with? And which men enjoyed dancing with you?"

"I hope all the men I dance with enjoy it."

Papa gritted his teeth. "But were there any men in particular . . ." His words faded. He was *not* used to these types of conversations. None of them were, and frankly, she didn't know why they were having this one. She had been out for two years, and during those years, none of them had worried about her getting married. She had a hefty dowry, and Papa was an earl. There was no need for a rush to the altar for someone in her position.

Were her parents just finally ready to have the home to themselves?

She supposed she could be happy for them. No two people loved each other more than Mama and Papa, save for perhaps Rosalind and Richard.

She sighed. "Mr. Beauford is always pleasant to dance with, and I was very pleasant with him." Papa nodded, and Mama stopped her tapping. "Lord Dowdle and Lord Buckley also received more than their fair share of my attention last night and didn't seem to mind it."

Mama smiled and Papa sat back against the chair. "That is good. You are not only beautiful, but also . . . enjoyable to spend time with. I can't imagine any man minding your company." He reached over the table and covered her hand with his. "We have been very blessed and, frankly, selfish keeping you to ourselves these past years, but, Mercy, it is time you started looking more seriously at finding a man you would like to marry."

She was only twenty. Rosalind had been twenty when she married Richard, but the two of them were so in love. Mercy had grown weary of them taking advantage of being engaged by stealing kisses every chance they got. There was no man of her acquaintance she felt that strongly about. "Why now? I've never felt the need to look seriously before, not from you or Mama. What's happened?"

Papa shook his head. "Nothing has happened. However, there are ideal times for things, and there are less-than-ideal times for things. I've seen this throughout my life. Your mother and I have been talking, and this year—it is your ideal year. I feel it strongly."

Her ideal year? "But what if I don't find an ideal man?"

Papa tipped his head like he hadn't considered that. "Well, then, perhaps it won't be your ideal year. Of course, more important than the timing is the person you will marry. We are just asking you to be open to the thought of marriage. It seems to be something that hasn't been at the forefront of your mind. We don't want to rush you, but we also don't want you to lose out on opportunities that you may not have in the future."

Kate's soft knock sounded at the door, and she entered with a large bouquet of flowers. "Some flowers arrived for Lady Mercy." Kate's Irish accent made every word interesting, even in a small sentence like that. Mercy loved it best, though, when Kate got so involved in one of her stories while doing her hair that her voice grew animated and her accent become even more pronounced.

The flowers in Kate's hands were filled with peonies and roses. Mr. Beauford often sent flowers after they danced together, but he had never sent any quite so extravagant. Kate handed the flowers to Papa, and after Kate left, Papa read the note. "From Lord Dowdle." He smiled. "He's planning to call this afternoon."

Mama straightened in her chair with a grin. "That's excellent news."

Lord Dowdle was kind. A marriage to him would probably be a good one. She hadn't encouraged any men she didn't think she had at least some chance at happiness with. But he couldn't dance—not like Mr. Beauford could. Not that a marriage to Mr. Beauford would be a better choice.

Marriage.

How had that suddenly become so vital? How had she succumbed to thinking about the men around her as only future prospects? The last thing she wanted to do was assess what kind of husband Mr. Beauford or Lord Dowdle would be, but here she was, doing it. And why? She didn't even want to get married. She loved her life here. If she married, she would be a stranger in another person's home. The servants wouldn't know her, and she wouldn't know them. Everything would change.

She broke the bread in her hand into tiny pieces on her plate without eating them. Mama and Papa looked at each other but didn't say anything. If she married, she probably wouldn't be able to sit with her elbows on the table, sulking. She would have to sit straight and pretend everything was all right, even when it wasn't. Everything about the idea was about as appetizing as the drying breadcrumbs on her plate.

Kate knocked again and entered with another bouquet of flowers—white roses this time. Mama's eyebrows rose, and her grin grew into an outright smile.

Mercy sighed. "You did ask me to be agreeable to three men. I was, and it seemed to make them happy. I assume there will be another bouquet and note soon. Who are those from? Lord Buckley?"

Roses seemed like something Lord Buckley would send. They were a respectable choice, and the white color was non-threatening. Lord Buckley was a careful man—one who would tread softly in a courtship.

Of the three men she'd chosen, Lord Buckley was the least likely with whom she would progress to marriage. Careful was the last thing she wanted in a courtship.

Papa read the note. "Yes, they are from Lord Buckley." He raised his eyes from the page. "Well done, Mercy." She ground her teeth together. Papa was not one to hold back compliments. He had always been proud of her for the things she had done. But for some reason, having him use the same phrase for receiving a bouquet of flowers from a lord as he had for some of her earlier paintings and her better-performed pianoforte pieces simply felt wrong. "He will also be paying you a visit this afternoon."

Mercy started ripping the small pieces of bread on her plate into smaller ones. She took a bite of cheese, but it was dry, and the flavor was wrong. She swallowed it down but didn't enjoy it.

Papa slid both of the cards across the table to her so she could examine them. The messages were nearly identical, although the handwriting was not. Lord Buckley's letters were small and tightly packed together in neat lines, whereas Lord Buckley's lettering was elaborate, like he had taken pains to make certain each flourish was noted.

A few minutes later, a third soft knock sounded. Mr. Beauford's flowers must've arrived. He typically sent a small bundle of wildflowers, and although not as expensive as what the two lords had sent her, she preferred them for their delicate blossoms. She loved that they fit on the small side table near her bed.

Kate opened the door, but Mercy didn't bother to turn and look this time. Mama gasped, and Papa's eyes widened, then slid to hers. Mercy spun in her chair and made a similar sound to Mama's sharp intake of breath. Kate's face was completely hidden by a bouquet of flowers so large she couldn't hold it in her hands. Instead, her arms were wrapped around the base of it. There *were* wildflowers, but there were also lilies and dahlias and probably every other flower a shop could carry.

Mercy grabbed the side of the table, her mouth even dryer than it had been when she had forcibly swallowed her cheese.

Mr. Beauford had most definitely noticed the change in her last night.

And he had taken it to mean something he shouldn't have.

"Oh my!" Mama blinked. "Where in the world will we be able to place those?"

Not on Mercy's bedside table. That was for certain.

Instead of handing the bouquet to Papa, Kate bent over so he could reach the card tucked inside. "I'll take these to the kitchen. Perhaps Mrs. Brooksby can divide them into several vases."

"That is a good idea, Kate. Thank you." Papa opened the card, and his face went pale.

What in heaven's name had Mr. Beauford written? He wouldn't have proposed with a note in a bouquet of flowers, would he?

Of course, he wouldn't. She and Mr. Beauford were friendly, but there had been no courtship, no time together other than consistent dancing at any ball they both attended. It would take more than a few extra smiles to make Mr. Beauford propose.

But those flowers . . .

They must have cost a fortune.

She swallowed and eyed Kate trudging out of the room with her large burden. Mercy hadn't even had the time to examine it properly. Not that it mattered. She wouldn't agree to marry Mr. Beauford simply because he had sent her a table full of flowers. She ignored her sudden desire to rush out of the door behind Kate to take in the bouquet as a whole before it was divided. It truly was magnificent. But the last thing she wanted to do was make Mama and Papa think she was sentimentally attached to Mr. Beauford's flowers.

She turned to Papa, who was still examining the card, turning it over and back as if he didn't believe what was in his hand. She closed her eyes. This is what listening to Mama had done. She shouldn't have done it. "What does Mr. Beauford write?"

Papa tipped his head slightly. "It isn't from Mr. Beauford."

Not from Mr. Beauford? She had thought . . . but there were wildflowers . . .

Mama leaned toward Papa and read the card over his shoulder. She gasped, grabbed the card from his hand, and flipped it over just as Papa had done. Mama's eyes scanned down the words written on the card for a second time before turning to Papa. "The Duke of Harrington?"

Mama and Papa locked eyes.

Who? Mercy jumped from her seat and strode around the table. She snatched the card from Mama's hand. It was true. The Duke of Harrington had sent her that massive bouquet. But why? She didn't even know the man.

His note was different from the others. The back was embossed in thick gold swirls with a coat of arms in the center. And he hadn't written to request calling on her this afternoon. He'd instead asked for an introduction to her and invited them to his home.

"Did you speak to His Grace last night?" Papa asked. "Catch his eye?"

Mercy stepped back, the thickness of his card heavy in her hand. How could she have? The note was asking for an introduction. They didn't know each other. So why would he send her flowers?

Curling dark hair, a clean-shaven face, and an impeccable coat highlighted only by the dim light of the corridor flashed into her mind. Certainly, he couldn't be . . . no, he would have said something about it. The two of them had spoken of the duke for heaven's sake. "Beyond his reputation, I don't even know who he is." What *exactly* had the man said about the Duke of Harrington? She had asked if he were a friend of his, asked if the duke was serious about marriage, but his answer had been vague, and then he'd suddenly walked away. Even if he were the duke, she couldn't have made a good impression on him, listening at the doorway.

Mama spun in her chair and craned her neck to look at Mercy. "I *knew* I was right to have you wear the emeralds."

Papa tapped his fingers on the table as if he were considering. "There was talk last night that Harrington is finally looking for a bride."

"Finally?" Mercy asked. She'd thought part of the excitement over him was his age. What was considered young for a duke? Forty? Was he contemplating a second marriage? "I thought the Duke of Harrington was a young man."

"He is young. Quite young. But he was in mourning for his father for two years and hasn't shown any particular interest in any woman for years after that. London has been holding their breath for this." He glanced up at Mercy, his eyes shining. "This truly could be your ideal year."

Papa reached for Mercy's hand, and she didn't have the courage to protest or pull away. Mercy had had two years of dancing, attending plays, and meeting with the people of the *ton* without having to worry about finding a match. That was more than most women were given. She should be grateful.

But instead, it felt as though she were a canary that had spent its life flying free, only to wake up one morning to find a cage, gilded and thick, slowly gliding toward her, ready to trap her and put her on display.

She had nothing against the Duke of Harrington, whoever he was. But the look in her parents' eyes and the warmth of Papa's hand covering hers . . .

There would be no escaping his interest. Just as she'd told the man in the corridor, one did not turn down the attentions of a duke.

She could ask Papa about Harrington's looks and try to discover if she meted out that wise proclamation to the duke himself, but the last thing she wanted to do was appear to be more interested than she was. What a disaster.

Kate's fourth knock was as soft as her others, but Mercy started at the sound of it. Kate walked in with a small bouquet of wildflowers. These were definitely from Mr. Beauford—none of them even bothered to read the card.

CHAPTER 8

MERCY HAD ASSUMED THE DUKE'S London residence would be in one of the most fashionable parts of Town, but she had been wrong. Apparently there wasn't a brilliant enough neighborhood for the duke. Instead, he lived just outside of Town on an estate. The advantage of his residence being on the outskirts of London was that she had plenty of time to think through her plan for the afternoon.

Her first item of business was to discover whether the man from the corridor was, in fact, the duke or simply a friend of the duke.

It could be accomplished immediately upon their introduction.

And whether the man was the duke or simply the friend of the duke, she assumed the duke's interest in her must have stemmed from that one interaction. Mama insisted that the emeralds were the reason he begged an introduction. While they had caught the man's eye a time or two, Mercy remembered him dragging his eyes away from them, as if in disapproval or disgust. They had been too gaudy, if not for a duke, then at least for the duke's friend. It wasn't the jewels or even her figure that had caught his eye. He had barely glanced at her in *that* way.

No, something else must have intrigued him, and the only possibility was her strange behavior. Who sneaked about, listening in to men's conversations during a ball? Who had full conversations in hushed tones in corridors with men they hadn't been introduced to? No one proper. Some men seemed attracted to women who didn't behave as they should. She had the sneaking suspicion the Duke of Harrington was just that type.

The man's eyes had sparked when she suggested listening at the wall, even though he had first refused. He definitely enjoyed teasing her about who the duke could be and what a duke would want. Which, in hindsight, made him almost interesting. After he left her, haughty and supposedly indifferent, she had caught him glancing her way several times during the evening, his dark eyes following her as she danced with Lord Dowdle. She had thought he might even ask her to dance, but he left the ballroom after dancing with only a few women.

Mercy had been following Mama's instructions by being her most vibrant while dancing with Lord Dowdle, laughing and listening intently to anything he had said. Once again, that wasn't necessarily the behavior of a demure woman. If her behavior was what had attracted him, it would be easy enough to act the opposite after their introduction. She would be demure, perfectly behaved, timid, and unsure of herself.

And the duke would lose interest.

Mercy could return to her carefree self, and her parents would have one less reason to push her toward the altar before she had the chance to meet the man of her dreams. The carriage pulled to a stop, and Mercy tugged at the three strands of pearls at her neck. Mama had insisted she wear them, and Mercy didn't protest. They wouldn't make a difference.

The carriage was silent as they waited for the servants to announce their arrival at the duke's estate. Mama hadn't taken her eyes away from the window since they'd arrived, but Mercy forced herself not to look.

She wasn't ready to marry, and no estate would change that fact.

A larger home would simply mean more work for her to oversee, and she would much rather dance, sing, or curl up on a sofa with a nice thick book. Those were all activities that could be done in any home.

The door opened. First Mama left the carriage, then Papa. She took a tentative step out and looked up. Her step faltered, and her traitorous breath caught in her throat.

Blast.

The home in front of her was not a home at all. It was a palace. Columns of white rose from the ground, topped with statues of Greek gods and goddesses near the roof line. The tall windows were crowned with arches and framed with the same white of the columns, but the rest of the home was painted in a pale yellow. There were no neighbors to be seen in any direction, and sweeping grounds fell away into a forested patch of land behind the home. Mercy swallowed. One would get lost in such a home. She could begin reading one night, get locked in by some unobservant maid, and never be seen again.

Mama said something under her breath, and Papa's shoulders straightened as if he were already trying to impress the duke. They walked slowly toward the front door, taking in the well-manicured flowers and shrubbery, guessing at which gods adorned the roofline, and at last, admiring the marble steps leading up to the entrance.

Mercy had grown up with wealth, but other than royal palaces, this was unlike anything she had ever seen. The door opened for them, and they stepped into a wide-open entrance hall, covered in a different, lighter marble. A double staircase adorned the entry, along with one of the largest chandeliers she had ever seen. If this is what the entry of the duke's home looked like, how would he furnish the ballroom? What could outshine this brilliance? And all of this for their home in London? What would the duke's country estate look like?

Or estates. He most likely had multiple estates.

They followed a footman to the drawing room, and when he opened the door, she struggled to not bite her lip.

He was there, tall and statuesque, with his dark hair styled as neatly as a man with a bit of curl in his hair could tame it. His clothing was less formal than what he had worn to the ball but was just as impeccable. A perfectly tied cravat made his neck appear long, and his head tipped in the superior manner of a man who always knew he was the highest-ranking man in the room. How had she missed that?

Perhaps he was only this stiff when there were other men around to out-rank, and there hadn't been any other men in the corridor. It had been just the two of them. Alone.

He was not alone now. Another man joined him, looking even sterner, but his hair was blond and his shoulders wide enough to make him intimidating. She'd seen the two of them speaking together at the ball.

One of them was the duke, but she still wasn't certain which. She should've at least asked Papa about the color of his hair. Why hadn't she asked someone at the ball to point him out? She had heard him spoken of several times but had wanted to remain disinterested. All she knew of him was that he was young, handsome, and looking for a wife. Both men could fit that description, although her man from the corridor was decidedly the more handsome of the two.

Whichever one he was, it looked as if the whole household had shown up for the introduction. Two beautiful women with dark auburn hair stood as they entered—mother and daughter, she assumed. The daughter stood next to the serious-looking blond man. Corridor-man stood near the heavily adorned fireplace. She had only seen him in a dim lighting and then later across the ballroom from each other. She remembered him to be handsome, with a full head of dark hair. But as their eyes met from across the room, his assessing—examining her clothing, her hair, and her face—she was struck by the fact that her memory had not done the man justice.

Double blast.

Mama curtsied, and Papa bowed his head not to the blond man but to Mercy's dark-haired comrade.

The Duke of Harrington.

Mercy's breathing shortened, but through sheer force of will, she kept her face neutral. The amount of effort she had to put into keeping her face bland probably meant she had the frozen look of a taxidermized deer. Mercy had been harebrained at the ball, trying to listen at a wall for clues as to why her parents had started acting strangely and then discussing the seriousness of marriage with one of the most powerful men in all of England. Not her finest moment.

Much too late, Mercy hastily curtsied, then raised her head. The Duke of Harrington's shoulders, stiff and straight like a soldier's, were nearly as impressive as his home. His eyes flashed with interest, and something else. Amusement? He was enjoying himself. Perhaps she had been too rash in determining to dissuade his interest. She didn't *need* a large home, but in reality, would she truly get lost in it?

She almost raised a friendly eyebrow at him in response but paused the treacherous muscle mid-lift. The duke lived in a perfect house with perfect manners, and there was absolutely no circumstance in which Mercy could belong here. Not because of her station. As the daughter of an earl, she was in a better position to "catch" the duke than most of the women whom she had overheard discussing him at the ball. But her parents had raised her to marry for love, to choose her own path, and to live life free of the most restricting parts of Society.

The most restricting part of Society stood next to the mantle.

She had two choices. She could do as Mama would choose and be her most beguiling. She had caught the interest of a duke, but it would take an overabundance of smiling and laughing to reel him in. She *could* do that. It wasn't that she didn't like laughing and smiling; she simply resented the fact that her mother felt compelled to tell her she must do it.

Or she could become the opposite of the woman she had been at the ball and cause him to lose interest. That would be the easiest plan by far. After all, what were the chances that out of all the men in England, *he* was her soulmate? If she encouraged him, she would have no other chances. Her parents' happiness about her catching the interest of a duke was as boundless as would be their disappointment if she rejected his advances.

She tried to picture the upright duke pulling her around a corner and kissing her just out of sight from a large picnic party. She had only two meetings to judge him by, but she couldn't. The man had practically run away from her in the corridor after admonishing her for not being tied to her chaperone. How many times had Richard and Rosalind escaped chaperones? Easily over a hundred.

She needed a man capable of passion. Someone to make her feel like she was the only woman in the world. Someone who would let her know that he couldn't live without her. And this man, with his ramrod-straight back and perfectly tied cravat, didn't seem the type who would kiss her knuckles, let alone her mouth, unless her father and the Queen had given him permission.

She pulled her eyes away from him. She shouldn't show interest. Not yet. Not until she had decided how to proceed. She was not ready to give up on having the type of mad devotion her sister had found with Richard, and she had no idea if the man in front of her was capable of such a thing. She pasted a bland smile on her face and walked forward.

Introductions were made. The red-haired women were, indeed, his mother and sister. The serious blond man was his brother-in-law, Lord Ottersby.

Everyone was so solemn and serious, her ears screamed for any sound other than the ticking of the mantel clock. The duchess motioned for them to sit at the tea table, and they all moved wordlessly to do so.

Tea was a tedious thing. Lady Ottersby started several conversations, and Mama and Papa tried to join them, but the two young men seemed unprepared to speak at all.

At one point, the duke leaned toward her and said, "This wouldn't have been a very exciting conversation to hear from the corridor."

She turned. He was looking at his cup as if it were the most interesting piece of ceramic in the world. She opened her mouth to say, "How could we compete with the thrill of a duke finally showing interest in marriage?" But then stopped herself. She couldn't mention marriage to the duke. He might misinterpret her meaning. It was one thing to discuss the duke and his marriage prospects in the corridor with a man she thought was unrelated to the subject. But now? Impossible.

So, instead, she simply nodded her head. "True."

The duke looked up, his eyebrows furrowed slightly, as if he were trying to decipher what kind of woman she was. Good luck to him. She didn't even know that herself. It was the one and only time he addressed her personally throughout the visit.

Nicholas paced in front of his drawing room fireplace. Mother, Ottersby, and Patience sat silently at the card table near the door Lady Mercy and her family had exited just moments ago. Patience coughed, and Mother started to make soft humming noises. He had half a mind to storm out of the room and swear off this blasted idea of getting married. Instead, he stopped and put both of his feet together like he was standing at attention. "That was an unmitigated disaster."

Mother's humming stopped, and her head shot up. "What do you mean? I thought Lady Mercy was lovely."

Nicholas scoffed. She *was* lovely. He had seen her be lovely to nearly every man at the Stafford ball. But the person she had become inside his home was a pale comparison. She'd barely spoken to him. His title, his home, and the pressure of meeting his family had turned her into a version of herself he didn't recognize. Lady Marion, in her white dress, had been more interesting than the Lady Mercy who had arrived at his home this afternoon. "Lady Mercy is lovely. But she clearly has no interest in me."

Ottersby frowned. "You have no proof of that. Besides, you are a duke."

Patience shook her head and laid a hand on Ottersby's shoulder. "Not everyone is a social climber, my dear, even if you were."

Ottersby tipped his head toward his wife. "And what a rotten one I turned out to be. In the end, I ended up proposing to my bewitching maid."

Patience smiled, and her eyes lit up as she leaned toward Ottersby. Nicholas knocked a knuckle against the fireplace mantle. This was not the time for him to watch his sister go moon-eyed over Ottersby. Nicholas went back to the figurative drawing board. Lady Mercy, despite her parents' encouragement, had been incredibly bored or disinterested during her introduction to him. He would have to find someone else. He wouldn't spend the rest of his life with someone who would rather be elsewhere.

"I think she was simply nervous," Mother said. "The first time I met your father, I barely spoke three words to him. Perhaps meeting her here was a mistake. The home is a lot to take in."

That it was, but he had thought to impress her. Instead, he had scared her off. She had almost, *almost* connected to him when he had spoken about listening at corridors. He could see it, sitting at the tip of her tongue, but then she changed her mind.

The Lady Mercy he had seen dancing with Lord Dowdle, and even the Lady Mercy he had met in the corridor, would never have stopped to think about what she was saying. She would have simply said it.

Patience sighed deeply, bringing his attention back to her. "I thought she was extremely well-mannered. Isn't that what you are looking for?"

Ottersby nodded in agreement. They both looked undisturbed by Lady Mercy's obvious lack of interest in him. Perhaps because they hadn't seen her like he had. Ottersby tipped his head to one side. "She seems rather perfect for you, really. Demure, careful, attentive. A woman like that could make a fine wife. She would be an asset, to be sure."

Nicholas narrowed his eyes, and the spaces surrounding Ottersby grew dark. How long had his friend been such a blackguard and so . . . right? The Lady Mercy who had arrived today had been exactly the type of woman he had thought he was looking for. If he hadn't seen her broad smiles and sparkling eyes at the Stafford ball, he would still be interested in her.

He *was* still interested in her.

But she had given him no reason to believe *she* was interested in *him*. And he knew she was capable of showing interest. Had she, perhaps, an attachment to one of the men she had danced with?

He stepped backward and rested his back against the wall. Leaning his head so he looked at the ceiling, he tried to picture Lady Mercy smiling and encouraging him as she had Lord Dowdle, her lips turned up and eyes sparking with unspoken words. For a moment it felt as if he were falling, and he put his hand on the wall to make certain he wasn't. Perhaps thinking of how vibrant Lady Mercy could be was not the best of plans. Maybe it would be better for him to find a woman who didn't excel at showing emotion. Lady Mercy had been dispassionate at tea, but if her ballroom fervor reappeared? How would he handle one of her smiles? Would he be able to control himself? He didn't spend two years in the army learning self-discipline and control only to lose himself at the sight of someone like Lady Mercy beaming at him.

"I like her," Mother said. Nicholas jerked his head away from the wall. "I like her family as well. It might not have been a perfect meeting, but these things seldom are. Patience met Ottersby after climbing through his hedges. At least it wasn't as terrible as that."

Patience snickered and smiled at Ottersby. Then she turned to Nicholas. "I like her too. Why don't I invite her to the opera? There is room in our box for both of you, as well as her mother."

The opera? If they sat near each other, it could be an opportunity for the two of them to speak. If she spent more time in his company, perhaps he could meet the woman from the ball instead of this stiff, empty version of her. But sitting together in Ottersby's box would also lead to speculation about their relationship. He had seen what one dance at a ball had done to set tongues wagging, and he would not subject either of them to that at this early stage of courtship. "No. Not the opera. It is too public. I don't want all of London gossiping about her. And you all know that's exactly what would happen. For now, I'll wait."

Patience didn't seem happy with his answer, but she never thought things through completely. That was Nicholas's job. And he was good at it. He wouldn't show more interest in Lady Mercy until he saw some evidence that she welcomed it, and if today's tea was any indication, his wait would either be very long or, more likely, infinite.

CHAPTER 9

It had been two weeks since the tea, and although Lord Dowdle and Mr. Beauford had both called on Mercy's family, she had heard nothing from the Duke of Harrington. Her plan had worked decidedly well.

However, Lord and Lady Hafton were hosting a ball this evening, and the Duke of Harrington was a likely guest. If at any point during the ball Mercy forgot that fact, the weight of her enormous drop earrings would serve as heavy reminder. Mercy held the skirt of her forest-green gown and carefully navigated the stairs until she met Mama at the bottom. Mama took her hand immediately. "Remember, if His Grace is at this ball, you must smile at him. Promise me you will smile at him."

How many more promises would Mercy need to make to Mama this Season? She had half a mind to suggest retiring to the country, but Papa had not stopped speaking of what an opportunity this year was going to be for Mercy. She couldn't do it. "I will."

"And you won't act standoffish toward him as you did at his home?"

Mama had been horrified at how Mercy had behaved at tea, despite Mercy's professions of shyness and awe. And she had been awed—by his home, at least. But Mama hadn't forgiven her for not being more flirtatious with him.

He mustn't have been very serious about pursuing her if one dull afternoon had snuffed out any flames of interest.

"Mama, I hardly know him."

"And how will you get to know him if you don't at least try?"

Mama had a point. It wasn't as though there was anything wrong with the Duke of Harrington. It was simply that . . . "He is a duke."

Mama's eyes sparked, and her smile widened. "I know."

Mercy had never, not even once, thought Mama had fallen in love with Papa for his title, but for the first time in her life, doubt crept in. "A duke can marry anyone. There is no reason for him to fall madly in love with me."

"Why wouldn't he? You are a lady, the daughter of an earl. You would make a wonderful match for a duke. And his station would be a protection for you from any storm. A duke could weather anything."

Mercy laughed. "Do you plan on many storms heading our way?" It wasn't as though her family had needed protection. An earl wasn't a duke, but they were certainly free from troubles and had enough clout not to need to worry about the whispers of others behind their backs.

A shadow crossed Mama's face, and she shook her head. "Of course not, darling, but what parents wouldn't want a secure future for their children? You won't find anyone more secure than a duke."

Security had *never* been an issue before. Mama had no complaints about Rosalind marrying Richard, and he was not wealthy, nor was he socially popular because of his Irish heritage. "Perhaps a foreign prince?"

Mama shook her head and frowned. "A foreign prince would take you too far away from us." Mama stroked her cheek—her soft, delicate fingers cool on her skin. "The Duke of Harrington will have to do." Mama's smile completely erased the earlier shadow on her face. Perhaps there hadn't even been a shadow.

The moment Mercy set foot in the ballroom, the duke was impossible to miss. He stood in the middle of a group of young men, a few inches taller than the tallest of them. His eyebrow was arched at one of them as if asking the question, *What could you possibly contribute to this conversation?* For a moment, his eyes left those of his companions and searched the room. When they landed on her, his face froze for half a heartbeat, then his superiority disintegrated into a friendly smile.

Her breath hitched slightly. Just slightly, nothing to write Rosalind about, but *have to do,* was suddenly a massive understatement. The opulence of the duke's home had been eye-opening, but his person was equally as impressive and conspicuous. The noises of the ballroom faded as he continued to hold her gaze, and then suddenly his eyes were gone, looking elsewhere. Mama bumped her with her elbow and frowned. "What?" Mercy mouthed, and Mama tipped her head and gave Mercy an overexuberant, very fake smile.

Blast. After all her promises to Mama, she had forgotten to smile.

And Harrington hadn't waited long for her to remember. His eyes had moved on to others, just as he had moved on after her one invitation to his home.

This was what she wanted, wasn't it? Mercy tipped her head toward Mama. "What about Lord Dowdle and Mr. Beauford? At the last ball you wanted me to smile and encourage them. Should I continue to do that as well?"

Mama took a deep breath—almost a sigh. "Of course, Mercy, if you would like."

"But I should smile at His Grace whether I would like to or not?"

Mama frowned and turned her head to Mercy. "If you don't like the duke, just tell me. Of course, your father and I wouldn't force you to pursue someone you aren't interested in."

If she didn't like the duke? How could she be expected to know whether or not she liked him? The problem wasn't His Grace, not precisely. It was . . . the pressure of the rest of her life looming over her. She had always thought she would feel compelled and desperate to spend the rest of her life with a man before she gave him any sort of commitment. Everything about her interactions with the Duke of Harrington felt rushed and forced. She was forced to smile, forced to visit him, forced to consider him when she barely knew the man.

Mr. Beauford strode through the ballroom and came to her side. He was not as striking as the duke, but he was handsome in his own boyish manner. His black hair was never completely tamed, and he never held back his smile. He was lean and lithe, which made him quick on his feet. Immediately, he asked her to dance. Mercy pushed away any thoughts of the duke. Balls were her absolute favorite form of entertainment. Dancing always brought her a rush of pleasure. Within the first few strains of the quick, bounding notes from the quartet, the duke was forgotten. Mama was forgotten. There was only music and dancing. Something about dancing centered Mercy. It always had. She closed her eyes and took in a deep breath but was pulled out of her quiet space when Mr. Beauford pushed her gracefully away from him with his right hand, swinging away from her with a dance variation he had never used before. Her smile grew, and she copied his lively motions. When she had only just perfected the motion, he spun her and pulled her back to him.

"I've been working on that," he said.

"I can see."

"Should I add it to our repertoire?"

She laughed. "We have a repertoire?"

"Of course we do. After nearly two years of dancing together, we could hardly not have one."

Mr. Beauford's pale-blue eyes gleamed with mischief and familiarity. Mr. Beauford knew her. He knew her likes and her dislikes. He knew she was completely uninterested in developing a serious relationship at this time in her life, and he had never pushed for more than what she gave him—one set of dances at any ball they attended together.

Perhaps she should rethink her resolve to see him as merely a dance partner and never anything more. At least she knew Mr. Beauford. "Yes, add it to the repertoire. I will practice it at home so the next time we execute it, I will be proficient."

"You were proficient today with no practice at all. At the next ball, you will be magnificent."

She laughed, and Mr. Beauford's eyes brightened once again. "I would hardly call my dancing magnificent, but I look forward to it all the same."

The strains of the music slowed slightly as the dance came to an end. She gave Mr. Beauford a curtsy, and he held out his arm to escort her back to Mama on the other side of the room. They turned together, and the Duke of Harrington stepped out from the crowd, cutting them off.

She was still slightly out of breath, and her blood coursed through her veins in a beat that matched her earlier steps. The room was bright and full of possibilities. She smiled broadly at the duke without even remembering her promise to Mama.

The duke's head tipped slightly to one side, as if he were surprised by her open friendliness. He probably was. She had acted distant at his home, and here in a ballroom after her first dance, her fears seemed foolish. Mama and Papa would never force her to marry someone she didn't know, and the duke had only wished to become acquainted. It would do neither of them any harm if she were friendly toward him. She'd been friendly with Mr. Beauford for over two years, and nothing had come of that relationship.

Perhaps her friendship with His Grace could be similar.

The Duke of Harrington gave a serious nod to Mr. Beauford, which Mr. Beauford returned just as seriously. Seriousness was an expression she was not used to seeing on Mr. Beauford, and she pulled her lips tightly together in order to avoid a laugh. The duke then met her eyes. "Lady Mercy, if you are not yet engaged for the next set, would you care to dance with me?"

His eyes were much darker than Mr. Beauford's—not a color she could name. They reminded her of a forest, filled with deep-green leaves and rough, dark tree bark. They were unfamiliar, and she couldn't tell what he was thinking. "My next set is taken," she replied, and the dark eyes changed from leaves and bark to moss and stone. His shoulders stiffened, and he gave her a nod, even more serious than Mr. Beauford's. She stepped forward but stopped before placing her hand upon his arm. Something told her the duke wouldn't appreciate any form of contact without permission. "But the set before supper is still unclaimed."

One edge of his mouth quirked slightly, as if he wanted to smile but thought better of it. His eyes came alive though, returning to their brighter forest version. "Until the supper set, then." He bowed to both of them, turned on his heel like a soldier, and strode through the crush, which opened up to make room for him.

Mr. Beauford stood for a moment, then must have remembered his task of returning her to Mama, for he started forward. "That was the Duke of Harrington."

"Yes." Mercy kept her voice unaffected, as if dukes asked her to dance every Wednesday and twice on Saturdays.

"Have you known him long?"

"Not long at all. We have only just been introduced." She said the words lightly, and she hoped Mr. Beauford took them that way. But she had offered him the supper set, which meant they would not only dance, but dine together as well. She had several other sets still free. Why had she offered him that one?

Because of Mama? Because of Mercy's atrocious behavior in his home? It had happened so quickly—she hadn't truly thought of either of those things. Although her behavior to him might have played a role in her quick decision. That, coupled with the way his forest eyes had darkened in disappointment. Dancing and supper would be her penance. Mercy wasn't a serious person, while the duke's whole persona was seriousness. Yet she wasn't normally cruel, and a small pit in her stomach had told her she had been cruel to the man while at his home. Despite his title, he was, in fact, a person. She may have forgotten that during their afternoon together, but she wouldn't forget now. It wasn't as though he was asking her to marry him. He was simply asking her for a dance.

CHAPTER 10

NICHOLAS DANCED WITH TWO OTHER young ladies and one older, married woman before his supper dance with Lady Mercy. Lady Mercy seemed to be much more comfortable in ballrooms than she was in drawing rooms. At least, *his* drawing room at any rate. Gone was the quiet young woman who didn't meet his eye. Instead she was smiling at nearly everyone.

Perhaps it was the music or her obvious love of dancing, but when he approached her and her parents to claim her for his set, Lady Mercy turned toward him with her lips turned up as if she were happy to see him. Two smiles in one evening. This may be his new way of measuring the success of an event.

Her mother smiled even broader, and her father's face was cautious but welcoming. Lady Mercy dropped a quick kiss on her mother's cheek. The movement caught Nicholas by surprise. It was almost childlike, but the decision to kiss her mother in front of a large crowd was also remarkably mature. Lady Mercy didn't hide her childlike nature to impress those around her. He had tried to understand what it was that drew him to her, and in that moment, it hit him.

Lady Mercy was secure and comfortable with who she was.

He wasn't sure he knew *anyone* who was comfortable with who they were. Patience was a prime candidate now, but before she'd married Ottersby, she'd run off to become a maid, for heaven's sake. That hardly showed an understanding of who she was. But Lady Mercy didn't shy away from her emotions or apologize for not acting as Society would have her act. Whether she was crying at a stranger's funeral, listening in at doorways, or losing herself as she danced, she displayed an indomitable spirit unfettered by expectations of the people around her.

He held out a hand, and when she reached for it, smiling in that way that lit up the space around her, he pitied the rest of the men in the room.

Their first dance was a Scotch reel, and as soon as they lined up, Lord Bryant and his wife lined up next to them, completing the foursome for the dance. He would have rather danced with strangers so he could focus all his attentions on Lady Mercy, but Lord and Lady Bryant weren't the type of couple that were easily ignored. Patience fancied them to be great friends. Nicholas could do without the pretentious lord who, before he'd married Lady Bryant, had managed to flirt with not only Nicholas's sister but his mother as well.

Nicholas stepped forward and tipped his head toward Lady Mercy. "Have you been introduced to Lord and Lady Bryant?"

She shook her head and raised an eyebrow at the couple. "He is dancing with his wife?"

Nicholas scoffed. "His reputation still follows him. I doubt his wife would want him dancing with anyone else."

Lady Mercy's eyes flashed. "It looks to me as though he wouldn't want to dance with anyone else either."

Nicholas turned to see Lord Bryant whispering in Lady Bryant's ear, his lips dangerously close to his wife's neck.

Nicholas blinked and looked away. "Lord Bryant has never been one to adhere to societal rules."

Lady Mercy pressed her lips together as if she were fighting a smile. "So I have heard."

"He is—perhaps unfortunately—a close family friend. I will introduce you."

Nicholas stepped back to his position across from Lady Mercy. He turned to Lord Bryant, who was now touching the bottom curl of his wife's hair. Nicholas cleared his throat loudly. Lord Bryant turned, and a devilishly crooked grin sprouted on his face. "Harrington." He strode two steps forward and grasped Nicholas by the shoulder. But his eyes only held Nicholas's for a moment before shifting to Lady Mercy. One solitary eyebrow lifted before he returned his gaze to Nicholas, tipping his head to one side in anticipation of an introduction.

The man was married. Happily married. Still, a ridiculous urge to pummel him rose up in Nicholas's chest. Why had Nicholas offered to introduce them? But it was too late now. Rules of Society, like introductions, were to be followed, and Nicholas knew how to follow rules. Thank goodness, otherwise Nicholas might have been tempted to drag Lady Mercy away to the corridor again so he could have those smiles of hers to himself. That would put a hasty end to his pursuit of her. The last thing she'd want was a man who couldn't control himself. He pulled his shoulders back and remembered who he was. The Duke of Harrington. His father's son. "Lord Bryant, Lady Bryant, may I introduce you to Lady Mercy Rothschild, daughter of Lord and Lady Driarwood?"

Lord and Lady Bryant smiled warmly at Lady Mercy, but the music started forcing them to form a square and halt any more conversation. The Scotch reel was typically a favorite of his, as the steps were fast-paced and technical, and he was always precise with the bouncing movements. With Lady Mercy, however, he would have preferred a dance with more opportunities for speaking.

They took their first step, and Lady Mercy's feet flew to the beat of the reel, and her mouth blossomed into that radiant and inviting bow. How often had he snatched glimpses of that delightful curve of her lips as she danced with others? For the moment, her smile was his, and he wouldn't spend wasted time regretting the dance choice. He straightened his shoulders and paid particular attention to his feet. Lady Mercy was a dancing master, and at least in this, he would not disappoint.

He managed every step perfectly, until they formed a square with Lord Bryant and his wife. Lord Bryant's wicked grin, as he flashed his eyes toward Lady Mercy and back to Nicholas, made him misstep slightly. Nicholas cursed under his breath and redoubled his efforts.

The four of them took hands, and Nicholas found himself directly across from Lord Bryant. The man didn't take his eyes off him as they circled. Then, the dance changed, and for a brief moment, Nicholas had Lady Mercy to himself as they rotated a few quick turns, her hands in his. It was his moment to speak to her, if he wanted it. And he did want it. But apparently his brain had stopped functioning, and he could think of nothing to say.

The moment was gone almost as soon as it appeared, and instead he found himself with Lady Bryant's hands. "Lady Mercy seems lovely," Lady Bryant said, her smile broad. Nicholas nodded in agreement, but he was hardly attentive. From the corner of his eye, Lord Bryant was laughing with Lady Mercy.

"She is," Nicholas managed before they switched partners again and Lady Mercy's hands were back in his own.

Lady Mercy leaned forward while she danced. Apparently keeping track of her feet was not as hard for her as it was for him. "Lord Bryant thinks the world of your mother and sister. He is quite taken with them."

That was what Lord Bryant had been talking to her about? The women in his family? Nicholas cared about women. Ottersby and his father cared about women. But Lord Bryant had some strange obsession with them. "Lord Bryant seems to be taken with most women."

Lady Mercy laughed. "I'm not certain that's fair."

Lady Bryant laughed to his side, and he glanced once at the two of them. At least the look in Lord Bryant's eye while speaking to his wife was quite different from the one he had given Lady Mercy. "Whether it is fair or not, it is generally true. However, I must begrudgingly admit there is no woman he cares about as much as his wife."

Lady Mercy snuck a glance at them and then returned her steady gaze to Nicholas. "I'm certain that *is* fair."

Then she was gone, and Nicholas found himself dancing across from Lord Bryant again, empty-handed. Their feet pounded out the last few bars of the reel, with the women laughing softly and he and Lord Bryant both perfectly executing the quick steps.

When the music stopped, Lady Mercy bowed to each of them and clapped her hands together. "That was wonderful. It was lovely to meet you, Lord and Lady Bryant." She walked toward Nicholas and took him by the arm.

Whatever distance Nicholas felt from Lady Mercy in their past encounters had melted away while dancing with her. With the music playing and their feet tapping out rhythms, Lady Mercy seemed wholly at ease.

He still had one more dance with her before dinner, and this one was a waltz.

He would be able to say more things to her during a waltz, and he would be the only man to make her laugh. But could he make her laugh? He could sometimes coax a laugh from Patience—however, it was often an unintentional occurrence.

Other couples were finding space on the floor, and some were headed to the refreshment table. He hadn't seen Lady Mercy stop dancing since the music began earlier in the evening. "Would you like any refreshment before our next dance?"

"Oh no." She shook her head with a smile. "I don't want to miss any of the dancing. Supper is directly after this one, and I'll have plenty of refreshment then."

She wanted to keep dancing with him. Her words lifted him even more than the bouncing notes of their previous reel had. He didn't want to miss any of their waltz either, although it was certainly not only because of the pleasure of dancing. He wanted his hand on her back and her arm on his shoulder. He wanted her mouth next to his cheek while she spoke to him, and most of all, he didn't want that time interrupted or shared.

They said their farewells to Lord and Lady Bryant. The eyes of the men and women nearby followed Nicholas and Lady Mercy back to the dance floor. Nicholas tried very hard to ignore the glint in Lady Bryant's eye. Nicholas couldn't remember the last time he had been anywhere near Lord Bryant, and the focus had remained on Nicholas. There was no reason anyone should be paying him more attention with Lady Mercy than they had with any of his other dance partners. He had paid all of his previous partners the proper respect.

But dancing with Lady Mercy *was* different, and apparently he wasn't hiding his feelings very well.

She smiled at him as he led her to a new location, away from the dancers already eyeing them. The outer edge wasn't much better, for here, not only the dancers, but the rest of the room watched them as well.

No matter. He would ignore them.

The quartet readied their instruments. Nicholas took a deep breath and placed his palm against the upper curve of her spine. The silk of her ballgown was warm even though his gloves. Lady Mercy settled in closer to him and placed one hand in his and the other on his shoulder. She smiled unabashedly up at him, as if he weren't a duke, not a suitor, not a friend. Simply another dance partner, and the person she was going to share her joy with for every single second the music played. That smile . . . that smile was making it difficult for him to remember to breathe.

The first strains of music started, and at the slightest movement of his leading hand, Lady Mercy was off.

Gone were any thoughts about their strange afternoon together, and gone were the thoughts of marriage and propriety. Nicholas's breath came back in full force. It had to. Lady Mercy was here to dance, and he would do his utmost to ensure she was not disappointed.

Nicholas had missed many dance lessons in his youth, but after he returned home from serving in the military, he'd hired a dance instructor on his own and had worked and rehearsed until he had every dance down perfectly. His waltz was flawless.

But dancing with Lady Mercy made his flawless steps feel stiff. While he executed steps and turns, she breathed life into them. Dancing was life. He had no doubt that after only a few bars, Nicholas faded from Lady Mercy's mind, and she was simply living and breathing the waltz.

He'd looked forward to speaking with her, but he hated to interrupt.

So, he didn't.

Instead, he closed his eyes for a moment and tried to imagine what she was experiencing. A place of music, movement, and discovery. With his eyes closed, there was only her hand in his, his hand at her back, and her other hand resting feather soft on his arm.

He forgot his lessons, forgot to count the steps in his head. Instead he moved the two of them in circles drawn with sentiment instead of precision. It was as if they had the floor and the instruments to themselves, and nothing in the world could infiltrate their space.

Until a woman's skirt brushed up against his leg.

Nicholas whipped his eyes open. They had narrowly missed one couple, and another was angled in their direction. He quickly navigated a turn before he ran into anyone else.

What had he been thinking, dancing with his eyes closed? How was Lady Mercy supposed to enjoy her dance if he had them knocking about the room, disturbing other dancers? He glanced at Lady Mercy. The corners of her lips were lifted, and her eyes sparked with a look he knew all too well from Patience. His desire to make her laugh was about to be fulfilled.

"Do you often dance with your eyes closed?" Her voice was lilting, but at least she didn't laugh outright.

"No, I do not." His spine stiffened, and he started counting beats again.

She didn't press him, and after a moment, she relaxed back into the place she had been before—unaware of the world around them, simply following his lead and taking pleasure in the moment.

Nicholas did not follow her there. One of them needed to be mindful of those around them. And it had to be Nicholas. He went back to his counting and perfect steps. He'd have time to speak to her later, at dinner. For the moment, he'd concentrate only on executing a flawless waltz. Lady Mercy remained fluid, turning and dipping at the slightest of suggestions from Nicholas's fingers. Waltzing wasn't hard for Nicholas, but Lady Mercy made it particularly easy, as if moving to the beat of three counts was as simple as breathing.

The music stopped long before he was ready to finish dancing and long before he'd expected it to.

Nicholas led Lady Mercy to the dining hall. She had been at his side for two dances. Her delicate hand resting lightly on his arm should be familiar by now, yet it was anything but. The smallest of movements from her heightened his senses. Every place she touched him felt as though the universe lived in that space. If Mother's singing had kept him from concentrating on his work, what would having a lovely, vivacious woman in his home do to him?

Perhaps this whole marriage idea was a terrible one.

But a connection to Lady Mercy's family and the legitimacy a wife would bring to his title must outweigh his discomfort. Especially since he didn't want to give up the chance to connect himself to the brightest spot in any room.

He pulled back Lady Mercy's chair, and after she sat, he took the seat next to her.

She tipped her head toward him. "Thank you."

Two simple words, but whispered only to him. "You're welcome."

It was as if the two of them talked off a script. He was going to have to ask Ottersby for conversational advice. No, that was a terrible idea. Ottersby wasn't any better at conversation than he was. Worse, perhaps. But who else could he ask? Lord Bryant?

He would rather spend the rest of his life as a bachelor, listening to his mother sing.

Lady Mercy started removing her gloves, and his brain malfunctioned again.

She didn't do it gracefully. Instead, she ripped each glove off as if they had been suffocating her hands. She dropped them on the table without a second thought. He had a sudden vision of her arriving home after any outing, exuberant and impatient, pulling her gloves off with her teeth. He shook his head. It was a ridiculous thought, as if he could know how this woman acted in her own home. Still, he let his eyes dip to the tips of the soft leather of her gloves, and sure enough, there was a tooth-sized mark on the index finger of her right-handed glove.

Lady Mercy removed her gloves with her teeth. Was that the type of woman he wanted to marry?

She reached for her gloves and then set them in her lap gently, as if she had remembered where she was, and smiled up at him as though she hadn't just exposed an intimate detail about her life.

A tiny, delicate chain of silver hung on her wrist. It was so different from the bulky jewels she typically wore. Throughout supper, the bracelet continued to catch his eye. He asked if she would like meat and served her when proper, but other than that, they hardly spoke to each other. As he placed a pudding on her plate, he turned to her. "Your bracelet."

Her hand covered it, and her eyes went wide as if she were surprised it was even there. "Yes?"

"I like it."

And then she laughed.

Men and women turned at the sound of it. They always did. He always did. Lady Mercy's laugh was like a spring bubbling up from out of a mountain side. As surprising as it was refreshing.

He tipped his whole body to one side in the chair and lowered his voice. "What is so amusing about me liking your bracelet?"

She tried to soften her smile, but pulling her lips together simply made her cheeks tighten in a cheeky, conspiratorial manner. "Mama is convinced the only reason you noticed me at the Stafford ball was because of the emeralds."

Ah. "I suppose you didn't tell her about our other meeting then? In the corridor?"

"Heavens, no. I was trying to listen in on Papa. I couldn't tell her about that."

She had been trying to listen in on her father? Why? Was the man trying to be rid of her? That is what she'd been listening for, wasn't it? Parents trying to get rid of their children. "It wasn't your jewelry that made me notice you." Not any jewelry that was made by man, at any rate.

Lady Mercy's eyebrows lowered, and she tipped her head to one side like she was expected him to expound. But he'd burn down this building before admitting that her skin had kept him up at night. She raised an eyebrow, and he suddenly found the silverware to be quite fascinating.

A moment later, Lady Mercy sighed and continued on without her answer. "Well, Mama and Papa are very grateful you did notice me. Even if you do like my maid's gift better than the emeralds my father gave Mama."

Her voice had the slightest hint of sharpness in it when she mentioned her parents. Lord and Lady Driarwood had seemed extremely loving. Not at all the type that are in a hurry to rid themselves of a daughter. But if they were? He caught her face in profile as she smiled at a woman across the table from her. What if he hadn't been there in that corridor that evening? What if she had met someone else? Whoever it may have been would have become enchanted by her. It was impossible not to be.

That man might have been sitting next to her now, glancing at her gloves and thinking about how delicate and dangerous her hand seemed in his, like he'd caught a fledgling sparrow and was holding it, concentrating on not gripping too tight or too loose, because either option could lead to disaster.

He wasn't holding her hand anymore, and yet that fear, fear of losing her, still hung thick in the air around him. He took a deep breath and shoved those fears aside. She *was* here with him, and he should be enjoying it. As long as his manners remained impeccable, she wouldn't have any reason to see behind his facade of propriety and glimpse the uncontrolled man of overzealous passion he'd been with Lady Plymton. He cleared his throat and nodded toward the line of silver. "Your maid gave you a bracelet?"

"Yes, although I begged her not to. The little imp probably knew what she was doing though. There is no possibility of her losing her position as long as I have this present."

"So it was a bribe?" An expensive bribe. The bracelet could be sold for months' worth of work.

"No. She isn't really an imp, and she knows her position is secure. It was a gift from her heart when I promoted her from maid-of-all-work to my lady's maid. Her mother had given it to her as a means to feed herself if she couldn't find a position here in England. Once she became my maid, she no longer feared going hungry and wanted me to have it." She stroked the chain softly with her thumb. "I wear it always, even when Mama claims the silver doesn't match the other jewelry she wants me to wear."

"A woman who despises emeralds but loves a chain of silver. Must you always surprise me?"

"Did I say I despise the emeralds? I love them. They were a present for Mama, given long before it would have seemed proper." Lady Mercy smiled. "I could never despise anything that represented my parents' love. If I showed them any disdain, it is only because they are difficult to dance in. That is their only flaw."

"A grave blemish indeed."

Lord Bryant was the only man foolish enough to remove Nicholas's gloves from the seat across from him in the cardroom after supper. "You don't mind, do you? You weren't saving this seat for any reason?"

Nicholas lifted his paper back up to reading level and grunted. "Only for some peace and quiet."

"Oh well." Lord Bryant scoffed. "I can provide that."

Nicholas raised an eyebrow at the baron but didn't bother refuting the man's unsubstantiated claim.

Lord Bryant was quiet for the space of one paragraph before his hand reached to the top of Nicholas's paper and pulled it down. "Tell me about this Lady Mercy you were dancing with. She seems lovely."

"Come to think of it, I *was* waiting for someone. Ottersby. He should be here any moment. Perhaps you could torment some other person in this room."

"I don't think I particularly like anyone else in this room."

"How fortunate for me."

Lord Bryant gave him a dashing grin, as if to say, *True. You are fortunate*, and then he leaned forward over the table. "But I did like Lady Mercy. I wasn't certain you did though. Or, rather, I was quite certain you did. I just wasn't certain the young lady would be able to deduce your intentions from your actions."

Nicholas sighed heavily. This was the last thing he needed. Advice from a rake. "I don't think there is another man in England who possesses your ability to make their interest so blatantly obvious to the women around them. Do not hold me to your standard on that. You and I are very different creatures."

Bryant cocked an eyebrow. "Are we?"

Nicholas went cold. His past indiscretions were public enough at the time, but since the death of his father, no one had dared mention them to him. "We are. I learned my lesson from the follies of my youth. You, however, learned a very different one."

Lord Bryant stilled, and his ever-present smile faltered. "Our lessons were very different ones, Harrington. It is no wonder they yielded dissimilar results."

Blast. He was correct. It was a simple matter to forget how serious Lord Bryant had been before his first wife had died. The person he'd become soon after her death was so much louder than the quiet young man Nicholas had known in his youth. Still, the fact that Lord Bryant's follies had started when he was older and wiser did not make the two men similar. Not at all.

"I don't claim to know what you went through in your past. Only I in mine."

"And I don't claim to know all that happened in yours, but I will say this: if you want to marry that woman, you are going to have to woo her, and I'm not certain you are doing that yet."

Nicholas took another quick glance around the room. "You speak too freely."

"And you don't speak freely enough."

"I never will, not when it could damage a young lady's reputation."

"Or your reputation."

"Yes. Unlike you, I need mine."

"Oh, I needed mine as well. But reputations aren't what we should be worried about damaging. It's the people behind the reputations who need to be protected."

Now the man was talking gibberish. Wasn't that the same thing? How could Nicholas protect a person without protecting their reputation? He should have put more than his gloves down on the chair to dissuade anyone from sitting near him. "Are you insinuating that I might take advantage of Lady Mercy's person?"

Lord Bryant scoffed. "Don't be ridiculous, Your Grace. I'm insinuating that you will ignore her person completely in order to pay homage to her reputation."

"Trust me. No part of Lady Mercy is at risk of being ignored. On the contrary. Which is why I must always be diligent in protecting her reputation. If I am not, I fear a repeat of the mistakes of my youth could damage both her person *and* her reputation. Not that it is any concern of yours."

"I do tend to concern myself a bit too much with matters of the heart. My wife would tell me to leave you in peace."

"I've always known your wife was an intelligent woman. Her only lack of judgment was marrying you."

"Now, that is something we can unequivocally agree on."

CHAPTER 11

THE DUKE OF HARRINGTON SENT flowers to Mercy the next morning, but this time, instead of an enormous bouquet, he sent only three delicate white roses with a note. Kate brought them to the breakfast table. After Papa read the duke's note, he smiled and handed it to her. Her eyes were still blurry from the late night of dancing, but the Duke of Harrington's script was clear and easy to read: *I may have overdone the flowers last time. My instinct tells me Lady Mercy will enjoy this simple bouquet more than the first. Or, at the very least, that she would appreciate both.*

His first bouquet had been stunning. She hadn't minded the mountain of flowers at all, and she adored the wildflowers in it. However, the three white roses were perfection, as if he had stood in the florist shop and handled each and every rose until he found only the most perfect ones.

She scoffed at the thought of a duke agonizing over his choice in a flower shop and handed the note to Mama. She'd been hovering closer and closer to her, in obvious hopes of getting a glimpse of His Grace's words. Mama snatched the note and read it like she'd never had any correspondence before.

Mercy ignored Mama's reaction to the note, instead inspecting the long stems and tightly coiled buds of the roses. The duke wouldn't have visited a florist, especially so early in the morning after a late night. More than likely, the florist always made certain a duke's roses were perfect. Still, for a duke, one would think the florist would send the largest and most impressive flowers. These were not only modest in size, but their blooms were still curled tightly together—rosebuds, waiting to bloom.

Was the Duke of Harrington being romantic?

For the first time since she had come out two Seasons ago, Mercy had no callers after the ball. And the duke's flowers were the only ones to arrive. It was as if the world had noticed His Grace's attentions, and now everyone, including some of her closest male friends, were waiting to see exactly what would happen.

Three days of quiet later, she woke to three roses blooming on her bedside table. The sight of them made her pull her coverlet up to her chest and sigh. They were just as beautiful as she had imagined they would be. When she joined Mama and Papa at breakfast, a note arrived from the duke.

He would be calling this afternoon.

First on her father and then her.

Mercy didn't get to examine his neat handwriting, as Papa had simply read it aloud. Mama made a sound not unlike a squealing pig, and Mercy snorted. "I'm sure it is nothing, Mama."

Papa tapped his fingers on the table, something he did when deep in thought. "It could be a proposal."

"Certainly not." The words were out of Mercy's mouth before Mama's second squeal ended. Since when did Mama squeal? "We have had almost no chance to speak or get to know each other. Why, it has been barely over two weeks since we were introduced."

"Sometimes that is how these things work," Mama said.

Any pleasant thoughts she had had about the Duke of Harrington when she saw those blossoming roses flew out the window. "Not with me, they don't."

"But perhaps with the Duke of Harrington they do." Papa met her gaze. "I believe his father's courtship of his mother was, indeed, short. And if I know anything about the duke, he respects and tries to live up to who his father was."

Mercy groaned. Papa wouldn't understand. He wasn't the kind of man who needed excitement in his life. Mercy turned her attention to Mama. "The man dances perfectly, not a step out of place, not a single movement missed."

Papa's forehead furrowed. "I should think that would recommend him."

"No." Mercy threw her hands above her head. "He makes no mistakes, but he has no soul for it. How can I marry a man who treats dancing like a formula to be memorized and mastered?"

"That would make him a better dancer than me."

"No, Papa, it doesn't, for at least you can enjoy dancing. There is no room for enjoyment in perfection." Papa didn't seem convinced. Rosalind would understand, but she wasn't here. Mercy tried to think of something, anything else, to say. Neither of her parents seemed appalled by the idea that a man she hardly knew might be coming to ask for her hand in marriage. And while his roses were beautiful, that did not make up for the fact that he knew nothing about her. "I cannot marry a man I have only spoken to a few times, no matter what his father did. Do you know if that marriage was even a happy one?"

Papa paused at that. "I do not."

Mercy raised her chin. "I won't settle for a marriage I'm not *certain* will be happy. And I definitely won't settle for a man who proposes without being in love with me."

"Oh, Mercy." Mama shook her head like she was speaking to a child. "You can *never* be certain you will be happy with someone. And you will never know them fully until you are married. Perhaps not even then."

"But you and Papa were different. You loved each other deeply when you married."

"That is true," Mama said. "But—"

"And Rosalind was practically mad over Richard."

Mama took a deep breath. "I did love your father, but that didn't mean I wasn't scared about what I was getting myself into. I knew happiness wasn't guaranteed simply because we loved each other."

"Why did you marry him, then?"

"Young lady . . ." Papa's eyes were furrowed, but his disapproval was playful.

Mama rose, stepped behind Papa's chair, and placed both of her hands on his shoulders, then kissed him on the top of his head. "That is easy to answer. As scared as I was, I couldn't imagine living my life without him."

Papa reached up and squeezed her hand. Normally, Mercy would be moved by such displays, but not this morning. Not when the life she had made for herself, as well as the future she had planned, were being threatened by a small scrap of thickly embossed paper. "Well, I can most certainly imagine my life without the duke. He only entered it a moment ago."

Papa handed her the note. Just as before, the handwriting was careful, straight, and without flourish. Even the way he wrote was proper and uninspiring. How could her parents be so blinded by the man's title that they didn't see how unsuitable he was for her? She needed more than straight lines and perfect flowers that blossomed exactly on schedule.

Papa cleared his throat. "So, if he asks for your hand, would you like me to say no?"

Mama sucked in a breath and looked as though she might faint, but a wave of relief washed over Mercy. Papa was Papa again. She reached across the table and grasped his hand. "I hardly care what you say to him. If I don't want to marry him, I will tell him myself. But thank you, Papa, for being willing."

Papa tipped his head to one side and squeezed her hand in return. "Of course. Your mother and I would like to see you settled down. But more importantly, we want you to be happy. We are excited about His Grace's interest in you. I know him to be a good man, he is proper to a fault and would never dream of doing you harm, and as much as your mother and I have talked about love and happiness in our marriage, goodness is at the root of all of those things."

She couldn't deny that. She had never heard a bad word said about the duke. And every interaction with him thus far had been decent and good. But even though she knew Papa was correct, goodness wasn't the easiest thing to get excited about. A man who didn't leave a blot or a smudge on his letters certainly was not the kind to seek a stolen moment during a party and pull her out of sight and kiss her. "I suppose we will simply have to find out what he has to say this afternoon."

The air in the house felt different all morning. If she didn't know better, she would say it was humming. Mama was in and out of Mercy's room while Kate pinned her hair and helped her dress. At first Mama had insisted Mercy wear the only short-sleeved, low-bodice afternoon dress she had, but then she changed her mind, and Mercy had to start the dressing process all over again.

Kate fastened the last button high on Mercy's neck, and Mama gave them both a nod. The deep-blue dress only had a bit of lace at each sleeve and covered nearly every inch of Mercy, but the cut and quality of the dress were masterful, with pieced diagonal fabric on both sides of her waist, creating a figure where she barely had one.

"You always look stunning in this dress." Mama nodded and put her fingers to her lips. "I'm only debating what necklace will look good over the high neck."

"None, Mama. It isn't as though we are going to a ball or the theater. Who wears large pieces of jewelry at home?"

"Typically, no one. But the Duke of Harrington isn't a typical visitor."

Mama unlocked the jewelry case she had brought. The three of them peered inside. The emeralds were obviously not correct. And while the pearls might work, she had already worn them. Truly, any necklace would look out of place. Kate tentatively pointed to a pair of earrings at the back of the box. The earrings were a perfect compromise of excess and class. Mercy had always loved wearing them. Grandfather had brought the stones home from a voyage to Russia. They were a unique stone of glossy yellow, found only in the Ural Mountains. The large stones were polished but still had some of their natural curves and edges, and when worn, they hung from her ears like two rough-shaped stars.

Mama nodded at Kate, and after the earrings were put into place, Mama finally left the room to finish her own preparations for the evening.

Kate laid rejected ribbons and trimmings neatly back into Mercy's dresser. Every few seconds, she would look up at Mercy as if she wanted to say something, but then she would wince and go back to her work.

"Do you need something, Kate?" Mercy asked.

"I hate to ask." Kate's voice was soft and careful, as if she were trying to cover her Irish accent. "I spoke to Mrs. Brooksby, but she said I should speak to Lady Driarwood, but I thought perhaps speaking to you first would be the best idea."

"Speaking to me about what?"

Kate dropped the last of the ribbons into the drawer and turned to Mercy completely. "I've a cousin—her ma and pa just died. The family is planning to send her to Canada in hopes that she can find work there."

Mercy stilled. To hear Kate, whom she saw every day speak of death so stoically, made her heart sputter. "Does she want to go to Canada?"

"What she wants is work. But, ma'am, she'd be going on a coffin ship. They're affordable, but not safe." Kate shuddered. "Bridget is good and strong. I know she is a hard worker. I thought perhaps your family could use another scullery maid."

Mercy's shoulders lifted. This, at least, was something she could do. The coffin ships were built to bring lumber from the New World and were never meant to be passenger ships, especially not to passengers who couldn't afford to bring enough food for the long ocean voyage. The thought of any family member of Kate's making such a journey made Mercy's stomach queasy. Mama would feel the same. "Of course we could use a scullery maid. I'll speak to Mama about it tonight."

Kate put her hands to her chest. "Truly?"

"Truly."

"You'll be employing half of Ireland if word gets out you are taking more servants than you need."

"Kate, I just told you we do *need* a scullery maid. And if your cousin is anything like you, well, then, we can't afford to pass her up."

After Kate left, Mercy lay on her bed and stared up at the ceiling. Everything seemed out of her control. Ireland, Mama and Papa, and now she had a duke to worry about. She wanted nothing more than to write to Rosalind. No, she wanted nothing more than for her sister to come and visit. She loved her brother-in-law, Richard, but he did have one extreme flaw: he lived in Northampton. And he couldn't live without Rosalind. Though not being able to live without Rosalind wasn't a flaw; their devotion to each other was a beacon of hope. Proof that somewhere out there Mercy had a Richard waiting for her.

She had never once thought that perhaps her Richard would be a duke. His visit had all of the whirlwind and excitement of Rosalind and Richard's romance, but none of the actual romance. If Mercy were going to fall madly in love with the man, shouldn't she feel a bit more . . . well, shouldn't she just *feel* a bit more of . . . *anything*?

Mercy sighed, pushed herself up with both hands, and went to her writing desk to start a letter. But before she could even begin to explain her situation to Rosalind, a knock sounded at the front door downstairs. Her pen wavered. She bit her lip and forced herself to continue. The duke wanted to speak with Papa first. Not her.

How long would their meeting take? And what in heaven's name would they be talking about? Papa would probably ask him to sit, and he would choose the large, leather chair across from Papa's desk. How many times had Mercy sat at that same chair and listened to Papa speak of his plans for the day or the month or the year? Now he would be discussing plans with one of the most powerful men of England, and those plans might include her.

No, not might. They did. The Duke of Harrington had plans for her. For them.

A blot of ink dropped onto her forgotten letter. She rubbed her forehead, then slowly and carefully put away her writing utensils. She couldn't write with the duke in her house. Her room was suddenly stuffy. She needed to escape, but she had no reason to rush downstairs.

But she also didn't have a pressing need to remain in her room. This was her home, after all. She could go where she wanted. Mercy tucked her unfinished letter into her desk and quietly padded across the room. The doorknob was cold in her hand, which made her pause. So many things could happen before she returned to this room. The conversation happening downstairs could change the course of her life forever. When she finally stopped studying the wood grain in front of her and yanked the door open, the knob had warmed to her body temperature.

Papa's study was at the bottom of the stairs on the left, but as soon as her foot touched the landing, she turned right. It wasn't ladylike to listen at doors. She would simply sit and wait in the drawing room.

She opened the door, but her thoughts and feet skidded to a halt just as she was about to step in. Hadn't she first met the Duke of Harrington outside of a door? He'd been listening to the conversation happening in the cardroom before she'd arrived. If the mighty Duke of Harrington could listen at doors, then why couldn't she?

She placed her hand against the door casing and eyed the thick, dark wood door to Papa's study. She shouldn't eavesdrop. She wouldn't. With a door like that, even if she wanted to listen in, she would be lucky to catch anything more than a murmur. But since that was the case, it wouldn't hurt to simply stand nearby. If she happened to overhear a word or two, well, then, it would be an accident.

Besides, the drawing room wasn't much better than her room. Either way, she would be stuck waiting. She stepped toward the study, but just as she did, the door cracked open. Mercy jumped backward and dashed inside the drawing room. She shook her head and took a deep breath as her heart pounded in her ears. Calm . . . she must be calm. This was her home. She could be wherever she wanted to be. She scurried over to the small chess table that sat on one side of the fireplace and stood behind one of the chairs. A moment later, the door opened, and Mrs. Brooksby led in the Duke of Harrington.

Mrs. Brooksby made a small noise at the sight of Mercy. The duke furrowed his brows in confusion.

Mercy raised her eyebrows in what was certain to be a terrible impression of surprise. "Oh, hello," she said in a voice that was anything but convincing. "I was . . . here . . . um . . . in-inspecting the table." She made an equally bad impression of someone running a finger on top of a table to search for dust. Never, in all of Mercy's lifetime had she critiqued the staff's work. Still, the Duke of Harrington didn't know that.

Mrs. Brooksby did, but she had already packed away her surprise, and Mercy's strange behavior went blessedly ignored. "Shall I have His Grace wait in the small parlor?"

"No, no." Mercy made a show of rubbing her finger and thumb together as if she might feel dust between them, then she strode straight toward the door. "I will go fetch Mama and return in a moment."

The only problem with leaving the room was that the Duke of Harrington still stood just outside the doorway. She would have to pass within a few inches of him. Mercy kept her head down and marched forward, but when she stepped through the doorway, her eyes shot up to his for the briefest of moments. His eyes roamed her face, asking questions she didn't have the answers to; she didn't even know what the questions were. She paused her death march and gave him a quick bob, which he answered with a slow bow of his head. He was so proper, so commanding and rigid but—also— so blasted good-looking. Michelangelo should carve this man and call the resulting piece *Untouchable*.

He looked away first and followed Mrs. Brooksby's outstretched arm into the drawing room. Mrs. Brooksby shut the door behind him and raised an eyebrow at Mercy. What? Mercy wasn't allowed to inspect the table in the drawing room? Simply because she had never done so before? Mercy grimaced. It *was* strange. But then again, *none* of them were used to a duke coming to visit. Mrs. Brooksby couldn't possibly feel as calm and collected as she seemed. Mercy threw a smile and a shrug at Mrs. Brooksby before dashing up the stairs to find Mama.

Mercy muttered to herself as she walked down the corridor to Mama's room. What had she been thinking? Why hadn't she simply stayed in her room? And why the drawing room? Of all the places she could have gone, that was the worst. The look on His Grace's face was unreadable. It wasn't as though she had garnered any more information by snooping around downstairs. She knocked halfheartedly on Mama's door, then opened it without waiting for an answer. Mama stood in front of the mirror, and Papa sat on the bed. He jumped up when she walked in the room.

"Where were you?" Papa asked.

"I was downstairs."

"The duke is here." Papa's hands were clenched together, his eyes wide.

"I know." She didn't mention that she had seen him. "What does he want?"

Papa leaned forward, his mouth almost a smile, but a cautious one, as if he wasn't certain what Mercy would think of his answer. "He asked to court you." Caution lost its battle to excitement, and Papa grinned. "The Duke of Harrington has come here to court you."

Courtship.

Of course he was here to ask about courting. Why hadn't she thought of that? Her mind had jumped immediately to marriage, but of course he would court her first. It would be preposterous to ask for her hand in marriage so soon. But his determination in their few meetings had her skipping logical steps. Still . . . being courted by a duke would change everything. Would her regular dance partners dare to ask her to dance? Would other high-ranking men she had no interest in, whom she had managed to avoid thus far, seek her out? That was what had happened to Penelope when Lord Bryant had started showing marked attention in her. "What did you say to him?"

Papa schooled his features, his smile lines receding back into his face. "I said I would ask you."

Mercy closed her eyes and took a deep breath. Mama and Papa hadn't planned her whole life without her, then. They were still the kind of parents who had allowed Rosalind to marry the man she had found most desirable, and they would do the same for her. Despite feeling as though her life was spiraling out of control since her conversation with the Duke of Harrington outside the cardroom, she would still have a choice in the matter.

She opened her eyes to find Mama standing directly in front of her, her hands fidgeting with the large opal ring on her finger. "You said you wanted to get to know His Grace better. Courtship is the perfect opportunity to do so."

Mercy was slow to answer. "I suppose that's true."

"Of course it is true," Papa answered. "And he was extremely respectful when I spoke to him. If it were only his title recommending him, we might not be quite so hopeful. But it isn't only his title. He is an upstanding young man, and I'm certain I haven't met his equal."

He was upstanding. That was the problem with being courted by such a perfect suitor. She could find no fault in him, and neither could her parents. But she hadn't ever imagined marrying someone simply because there wasn't a better candidate. He was untouchable, and it just so happened that Mercy very much wanted to feel free to touch the man she would marry.

"I hate to leave His Grace waiting downstairs. I'm certain he would like to hear your answer sooner rather than later." Papa stepped toward the door. "Do you have an answer for him?"

Mercy swallowed. It was just courtship. She had been pursued by several men in the past; none of those experiences had amounted to anything serious. She had always been a distracted companion. Never willing to give only one man the attention he craved. But courtship with a duke would be different—other men would step aside. For the first time since her coming-out, she could be facing a decided lack of dance partners.

But her parents' eyes said everything. They'd given her a choice, but they weren't impartial in the matter. The duke was an opportunity not to take lightly. Why couldn't Rosalind be here? Perhaps the duke could be exciting, and perhaps she could fall in love with him. Stranger things had happened. He was extremely good-looking, better looking even than Richard. But his eyes didn't spark like Richard's. Harrington's eyes were shuttered, as if he didn't actually want Mercy to come to know him. Still, her parents were right about courtship. Mercy wouldn't be able to get to know the man behind those shuttered eyes unless the two of them spent more time together.

Mercy allowed herself one long steady breath, and then she met Papa's eyes. "My answer will be yes."

The relief on her parents' faces almost made up for the unrest in her stomach.

Mercy followed her parents downstairs and into the drawing room. The Duke of Harrington was standing in front of the fireplace, and he turned as they entered. His eyes went to her parents for the briefest moment, and then to her. For the first time since she met him, he seemed unsure. He stepped forward, then stopped, put his hands behind his back, and stilled. The room felt heavy, as if everyone was waiting on word from her. She waited as well. Waited for him to turn to look back at Papa for his approval, but he didn't. Harrington looked only at her. And he looked . . . worried.

He was the most eligible man in London, but he wasn't certain of her answer. And that uncertainty seemed to be burning him from the inside. "Did your father explain why I came?" His voice was quiet and hesitant. Not assuming and bold. He could have been assuming—most people in his position would be.

Mercy nodded. "Yes."

The Duke of Harrington tipped his head to one side and looked as though he would like to step forward again but didn't. "Yes, he told you? Or yes . . ." He paused as if hesitant how to finish the sentence.

She smiled. This was a side of the duke she hadn't seen before. He might not quite be touchable, but with that look on his face, he was, at the very least, approachable. It was a start. "Yes, to both."

The Duke of Harrington's shoulders relaxed, and a slow, boyish grin arose on his face. "Thank you."

The Duke of Harrington with a grin was very different from the Duke of Harrington without one. Whatever heaviness was in the room lifted. He was blazing with that grin, actually. How had she even thought to compare his looks to Richard's? It was unfair on an epic scale. She blinked slowly and wished for a chair to lean against. What exactly had she gotten herself into?

Mama stepped toward Harrington and motioned to the chess table Mercy had been pretending to inspect earlier. "Would you like to stay and play cards or chess with Mercy? Lord Driarwood and I have some reading to do, but we could keep you company."

His grin was still there, distracting her. Making her feel like all he had to do was smile at her and she would be the one pulling him around corners. He nodded. "I should like that very much."

The duke pulled out one of the chairs for Mercy, and she sat, his arm just missing her shoulder. He waited for Mama to take a seat in one of the club chairs near the bookshelf on the opposite side of the room, and then he came around to the other side of the table and sat across from Mercy.

It was silent for a moment, and Papa coughed. An obvious hint to Mercy to start some kind of conversation. But Mercy was still processing the strange sensations fluttering through her. One little smile shouldn't change everything. She needed to keep her wits about her. And she needed to think of something to say, or this courtship would be over before it even started. "Thank goodness I inspected this table earlier . . ." She pursed her lips together. That was not at all the right way to start a conversation. The duke simply tipped his head to one side in curiosity. She shook her head and tried again. "What type of cards do you prefer?" she finally asked. "Piquet?" The dark and light inlaid squares on the table inspired her. "Or we could play chess."

Brilliant speech. They would be married in no time at all. He wouldn't be able to keep his hands off such a conversationalist.

But the duke didn't seem to mind her uninspired suggestions. "Something tells me you would beat me at both."

She raised an eyebrow and smiled. "Unless you are quite inept, you're wrong."

"You aren't skilled at games?"

"I play, but in general, I would rather be moving about. My sister was always so much better at cards and chess than I was. I gave up on them quite early."

Harrington leaned forward, as if he had a secret. "Because you like to win?"

"Because I hate to lose."

He laughed, and his laugh was not helping Mercy remember why she wasn't at all certain about this courtship. His laugh made his grin look amateur. "Well, we have that in common. Although, I'm not certain I've ever met a person who liked to lose."

Mercy leaned forward. "So, our commonalities can be categorized by things that are extremely ordinary. Do you prefer a cold room or a comfortable one?"

"A comfortable one."

"And would you rather your inkpot be full or empty?"

"Full."

"No wonder you asked to court me." Mercy flicked an imaginary piece of lint of her hand. "We are practically the same person."

"If that were the case, we would be a very dull pair indeed. Asking to court you had nothing to do with the fact that we both hate to lose at cards or chess."

"It didn't?"

"No. You have other qualities that drew me to you."

First his grin, then his laugh, and now . . . was he flirting? Mercy tipped her head to the side. "What other qualities?"

The duke's eyes traced her face, then slid down her neck and landed on the spot where Mama's emeralds had sat during their first meeting. Had Mama been right? Was it the jewelry that had caught the duke's eye?

He blinked and jerked his gaze back to hers. Any trace of his earlier smile was gone. He'd schooled his face into bland propriety. "I think you and I can both agree that our stations in life are quite compatible. Your family is well respected, and your father has similar political leanings. I've worked tirelessly to try to bring aid to Ireland, and I simply don't have the kind of sway my father had. I think having a . . ." He paused as if not certain what he was about to say was appropriate. "An ally such as yourself would help improve my reputation in the House of Lords."

Whatever mirth Mercy had felt at the duke's grin left her. He wanted her to help him politically? Is that why he'd been looking for a wife? Not that he could even bring himself to say the word. Did he think he would be obligated to marry her if he spoke of marriage in such clear terms? For heaven's sake, did he even like her at all?

If the duke noticed her distress, he didn't show it. Instead, he looked down at the chess table. "Perhaps we can both get better at chess." His Grace raised his eyes, his thick lashes making him appear younger than he was. "Together."

"Today?" Mercy asked, still struggling to come to grips with the fact that the only reason he was here was because of her family's position in Society.

"Not only today. I imagine I will be here often now. We can work on improving regularly."

Weeks of playing chess and drinking tea with the duke flashed before her eyes. Definitely not the most romantic of courtships. She grimaced. "I suppose we can do that. But I think you are going to trounce me in chess."

He raised an eyebrow. "Why?"

"Because you don't strike me as the type of person to give up as easily. I, on the other hand, tend to give up as soon as trouble arises."

"How do you ever win like that?"

"As I told you, it isn't that I like to win; I simply I hate to lose. And I cannot lose if I stop playing the game." She shrugged and pulled out the box of chess pieces stored under the table. She opened it and motioned for the duke to start setting up his side of the table. "Thus, the giving up easily."

The duke eyed her carefully. "I do like to set a course and stay steady on it. And now that I know you don't like trouble, I will try to not to give you any." He spoke of chess, but certainly not only about chess. He'd set out on a course when he'd met with Father earlier, and now he was going to use her words to make even more certain their courtship was as uneventful as possible. This courtship was a mistake. She'd been blinded by the duke's good looks and her parents' words of encouragement, but there was no possible way she was going to fall in love with the man in front of her while they spent several weeks playing chess.

But it was too late now. Mercy started laying out her pawns. She would play chess with him, and then hopefully he would leave.

"Did you know that the first time I saw you was not at the Stafford ball?" The duke's voice was low.

Mercy had a hand on her queen and was about to set it into position. She paused. "What?"

"I saw you once before. Outside of Donald Young's funeral."

Mercy's heart went as still as her hand. She'd only ever talked about Donald with Rosalind. "You knew Donald?" How would Donald have known the duke? Her family was by far the best connection the Young family had, at least as far as she knew.

"I did." His eyes softened. "He was a very dear friend. How well did you know him?"

"I . . ." Oh dear. This was one of the most embarrassing chapters of her life. She'd never met Donald, but she had set him up as the most likely of men to run off with her. "I didn't. His brother, Richard, is married to my sister."

The duke nodded as if he had known. "You were . . . inconsolable. But I don't remember Donald mentioning you."

She had been heartbroken. At fourteen, she had known that when she and Donald met, the two of them would have a whirlwind romance just as her sister had had. It was the ridiculous fancy of a young mind. She would have seemed like a child to Donald, if he had made it home. Still, Donald, despite being more fantasy than reality, had been an important part of her childhood, and she wouldn't hide it. "I was fairly certain I was going to marry him."

The duke made a choking sound in his throat and knocked the rook he had been laying out on its side. "I thought you hadn't ever met him."

"Oh, I hadn't. But he was a soldier—sure to be handsome like his brother—and I just knew when we did meet, it would be fire and torchwood for the two of us."

The Duke of Harrington muttered something that sounded a lot like *lucky devil.*

"What was that?" Mercy asked, wide-eyed, as if she hadn't heard.

"Donald was one lucky devil, and he didn't even know it."

"Yes, very lucky. All until that bullet—" Mercy stopped. The duke's face had gone pale. Donald had been a fantasy for her, but he had been very real to the man sitting in front of her and to Richard. "Your Grace, I'm sorry."

The duke shook head as if to say it was nothing, but she knew better. "I'm all right. And I'm sorry for your loss. Donald would've been a much better man for you."

Mercy scoffed. "I'm not quite as delusional as I was at fourteen. He would have seen me as a child."

"I didn't. It was as if I saw a bit of your soul that day."

"You saw my soul?" Mercy had been a mess, a deluded young woman who had built up fantasies around a man whom she had never laid eyes on. "I'm afraid my soul was very naive."

"It was beautiful. And I'm glad Donald had someone to cry for him like that. Even if the two of you never met." The duke set up his last chess piece, and without thinking, Mercy placed her hand over his.

There was more to his interest in her than simply that one strange meeting in the corridor. He'd seen her once years ago and still remembered her. It wasn't the same as being whisked away for stolen kisses, but it was something more than political aspirations, at least. Harrington went still. All the connection of the past few minutes dissolved in an instant. His eyes went to hers, then to her parents at the other side of the room, and he slowly withdrew his hand.

Any warmth Mercy had felt was gone. Didn't he want her to touch him?

The duke cleared his throat and motioned for her to make the first move. As if she could concentrate on chess after what had just happened. How could the man want to court her but not be willing to let her touch him? She blinked a few times and picked up a random pawn, moving it forward two spaces.

The Duke of Harrington made a similar move.

Then he leaned forward, his hands folded into his lap. "I want you to know I take this courtship very seriously."

She almost laughed, but he might not take that laughter well. However, there was absolutely nothing surprising about the duke taking anything seriously. "I know."

His words were low and steady. "I will always treat you with respect."

Mercy did chuckle at that one. She couldn't imagine the stiff duke treating her with anything *but* respect. "I would be shocked if you didn't."

And in that moment, she knew what her future would look like if she didn't do something to change it. The Duke of Harrington would spend the next month or two playing chess with her and dancing sterile but faultless polkas and waltzes with her at balls. They would have conversations that were interesting enough for him to think the courtship was going swimmingly, and then when whatever time he determined was the proper amount to spend courting was accomplished, he would propose. Just as he had told her, he set a course and stuck with it. Everything would be orderly and controlled, and she would have no idea if she had left another life, a better life, with a man she hadn't met yet—but who would bring her excitement instead of comfort and control—behind her, unlived.

The Duke of Harrington was dashing and ranked above anyone but royalty. He was hers for the taking—he had made that abundantly clear. His mind had connected the dots from introduction to courtship to marriage in one straight, unwavering line. He didn't expect anything to change that course.

And it was the least romantic thing she had ever heard.

Where was his passion? Where was his zest for life . . . for her? Why didn't he want to touch her?

As much as she admired the duke, she couldn't live the rest of her life in such controlled circumstances. She didn't need a courtship period to under-stand that. She shouldn't have listened to Mama and Papa. They were too enamored of his title to allow her to snub him or even not smile at him enough. It would break their hearts if she simply told him she was breaking off the courtship.

But she needed out of the courtship somehow. Social connections aside, Mercy was not the right woman for the duke.

He took one of her bishops. She should have seen that coming, even as bad as she was at chess. He smiled at her as he tucked away her piece, and she was struck again by how young and handsome he was when he wasn't so focused on being proper. Almost any other woman would be in love with him for his eyelashes alone. Why did the man have to choose her?

The Duke of Harrington should have found a more expedient woman for his plans.

Mercy's hand was midair reaching for her rook when the idea came to her.

It was a terrible idea.

But a terrible idea with the best of intentions. She quickly reached for the rook and slid it forward three spaces, completely unaware of whether the motion was strategic or not. Based on the way the duke raised his eyebrow, it was not.

But she didn't care. Mercy was already several steps ahead of him, just not on the chessboard.

There were plenty of women who would be a perfect match for the duke. Dozens with equal or better social standing than Mercy. The duke had made it painfully obvious he didn't entertain any deep feelings toward Mercy. She had simply been the best fit for his purposes on the night he'd decided marriage could help his political causes. It would be an easy matter to have him find another women he liked better than her.

Mercy would merely have to arrange it.

She started paying attention to her pieces after that. The excitement of having a plan to remove herself from this courtship adding fire to her movements. She and the Duke of Harrington were going to play a game, but not a game of chess. The most dangerous game of all: a game of courtship. And if she played it correctly, she might not win, but hopefully, neither of them would lose.

CHAPTER 12

NICHOLAS PACED IN FRONT OF Ottersby's desk. Patience was late, a fact that her extremely punctual husband seemed to take in stride. Ottersby was dressed impeccably, and although Nicholas had brought the carriage so they could ride to the Bensons' ball together, he wasn't certain when they were actually going to leave.

"I'm certain Patience will be down shortly," Ottersby said, but he pulled out a second sheet of paper and began taking notes on something he was reading in the paper.

"Are you?"

"Well, perhaps not certain, but hopeful."

Nicholas grunted, certain that was wishful thinking on Ottersby's part.

Ottersby jotted something down, then looked up. "How is the courtship with Lady Mercy progressing?"

"I don't know." He had been to her home twice since asking to court her. Usually they played chess, although neither of them seemed very interested it. But it did give them time to talk about their likes and dislikes, as well as what things were most important to them. Lady Mercy always gave him answers that intrigued him. She disliked clams and any dress fabric with too much yellow in it. His answers felt stilted and rehearsed compared to hers. They'd talked of his time in the military when he'd gotten to know Donald. Fortunately, she never asked why the only son of a duke had been in the military at all. "I enjoy her company. Perhaps too much."

Ottersby stopped writing and raised his head. "You can't like the woman you want to marry too much. Would you prefer that you didn't enjoy her company at all?"

Of course he wouldn't prefer that. He rubbed his face. "I just feel so . . . so uncertain. I saw this all going very differently."

"More like a business transaction?"

"Yes and no."

Ottersby cleaned his pen. "Which part yes and which part no?"

"Discussions with her father, they go as planned. He makes sense to me. I tell him I want to court his daughter, and he gives me a blessing along with a missive to decide quickly if she is the woman I want to marry. I understand his concern about long courtships and engagements, and I agree with him. However, Lady Mercy is harder to understand. I know she is capable of strong attachment. But . . ."

"She isn't attached to you," Ottersby said it as if it were painfully obvious.

"I don't think so, no."

"And how does she feel about the courtship?"

"She has agreed to it."

Ottersby raised an eyebrow. "It seems as though you don't want a business transaction at all. You want more."

"I don't think I know how to do *more*." Nicholas grimaced. He never considered himself a Casanova, but in general, women had been flattered to have his attention. Lady Mercy seemed . . . well . . . as if she were biding her time until he gave up on her.

Ottersby nodded as if he understood all too well. "Because in a business transaction you won't get hurt?"

It wasn't himself he was worried about hurting. "I don't care about being hurt. Heaven knows I've lived a life well protected while others faced harm." Donald could have attested to that. "I don't want her to be hurt, though."

"And you think you might hurt her by . . ." Ottersby put a hand out, palm up, waiting for Nicholas to fill in the last word.

Holding her too close in public, running a hand down her back while they danced, touching her hair, counting her freckles, forgetting himself completely and pulling her into an abandoned corridor and instead of speaking like they had the first time they'd found themselves in that situation, kissing her senseless. "Damaging her reputation," Nicholas said.

"And do you plan on damaging her reputation?"

"Of course not. What kind of man do you think I am? I've been nothing but proper with her."

"And you assume that by following all of Society's rules, you will be protecting her?"

"Isn't that why they exist?"

"Honestly, I don't know why half of them exist, but I suppose in this case, yes, they should allow Lady Mercy a protection from gossip and the like."

"And from me."

Ottersby laughed. "From you? No one needs protection from you. If you are this careful about protecting her, you may lose her." Ottersby stood up and strode around his desk. He took Nicholas by both shoulders. "Lady Mercy reminds me a bit of Patience, and if I had courted her like you are courting Lady Mercy, I don't think she would have given me the time of day."

"No one courts the way you and Patience did. Lady Mercy will not be applying to be a maid in my household anytime soon. And I don't know that it would have mattered with you and Patience. You should have seen how she went crazy over your long, detailed lists." Nicholas shook his head. Chess was a delight in comparison. "I simply know myself well, Ottersby. And the things that come to my mind sometimes . . ." The splash of freckles along the top of Lady Mercy's collarbone, the way her thin bracelet draped across the flesh of her wrist when she pushed it up to move a chess piece. The curve of her neck as it melted into a shoulder. "I don't want to lose control."

Ottersby's eyes flashed to his desk, and a half smile arose on his lips. Nicholas did not want to know what he was thinking. He had trusted Ottersby had been a perfect gentleman while Patience had lived with Nicholas. He didn't want to start doubting him now. It was too late, anyway. They were happily married.

"Passion can be a beautiful thing, Harrington. It is just as much a part of a relationship as respect and admiration."

"I'm not a complete dunce. I know that." He wanted that, but not until he and Mercy were engaged, at least, and she knew he was not taking advantage of her. If, at the end of all this, she decided to walk away, he wouldn't have anything tarnishing her name.

"Then perhaps at the Bensons' ball you could show her—at least a little bit—that you struggle to keep your hands off her."

"I don't struggle—" Nicholas started, but at the sight of Ottersby's raised eyebrow, he stopped. He did, and they both knew it.

Patience dashed into the room, a flurry of smiles and breathless excitement. "Shall we?"

Ottersby stood, and in a show of supreme superiority, or perhaps simply habit, he took his wife's arm in his and kissed her temple. "We shall."

CHAPTER 13

MERCY HAD TOLD EXACTLY NO one of the courtship between her and the Duke of Harrington, and yet, the moment she set foot into the Bensons' ball, she knew word had spread. The room quieted as she entered, and while she and Mama walked toward a group of Mama's friends, crowds seemed to part to make way for them.

"Mama, who did you tell about the courtship?"

"Almost no one." Mama made a noise in her throat as if something was stuck there. "Mrs. Jenkins was over for tea, and I might have said something."

"Mrs. Jenkins? No wonder everyone is looking at us." What started as silence was becoming a low murmur of whispers. Anyone who hadn't heard the news was certainly being informed of it now. They reached Mrs. Benson and Lady Chatsworth. Typically, they would acknowledge Mama first, but both of them gave Mercy a quick nod and smile before turning to Mama.

"The duke and his family haven't arrived," Mrs. Benson said, "but we heard they were coming."

There was no need to be specific about which duke they were speaking of. Mama simply nodded, and the two women regaled her with questions.

After a few minutes without being addressed, Mercy let her eyes wander. Mr. Beauford was across the room already dancing, and she didn't manage to catch his eye. A few other men who typically asked for her to save them a dance stood about the room, but none of them looked her way. Not a single one of them.

This was not an accident.

Blast. The courtship was already taking effect. By now she would have already been engaged for several dances, but it looked like instead, she was to stand and speak to Mama and her friends while the rest of the room enjoyed themselves.

If no men would dance with her, she might as well find some of her own friends to speak to. Penelope had sent a card last night to say that she and her husband, Lord Yolten, had finally arrived back in Town and that they would be at the ball. Mercy searched the room, but she didn't see her either.

She spent the next half hour listening to Mama and the other women speak about lace patterns and speculate about what would be served for supper. She tried to catch Mr. Beauford's eye, but he never looked in her direction, a feat that could only have been accomplished on purpose. Mercy nearly asked Mrs. Benson to dance with her when a polka started playing but decided against it. Mrs. Benson wasn't the most graceful woman while walking; dancing with her might not have been much better than listening to her talk about which butcher had the best steaks.

At long last, Mercy spotted Penelope. She'd just finished dancing and was headed toward the punch table. Mercy asked permission to join her and excused herself from Mama and her friends.

As soon as Penelope saw Mercy, her eyes widened, and she stepped away from her husband, whispering, "I'll find you later." Penelope grabbed Mercy by the elbow and steered her to a quiet corner of the room.

"I'm in the country for three weeks and look what happens. What is this I hear about you and the Duke of Harrington?" Penelope was never one to mince words. "I didn't realize the two of you were acquainted. You've never once mentioned him to me."

"I haven't known him long."

"Long enough, apparently."

"No." Mercy tried not to grimace, but the combination of keeping her voice down and the need to make Penelope understand exactly how confused she was by the whole situation had her face scrunched like she'd eaten underripe persimmons. "I don't know him very well. Do you?"

"Not at all. I only know *of* him."

"He is courting me, yet that is how I feel about him as well. That I only know *of* him."

Penelope's face formed an adorable pout. "This isn't an exciting development, then? I was hoping a man had finally turned your head."

"More like barged into me while I was caught unaware."

"But he is a duke."

"Oh, trust me, that is the one thing I know for certain about him."

"And a handsome one at that."

"Yes, I am aware. But—"

"But what?"

"We aren't in love. Not even a little bit. I feel like he met me, decided I would be a suitable wife, then proceeded on a course to make me thus without even asking what I thought about the whole situation."

"How *do* you feel about the situation?"

"Only that it is very rushed. And I am not used to being rushed. I always thought my situation would be like my sister's, with all the time in the world to find a man who suited *my* liking. Suddenly that option has been ripped away from me, simply because he is a duke."

Penelope tipped her head, as if weighing whether or not this was a justifiable concern. Mercy rubbed her temples. If even her good friend considered his title enough to recommend him, she was doomed. How would she ever get out of this situation?

"Are you quite certain you don't like him?"

"I don't dislike him. But I am quite certain we feel almost nothing for each other. It feels so arranged. So . . . unlike me. And so very like him."

"And you feel lost?"

As soon as the words were out of Penelope's mouth, tears threatened in Mercy's eyes. Yes. She was lost. She had struggled to put a word to what was happening to her, but gone was the Mercy who made her own choices. Gone was the carefree woman who would happily wait as long as it took to find a man who made her feel adored. And gone was the daughter who had complete confidence in her parents' desire to always do what would make Mercy most happy. She didn't even have dance partners anymore. "Yes." The word came out strangled. "I feel very lost."

Penelope immediately grabbed both of her shoulders and enveloped her in her arms. "I'm sorry." She rubbed Mercy's back. "We cannot lose you. You are one of the very best people in the whole of creation. If you want to fight it, we will fight it."

Mercy laughed. Fight? How did one fight against something that made everyone else in the world happy? Still, she was going to try. "I do have one idea, but it is, um . . . unusual."

"There is always a way. I got my Yolty, didn't I?"

"Yes, after a brief stint with Lord Bryant." Mercy had never understood how Penelope had fallen under the charming baron's spell.

Penelope jerked away from her. "Lord Bryant, of course, perhaps he could—" Then her face dropped, and her lips pursed together. "No, he is married now. And to Diana Barton, that lucky duck."

Mercy didn't know if Penelope was referring to Diana Barton or Lord Bryant when she made the comment, and she didn't dare press the issue. Lord Yolten and Penelope were one of her favorite couples. They had the kind of relationship that, like her parents' and sister's, gave her hope. Mercy had assumed her friend's brief time with Lord Bryant had been completely forgotten, but perhaps not.

"I don't see how Lord Bryant could have helped me with anything."

"Oh, no. He couldn't. I just—well . . . it doesn't matter now. We will think of something. Have you had any ideas of how you might extricate yourself from the situation? Could you simply tell him you aren't interested?"

"I could. I've thought about it. However, it isn't as though he has asked to marry me. And when I spoke to my parents about it, they rightly told me I hadn't given him much of a chance yet. But—"

"You want something more," Penelope finished. "And you should. I can't imagine my life with anyone else but Yolty." Penelope shuddered. "And if the duke isn't that for you, he isn't. You can't force it."

Couldn't imagine her life without him. Exactly like her parents. "I have a good family and a dowry large enough to tempt anyone. There is no reason I should settle, simply because the man is a duke."

Penelope smiled and then laughed. "We are quite the pair, you and I. What are we going to do?"

We. Such a small word, and yet suddenly her world was brighter. "I was thinking . . ."

Penelope leaned forward. "Yes?"

"Well, perhaps if he met someone else. He doesn't seem overly particular about who he marries. If we could push him in someone's direction . . . someone who wouldn't mind marriage being more of a transaction . . . then, if my parents could see his interest, I would be able to break the courtship without feeling like I have disappointed them."

"I didn't think your parents were the type to push you into a loveless marriage."

"They aren't. But, well, he *is* a duke."

Penelope nodded again. Mercy's life would be much simpler if she shared the same sentiment as most of London.

"So we need to find a match for the Duke of Harrington."

"Other than the woman having an influential position in Society, he isn't particular. He chose me without much of a thought."

Penelope looked at her as if she had said something ridiculous, but then shrugged. "What are his likes and dislikes?"

Mercy thought long and hard about the question. She had spent several afternoons and evenings with him; she should know something about him. "I think he dislikes singing and chess. He saw me crying once, years ago, and I think that may have left an impression on him. Mama thinks he is impressed by my jewelry, but I'm pretty sure that isn't the case."

"What do you mean?"

"The night I first met him, I was wearing the family emeralds. Mama thinks that is why he noticed me."

"Why do you disagree?"

"He's never mentioned my more elaborate necklaces or earrings. In fact, the only piece of jewelry he has ever commented on was Kate's silver bracelet." Mercy paused. "And Mama didn't know that he and I had had a conversation alone in the corridor that night."

Penelope's eyebrows rose.

"What were you doing alone in a corridor with a duke?"

"I didn't know he was a duke then. He was listening in at the cardroom, and I happened to come up behind him."

"What did you say to him?"

"Nothing of consequence. I didn't know who he was, and he didn't know who I was. The men inside the cardroom were talking about him finally looking for a bride. He turned and looked at me, and I suppose that was it. He needed a bride, and I walked into that corridor at exactly the wrong moment."

"Or the right one," Penelope murmured under her breath. Mercy narrowed one eye at her, and Penelope threw her hands up. "All right. I will ignore the obvious romance of that moment and help you with your quest."

"I thought, perhaps, getting him alone in a corridor with a different woman might work."

Penelope nodded. "Are you certain he has no interest in you personally?"

"Nothing that can be too enduring. He'll forget about me very quickly."

Again, Penelope gave her that look, as if she were saying something improbable. But Penelope didn't know the duke like she did. His feelings didn't run deep. He felt the need to get married, and she was a convenient match. There was nothing more to it than that. They simply needed to find him either a more convenient woman or, perhaps even better, someone for him to actually fall in love with.

"All right." Penelope nodded and looked toward the crowded ballroom. "For tonight, we shall simply keep our eyes open. Look for someone who catches his eye more than anyone else. We need to make a list of possible candidates and work through them to find the best match for him. Then you will be free, and you can go back to waiting for your Prince Charming."

"I'm not waiting around for a prince."

"Maybe not." Penelope laughed. "But if a duke wasn't good enough for you, who else is there?"

"A good man who loves me. That is all I have ever wanted. It is that or nothing at all."

"Good for you." Penelope winked at her. "Now let's get to work."

Mercy spotted Mama near a window with another group of her friends. "I should return to Mama."

Penelope nodded. "I'll talk to Yolty. He is certain to have some ideas." Mercy had no doubt that Penelope would tell her husband at least a portion of their plans, and as foolhardy as those plans may be, he wouldn't stop them. Mercy had seen him go along with much worse for his wife's sake. Penelope gave her a quick embrace, and they parted ways.

Halfway to Mama, Lady Bryant stepped out of a group of gruff-looking men and reached for her arm. "Are you a friend of Lady Yolten's?"

Mercy stopped dead in her tracks. Lady Bryant's dark hair and impeccable dress alone would be enough to make her stand out in a ballroom, but the fact that she owned a railway company truly set her apart.

That and the fact that she had been interesting enough to make Lord Bryant finally tie the knot. But Lord Bryant had had a short, but almost scandalous, flirtation with Penelope before either of them were married. Was she about to see a darker side of the beauty in front of her?

Still, she wouldn't deny knowing her best friend. "Yes, she is a dear friend."

Lady Bryant gave her a broad smile. "She is lovely, isn't she?"

Mercy fought the urge to rub her eyes in disbelief. It appeared that Lady Bryant was a kinder woman than Mercy would ever be.

Lord Bryant came up behind his wife. "Did you finally get rid of all the stodgy businessmen so you can pay some attention to me?" he said with a pout. Most of those businessmen were right behind him, and well within earshot. "And were you speaking of Lady Yolten? She is one of my favorite women of the *ton*. Top fifteen, easily." He gave Mercy a wink.

Heavens. Top fifteen? Did he rank every woman in London?

Lady Bryant shook her head and clicked her tongue. "Everton, stop. You will scare poor Lady Mercy away." Lady Bryant turned toward Mercy with a smile. "And I would like to get to know her better."

Lord Bryant glanced about the room. "It seems most of London is hoping to get to know her better." He smiled at her, and there was no flirtation behind it. The genuine camaraderie seemed foreign to his face and yet also very authentic. "I hope you are well prepared to be the most envied woman in London."

Because of a stiff duke's attentions? She would rather not be envied for that. "Thus far, all I have gained is a sad lack of dance partners."

Lord Bryant leaned toward his wife and whispered into her ear. She gave him a quick nod. Lord Bryant stepped forward. "I'm certain the last thing Harrington would want is for you to feel neglected. Would you dance this set with me?"

Mercy glanced between Lord Bryant and his wife. Since when did a seasoned philanderer ask his wife's permission to dance with another woman? Then again, she hadn't truly seen him act scandalously. The quartet was playing a polka, and her feet had been itching to dance ever since they set foot in the room. "I would be honored. Thank you, Lord Bryant."

Lord Bryant dropped the slightest of kisses on his wife's cheek and held his arm out to Mercy. Lady Bryant smiled at him the way Mama and Papa smiled at each other when they thought no one was looking.

The dance had already started, so as soon as Mercy and Lord Bryant reached the outskirts of the dancers, he pulled her into position, and they were off.

Lord Bryant was an excellent dancer, almost as proficient as Mr. Beauford. How had she never danced with him before he married? He had seemed to dance with nearly everyone. Actually, that wasn't true. He had danced with many women, but usually one or two more often than others.

He didn't bother with talking, either, and held her at what even the most prudish of mothers would call an appropriate distance. When the polka ended, they were both slightly out of breath. Lord Bryant smiled down at her—the genuine smile, not the flirtatious one—again. "I'm certain the news of your courtship won't keep you from dance partners forever. A woman who enjoys dancing as much as you do should never find partners in short supply."

Mercy smiled back. "I hope so. If I had known that was the result of a courtship with the duke, I'm afraid I wouldn't have agreed to it."

Lord Bryant's eyebrows furrowed slightly. "You wouldn't have?"

"No. If a courtship with Lady Bryant would have meant you could never again flirt with other women, would you have agreed to it?"

"First of all, I never agreed to a courtship with my wife. She manipulated me into it. And second, a thousand times yes. Despite my habits of spreading cheer with my charming smile." He sent her his devilish grin, and yes, it did spark something in her. Not desire—but the warmth that comes from having been noticed and singled out by a man who was arguably one of the most handsome in England.

The Duke of Harrington didn't smile at her like that, nor did he smile at her like Lord Bryant smiled at his wife. His smiles were not about appreciation or giving her joy. They were . . . she didn't know exactly what they were. She enjoyed his smile, especially when he'd smiled at her after she agreed to allow him to court her. But she didn't see it often. She got the feeling that the Duke of Harrington was as surprised by his smiles as everyone else was. As if he hadn't meant to smile; it had simply happened. They weren't given, like Lord Bryant's. They had to be teased out.

The strains to a slower dance started, and once again, the two of them fell into a comfortable dance pattern. The dance was an easy one, and she needed no concentration to speak. "What do you mean, your wife manipulated you into courting her?"

"I mean just that. I hadn't planned on it. I was involved with another young woman at the time . . ." He trailed off, and Mercy was left to try to piece together the two images of Lord Bryant. On the one hand, a devoted husband, but on the other, by his own admission, someone who had been pursuing many women before he settled down. "Sometimes," Lord Bryant said with a wink, "we can be a bit obtuse to what is standing right in front of us. I resisted Diana as long as I could." He tipped his head. "But that didn't actually turn out to be very long."

They finished the rest of the dance in silence, and Lord Bryant led her back to Mama. Lady Bryant still stood with the three women, laughing. Four other figures had joined them during their dance.

Mercy's shoulders automatically straightened, and she put another inch or two of distance between herself and Lord Bryant. The Duke of Harrington, his mother, and Lord and Lady Ottersby were waiting for their return. A muscle in His Grace's jaw tightened as he watched Mercy walk toward them with her arm around Lord Bryant's. That small movement was the most notable reaction she had seen from the duke since he'd laughed during their first game of chess.

His Grace might not be overly affected by her, but he was certainly affected by her dancing with Lord Bryant.

Men.

"Well, Harrington," Lord Bryant said once they were in earshot. "This lovely lady has been bored to tears without you."

"I have not." Mercy took back all the good thoughts she'd had about Lord Bryant.

Lord Bryant tsked. "I suppose not after I showed up. Still, ask her to dance, for heaven's sake, before she becomes a wallflower."

Harrington's eyes shot daggers in the baron's direction. "Lady Mercy would never become a wallflower."

"Tonight she nearly has been," Mama chimed in. "She hasn't danced with anyone except Lord Bryant."

Harrington turned to Mercy, and for the first time, their eyes met. "I'm sorry. I know how much you enjoy dancing."

He was sorry? She didn't know how to process his comment. "It's no trouble." But it was. Truly, it was. If this courtship ruined dancing for her, she would never forgive him.

The Duke of Harrington looked apologetic. "Is your next set free?"

"Yes."

"Would you be so kind as to dance with me?"

Mama looked like she was about to faint with happiness. Mercy nodded at him.

Mama clapped her hands. "Wonderful. The two of you dance so beautifully together. I shall look forward to seeing it often this Season. What are your favorite dances, Your Grace? Our annual ball is fast approaching, and I'd like your opinion on the music."

Every year Mama got excited about their annual ball, but this year felt different. She was sparing no expense and wanted to make certain everything would go according to her plan.

It was safe to say that Mercy dancing with the Duke of Harrington was high on Mama's list of priorities for the ball.

"I'm certain I'll be happy with whatever dances Lady Mercy chooses. After all, she is the expert." The duke held his arm out, and she took it. If the only men willing to dance with her were Lord Bryant and the Duke of Harrington, she had better take the chance while she had it.

Besides, it would be a good opportunity to spy on his reactions to the women around them.

Harrington still danced perfectly, but with an edge of stiffness that seemed to convey that he was worried he would somehow make a mistake.

"You dance perfectly," she said, hoping to relax him.

His eyes met hers suspiciously. "Somehow, that doesn't sound like a compliment."

"It is."

He pushed his lips together into a tight line. "Who is the best dancer partner in this room?"

"Mr. Beauford," she said, without thinking. He was. "Lord Bryant is a close second."

"And what makes them stand out above the rest?"

That was easy. "They don't think about the fact that they are dancing. They simply dance."

The duke nodded. "I think a lot about dancing when I am dancing."

"And therefore, you dance perfectly."

"But not well."

She laughed. "I don't mind dancing with you."

"If I forgot I was dancing, you might like it better. Though, the last time I did that, I closed my eyes and almost caused a collision."

"That was what you were doing?"

"I was trying to enjoy dancing as much as you do."

"And did you?"

"I don't think anyone can enjoy dancing as much as you do, but yes, I did enjoy it more. Until I realized I was about to crash into three different dancing pairs."

"What if we try it again, only this time with your eyes open?"

"How would I do that?"

"For starters, loosen your arms slightly. It feels as if you are trying to keep me an arm's length away."

After the debacle of a chess match where he pulled his hand away from hers, she half expected him to resist, but he didn't. His elbow fell slightly, resulting in her moving inches closer to him. His chest was directly in front of hers, and they spun about the room more smoothly, less controlled and more in tune with the music. "Much better."

He smiled and relaxed even more, so only his fingers at her back were left solid and unforgiving. They pressed her closer to him, and she allowed herself to comply. Only when her head was within inches of his did he soften his fingers as well.

"Much better, indeed." His voice was near her ear, and after days of sterile games of chess, the low melodic tones of his whisper sent a jolt of energy through her. Dancing with Mr. Beauford had never done that.

Still . . . there was no reason to get excited. Soon enough he would revert back to his steady, not at all exciting, self. She nodded, suddenly unable to find her voice.

"If our courtship has caused you to lose out on dance partners, the least I can do is make your dances with me more enjoyable."

Her fingers played with the fabric of his jacket on his shoulder. This dance was certainly enjoyable. Despite calling her chess games with the duke dull to Penelope, she supposed she had been able to get to know the duke better because of them. If nothing else, she knew the way he was holding her now meant something. More than it would mean if any other man held her in the same way. "*Mile buiochas*," Mercy replied without thinking. The new scullery maid, Bridget, barely spoke any English, and Kate had taught Mercy a few phrases.

The duke lifted his eyebrows. "What was that?"

"*Mile buiochas*. It is Irish. It means—"

"A thousand thanks," the duke finished for her.

"Yes, my lady's maid is teaching me some Irish phrases so I can speak to our new scullery maid."

"They are both Irish?"

Richard's mother's family originally hailed from Ireland, and Mama's great-grandmother was from there. It was not coincidence that so many of their servants were Irish. "Yes."

"It is a beautiful land. I spent some of my army time there, but that was before the blight."

Mercy relaxed. "I would love to go there. Richard has some family still there, and a branch of my mother's family used to live in Limerick."

"I never got to Limerick, unfortunately."

For the briefest moment, she had the idea to tell him they should go together sometime. It was ridiculous. What was she thinking?

"I hope you know, Lady Mercy—" His voice stopped mid-sentence, his eyes trained on something behind her. His arms stiffened, and the distance between them doubled. He went completely rigid, barely making the steps land as they should. If she had thought his jaw had clenched when he had seen her with Lord Bryant, now his teeth were crushed together with terrible force, making even the veins at the top of his neck stand out. His eyes darkened, and she followed his penetrating gaze.

A woman had just entered the ballroom. No, *entered* was the wrong word. *Invaded* perhaps described the way she stood looking over the masses as if they were a people to be conquered. She was stunning in a sleek and polished way Mercy would never be. Her dark hair was severe and pulled back tightly, without any curls to soften it. Her dress had a plunging neckline that exposed her shoulders. It was a deep, emerald green, with dark purple lace that looked almost black. She surveyed the room with one eyebrow lifted, as if she were assessing the worthiness of the company she would find.

"Who is that?" Mercy asked.

She thought he might feign ignorance or pretend he had not just been staring at another woman, but he did not. "Lady Plymton, the widow of Lord Plymton. It seems she has returned to London a month earlier than planned."

A month earlier than planned? Who was this Lady Plymton, and why did Harrington know her schedule?

He blinked and led her with his careful, perfect steps toward the opposite side of the room as far from Lacy Plymton as possible. Good or bad, this Lady Plymton had elicited an intense reaction from the Duke of Harrington.

Which meant two things. First, Harrington was indeed capable of fierce emotions; he simply hadn't felt them toward Mercy. And second, Mercy had found her first possible candidate for her plan to pawn her suitor off on someone else.

CHAPTER 14

WHAT WAS *SHE* DOING HERE? Nicholas had known Lady Plymton would be returning to London, but her uncle had said she would arrive next month. And to be at a ball? Her husband had only been dead just over four months. Six months was generally considered to be the minimum mourning period, and he had never understood how someone could only mourn for that long. Why had she rushed her mourning?

The answer was as obvious as her low-cut dress. One title would not be enough for her.

He steered Lady Mercy away from the crowds of people. For the most part, dancers gave them a wide berth anyway, and by the time they reached the opposite side of the room, they had a decent distance between them and anyone else.

"How do you know her?"

Nicholas wanted to laugh. He didn't know her. Not really. Lady Plymton was not the type of woman that could be known. She changed with whatever person she was around. Cold to some, warm to others, her supposed interests no different from the men she wanted to impress.

And he had fallen for it all. "I knew her when I was younger—much younger. Before she married."

Mercy nodded, her soft features a stark contrast to Lady Plymton's harsh, but beautiful, ones.

He had counted on at least another month of courtship with Lady Mercy before any conversation about Lady Plymton had to come up. He would have preferred to wait, but he would not hide anything from her. "But not before she was engaged."

"Oh." Lady Mercy nodded, then blinked, then glanced to the part of the room where Lady Plymton stood.

Already, a few men had ensconced her. He recognized some of them. Men he had considered rivals in her affection at one time.

How could he have been so foolish?

"And you . . ." Lady Mercy looked confused, as if she were trying to put him together with a woman like her.

Nicholas took a deep breath and closed his eyes for a quick moment. When he opened them, he allowed himself to take in the delicate angles of Lady Mercy's face, her soft trusting eyes, the texture and artwork that was her skin. How had he ever fallen for a woman like Lady Plymton when someone like Lady Mercy was on the earth? This could very well be the last time Lady Mercy looked at him without reproach, but he had to continue. "I pursued her with the passion of a young man who hadn't learned much about how the world works. I didn't care that she was engaged. I didn't care that my parents didn't approve. I didn't think about consequences at all. I lived only for my next glimpse of her."

The music stopped, and he dropped his hands to his sides. He wasn't a fool. He knew he cared for Lady Mercy much more than she did him. He had hoped . . . truly hoped to have more time to convince her of his steadfastness before stories of him at that age surfaced. But now that Lady Plymton was back in London, she was bound to hear them soon enough, and he wanted her to hear them from him.

She didn't step away from him, and her eyes were soft and curious, as if it were more important to her to know him than to judge him. A small part of him dared hope that woman's arrival would not mean the end of his relationship with Lady Mercy. And for the first time since he'd relayed the story to Donald, he found himself wishing to be understood. Not just wishing but needing. He needed Lady Mercy to see not only what he'd done but why he would never do anything like that again. He reached for her hand but then stopped and pulled his behind his back. This was most certainly not the time to throw decorum out the window. "I'm not the same person I was then. I have worked very hard not to be so naive. I was young, and when my father learned of the affair, I was sent to the army. I was a terrible service man for the first two months. Unruly. Proud. I thought myself above everyone and above every part of being under someone else's command."

"There aren't many future dukes who go into service."

"No. There aren't. I was an oddity."

"Did you write to her?"

A grim smile rose to his face. "I shouldn't have, but yes. I wrote to her."

"And did she write back?"

"She wrote to me a few times, telling me I shouldn't anger my father too much. And then communication stopped."

"What happened?"

"She married her fiancé." He didn't mean for his voice to sound so hard, but he still hadn't forgiven the stupidity of the young man he was. He hadn't expected her to go through with it. But she had never said anything about breaking off the engagement to him. Nor had he asked her to break it off. He had assumed. Assumed that the times they snuck away into gardens, the times he was able to pull her into a dark corner and kiss her, had meant the same to her as they had to him.

Everything.

He was certain he was ready for marriage, and she had never done anything to convince him otherwise.

Until she married someone else.

"You were in love with her." Mercy said it like a statement, her face emotionless.

"I thought I was. I was a fool."

She eyed Lady Plymton with curiosity more than ire. "Do you ever think—"

"No." He needed her to understand. He was not that person anymore. "After I heard that she'd married, I finally started listening to my superior, General Woodsworth. I changed. I grew up. I left such silly notions behind, and I hope you know that the mistakes I made with her will never be repeated."

"You mean falling in love?"

"No. Of course not. I mean letting my heart rule my head. Nothing about the relationship made sense, but I ignored all the warning signs, broke nearly every rule of propriety, and ended up disappointing my father and paying for my mistakes for years."

Mercy nodded. Another dance was starting, but the two of them had already danced twice. Until they were properly engaged, he couldn't ask her again. At least, not without invoking the ire of Society. He sighed. She would want to keep dancing. He couldn't drag her away to the cardroom for a game of chess.

He'd looked forward to seeing her all day, and now his time with her was already over. "I wish we could dance again. I would rather not leave you. Not now."

Her eyes met his, and for a moment, they were quiet. What was she thinking behind those deep-set eyes of hers? He'd run the gamut of emotions during that episode of his life. Euphoria, excitement, danger, longing, despair, and shame. He didn't think she would judge him as harshly as Father had. But he ached to wrap her in his arms and promise her that any feelings he'd had for Lady Plymton had burned out long ago.

One small corner of her mouth rose, slowly, softly, as if she were releasing him from his unease on the matter. "I'll be all right. You should dance with a few more partners today."

He shook his head. "If I can't dance with you, I'd rather watch you dance."

"Would you?" She raised an eyebrow at him. "I find that hard to believe. Besides, as the perfect gentleman you are, you should dance. There are poor wallflowers like me who need asking."

"You're hardly a wallflower."

"I felt like one today."

"I'm sorry about that." His shoulders drooped. "I'm sorry about a lot of things. I'll make certain a few men know I am not a jealous man."

Her smile dropped slightly but then returned. "That would be appreciated."

He led her back to her mother, bowed to the other women there, and asked the very next young lady he met to dance.

He would not be caught with a free moment until he went to the cardroom. He wouldn't risk giving Lady Plymton a chance to speak with him. He had no doubt that Lady Plymton would not reenter Society quietly. If that had been her plan, her uncle wouldn't have felt the need to warn him of her arrival.

He quickly danced three more sets with three different women, always making certain to stay far from the dark-haired woman who had ruined his relationship with his father. None of the women he danced with compared to Lady Mercy, though. Not in their grace and not in the way he felt like she belonged in his arms. For a man who had grown to respect rules and the things they protected, he was starting to despise the ones that kept Lady Mercy at arm's length.

CHAPTER 15

The next morning, Penelope came for a visit. Mama was still resting and Mercy was able to have her to herself. Mercy thanked Mrs. Brooksby for delivering the tea service and turned to Penelope.

"Any thoughts from the ball? Did you notice anything?"

"All I did was watch your duke last night. Poor Yolty. I think he was worried about me."

"And?"

"Truthfully, I didn't notice him paying serious attention to any of the women he danced with. None of them made him smile more than another. He didn't follow any of them with his eyes afterward. Well, except for—"

"Lady Plymton." Mercy jumped up and snapped her fingers. "Right?"

"I was going to say *you*."

Mercy shook her head and waved a hand away from her face. Of course, he would look after her now and again. They were supposed to be courting. "I don't count."

Penelope pulled her face into a disbelieving grimace and shook her head. "Who is Lady Plymton?"

"You didn't see her? The dazzling woman in the emerald dress?"

"Oh, her. I did notice her. But I never saw Harrington look at her."

"If he didn't, it was through sheer force of will." She took Penelope by both shoulders. "He was in love with her, but his father broke them up and made him join the army. The man does, indeed, have some deeper feelings. They have just been shut off due to a misunderstanding parent's disapproval."

Penelope set down her teacup. "Are you certain? I asked Yolty about him last night. He said His Grace is one of the most upstanding men he knows."

Lord Yolten said that? But how well would Lord Yolten *really* know the duke? And if he didn't know the story of Harrington and Lady Plymton, perhaps it wasn't one Mercy should be blabbing about. But Harrington had told her so quickly, she'd assumed the whole business had been fairly well-known. "The Duke of Harrington told me the whole story himself. And he used it to explain why he is so stiff and proper. He will never make those mistakes again, etcetera." She waved her hand about. "Don't you see? This is our opportunity. I can get out of the courtship, and he can return to the woman he loves."

"Once loved."

"Please." Mercy flopped down into her seat. "Could anyone be more stalwart and steadfast than that man? His whole persona is a direct result of the pain she caused him when she married someone else. Lord Yolten may be correct, that he is upstanding, but at one point, she enticed him, and I don't think anyone has done so since."

Penelope didn't look convinced, but as Mercy lay in bed after the ball, the more she thought about it, the more she became certain the duke must still have feelings for Lady Plymton. The Duke of Harrington had never shown her a tenth of the emotions that Lady Plymton had evoked in him. "I tell you, I have never seen him so impassioned. It was like he was another person. I don't expect you to understand, since Lord Yolten has always been passionate about you. You didn't have to resort to anything devious in order to have the type of match you deserve."

Penelope's hand dove to her tea, and she took a quick sip, a mite too fast for how hot it still was. After blowing through her lips for a moment, she set down her cup. "I suppose we could try to give him a chance with her. Make him face her so he can decide." She tipped her head from side to side, considering. "It isn't as though we would be harming anyone, and sometimes love does need a bit of a push."

"Yes." Mercy couldn't believe Penelope was actually starting to believe her idea had merit. "Then I will approach him about releasing him from the courtship. I'm certain, if given a chance, he will make the choice that was robbed of him when he was younger. He just needs to be taken away from Society and its prying eyes to see what he wants."

Penelope tipped her head to one side. "So you want to get him alone with Lady Plymton. How will we manage that?"

"He made it quite clear that he managed it plenty when he was pursuing her."

"Yes, but he isn't pursuing *her* now. He is pursuing *you*."

Mercy waved her hand. "A minor detail."

Penelope pushed her lips to one side. "One of us will have to become acquainted with Lady Plymton."

"It might be strange if it were me." Meeting an old flame of the duke would be not only awkward, it might give away what she was trying to do.

"I could do it." Penelope shrugged. "I don't mind meeting new people." She didn't. Penelope was one of the most unassuming people she had ever met. Mercy could hold conversations, but Lady Yolten could steer them like she was a naval captain. "Step one, get an introduction to Lady Plymton. Step two, create a situation where the two of them can be alone together."

"For now, let's concentrate on step one."

Penelope nodded and returned to her tea. Mercy rested her back against her chair and sighed. With any luck, she would be free of the Duke of Harrington and the enormous pressure this courtship had put on her. She could go back to dancing and enjoying life until a man she couldn't live without came along.

There was a soft knock at the door, and a footman entered. "A Mrs. and Miss Morgan to see you, Lady Mercy."

Morgan? Mercy glanced at Penelope and raised her eyebrows, but Penelope shook her head. Mercy had been introduced to a Morgan family the previous year, but other than their short introduction, they'd had no further interaction.

"Could you let Mama know they are here and send them in?" Mama must be more acquainted with the Morgan women than Mercy was. Otherwise, this would be a strange morning call, indeed.

The footman nodded and returned a moment later with the two women. It was the Morgans she had met, although she only vaguely remembered them. What were they doing here? Mercy was never one to stand on tradition, but when others didn't follow it, she was taken by surprise.

"Mrs. Morgan, Miss Morgan. My mother will be here shortly. She is still resting after the festivities last night. Have you met Lady Yolten?"

Mrs. Morgan's eyebrows rose slightly at the mention of Penelope's title. "We have not but would be very pleased to be introduced."

Mercy managed the introductions, though it was a task she was seldom required to do. Mercy motioned to the two chairs not in use at the tea table. "Won't you join us? Mrs. Brooksby will bring more tea things."

Mrs. Morgan took her seat with force while her daughter shuffled shyly to the seat next to her. She only made eye contact a few times before quickly looking away. She was either painfully shy or mortified by the questionable propriety of their visit.

No one spoke. Mercy should be the one keeping the conversation civil, but her mind went blank. Why couldn't she think of a simply social nicety when she needed one? Penelope picked up her small gold spoon and stirred her tea, the metal scraping the sides of her cup as if she were purposely trying to break the silence. She probably was.

Mercy cleared her throat. "Are you and my mother well acquainted?"

"Lady Driarwood? No, not particularly well. Although, we would like to remedy that, wouldn't we?" Mrs. Morgan looked to her daughter.

Miss Morgan glanced down at her hands. "Yes, Mama," she said quietly.

Mercy's heart immediately went out to the girl. For some reason, her mother had dragged her here, and her discomfort couldn't be more obvious.

Mrs. Brooksby arrived with a tea tray and set a cup and saucer in front of each of their new guests. Mercy reached for the teapot, poured Mrs. Morgan a cup, and turned to Miss Morgan. She waved a hand above her cup. "No, thank you."

Mrs. Morgan scoffed. "Oh, have some tea. It will settle your nerves."

Miss Morgan shook her head. "No, thank you. But . . ." Her big doe eyes looked up at Mercy. "If you don't mind, I may sit in front of the window for a bit. I think the cool air coming through the glass may help me settle."

"Of course," Mercy said. She had never seen anyone be quite so uneasy in her home. Then again, most people did not come uninvited, unless they were very close friends or family. Miss Morgan gave her a shaky smile, then stood quickly and dashed off to the window.

"Don't mind my daughter. She has had a rough go these past few years, and she has become quite sensitive."

Penelope coughed, and Mercy caught her meaning. Anyone might be sensitive with a mother as graceless as Mrs. Morgan.

"Large groups are hard for her. She does much better speaking one on one with a person."

"I don't mind speaking with her. Do you think she would want company by the window?" Penelope asked.

Mrs. Morgan's eyes lit up. "She would love that. She does like people, and meetings like this never used to be a problem. It has only started lately. She has had a few disappointments."

Penelope started to stand, but Mrs. Morgan put a hand on her arm. "However, she might feel more comfortable with a woman closer to her own age."

Penelope blinked, then turned to Mercy. Mercy blinked back. True, Penelope was three years Mercy's senior and married, but it wasn't as if she were an octogenarian. If Mercy had to guess, Miss Morgan looked to be closer to Penelope's age. Mercy caught Mrs. Morgan's eye. "You think I should go?"

"Oh, could you? It would mean so much to her."

This meeting was getting stranger and stranger, and Mercy wanted nothing more than for Mama to enter the room so she could take over hostess duties. Perhaps Mercy should have waited to hear exactly how Mama knew them before allowing them into the drawing room. Still, if given the choice between sitting with Mrs. Morgan or her daughter, the daughter was definitely preferable. Mercy gave Penelope a sympathetic shrug and stood.

Mercy reached Miss Morgan just as she heaved a large sigh. She jerked in surprise when she noticed Mercy standing beside her. "Oh, you didn't need to come."

"I wanted to make certain you were comfortable."

"I'm much more comfortable here than at the tea table."

"Lady Yolten is rather intimidating, isn't she?"

Miss Morgan's eyes flashed in surprise, and then the corners of her lips turned up. "You are toying with me, aren't you? My mother is intimidating. Lady Yolten seems lovely."

There was only one chair by the window, and Miss Morgan occupied it, so Mercy sat halfway inside the windowsill. "She is, isn't she?"

"You're fortunate in your friends."

Mercy nodded, for she was, and she was extremely grateful for her good fortune. Perhaps this Miss Morgan needed a bit more fortune in her life. "How are you enjoying the Season?"

The hint of a smile that had been on her face earlier dropped. "I am enjoying it," she answered.

"But?"

Miss Morgan snuck a glance at her mother, but she and Penelope were deep in discussion about the quality of the tea. "I'm afraid I've become a bit of a disappointment to Mama."

Miss Morgan was a beauty, with her blonde curls and pert little mouth. She had a quiet demeanor that many men looked for. What on earth could have made her a disappointment? Her shyness, perhaps? "I find that hard to believe."

"It's true. I'm practically on the shelf."

"You are hardly—"

"This is my fifth Season. You don't need to pretend otherwise."

Miss Morgan couldn't be more than a couple years older than Mercy, and Mercy had not once worried about an impending *shelf*. But that was most likely a privilege Miss Morgan didn't share. She didn't know the Morgan family well enough to know their financial position or even their exact social standing. Perhaps Miss Morgan's plight was valid. But what could someone in Mercy's position say to comfort her?

"It is much better to be on the shelf than married to the wrong person."

"I can see how you would think that. But in your situation . . ." She very nearly blushed. "With one of the kindest, most passionate men courting you, I'm not certain you can fully grasp what I'm feeling."

Kindest and most passionate . . . Did she mean the duke? Kind, certainly, but passionate? She had *never* seen that side of him, even though he'd mentioned it in regard to Lady Plymton. "The duke? Do you know him?"

"I did. I had thought . . . well . . . I had thought perhaps he and I . . ." That little mouth of hers quivered. What was Miss Morgan trying to say? But then her eyes lifted, half full of tears, and Mercy knew.

Heavens above. She had a sudden desire to press her own forehead against the cool glass of the window. The Duke of Harrington and this sad little creature crouching in the corner of her drawing room? What had he done to raise her hopes?

"Oh," Miss Morgan said. "But I shouldn't mention that, not when he is so ardently pursuing you."

Ardently? Chess games and well-turned dances were hardly what she would call ardent. "I don't know that I would say he is ardently pursing me."

Miss Morgan raised one eyebrow. "Oh, I know how he is. Always extremely careful in public, but in private?" Miss Morgan smiled, and her eyes glazed over, as if she were reliving a *very* pleasant memory. "I am probably an awful human being for admitting this, and I shouldn't, for my own reputation's sake, but I do envy you."

Mercy was at a loss for words. In the course of two days, she had heard from the duke, and now this young woman, about his supposed escapades. True, she hadn't known the duke very long, but it was starting to seem like she didn't know him at all. "I'm sorry, but when did this happen?"

Miss Morgan glanced out the window. "Off and on for the past two years. But I see now what he was doing. I thought the secrecy was exciting, and I, well, I fell for his plan. I'm still not even sure I mind. I should have known the duke would never take someone in my position seriously. What do I have? A large dowry, for certain, and the Duke of Pemramble as a cousin." She looked up at Mercy as if to see whether she knew of the duke. Vaguely, she did. But it wasn't until recently that dukes had become a more common feature in her life. "I will also possibly gain a Scottish title someday, but still, compared to you? A lady? Of course, he would feel obligated, no matter his feelings toward me, to marry better than what my family can give him. It was such a disappointment to Mama."

Why was Miss Morgan telling her all of this? She barely knew the woman.

"I know what you must be thinking. Why are we here? Why did we come, when we are only the slightest of acquaintances? I will tell you. Mama was hoping to dissuade you. Then, perhaps, he would look at me again, like he used to. Like he hasn't allowed himself to do. But I know better, and I only wanted to let you know that—well . . . you aren't the only woman he has pulled into dark corners . . ." She let her voice peter out. "And perhaps you are all right with that, but on the chance that you weren't, well, I wish I would have known sooner. I was so certain of his love for me." Her voice broke, and she pulled a handkerchief from her sleeve, dabbing at her eyes.

Mercy sat dumbfounded, absently listening to a carriage that rolled down the street in front of their home, the cobblestones clinking as the horses' hooves marched forward. The Duke of Harrington had *never* pulled her into a dark corner. He'd *never* shown Mercy the type of passion Miss Morgan was speaking of. She knew Miss Morgan expected her to be angry, or perhaps indifferent, depending on the depth of her relationship with the duke. But she felt neither of those things.

She was extremely confused. And, perhaps, even a bit disappointed.

Which was ridiculous. If the man didn't want to pull her away from a crowd and kiss her senseless, then she didn't want him to do it.

"He wanted—" Mercy's voice came out a bit gravely, so she cleared her throat. "You mentioned he wanted to keep you a secret?"

Miss Morgan stopped dabbing her eyes and opened them in complete shock. "I shouldn't have said that. I know he had to give me up. No matter his feelings for me, it was necessary. He is a duke, after all, and a duke wouldn't marry a mere miss. It was foolish of me to even think." She shook her head. "I thought you should know, before you marry him. That's all."

"He is only courting me. We aren't engaged."

"But he has never courted anyone before, no matter how *interested* in them he was. You are perfect for him, so of course you will marry."

Mercy straightened her spine. There was always a recurring theme in her conversations about the duke. Surely Mercy *wanted* to marry him. He was a duke. "I wouldn't count on it."

"It doesn't matter." Miss Morgan waved her hand to the side of her face. "It really doesn't matter whether it is you or some other lady. He won't let his heart make his decisions for him—not any long-lasting decisions, anyway."

Mercy clenched her jaw. Miss Morgan knew the duke very well indeed. Miss Morgan tucked her handkerchief back into her sleeve, blinked a few times, and pasted an obviously fake smile on her face. "I should probably return to Mama. She hates when I spend too much time by myself."

They rejoined the two sitting at the tea table, and Mercy sipped her lukewarm tea. A few minutes later, Mama sent her regrets to Mrs. and Miss Morgan, stating that she still had not recovered from the ball.

Miss Morgan's initial shyness wore off, and by the end of their conversation, she had turned into a lively young woman. One the Duke of Harrington would have certainly enjoyed kissing.

After they left, Mercy turned to Penelope. "Well, we can add one more name to the Duke of Harrington's list."

"Miss Morgan?" Penelope's eyebrows rose.

"Apparently he was quite taken with her a few months ago."

"Exactly how taken?"

"Quite," was all Mercy said.

Penelope eyed the window where the Morgan carriage was waiting for its passengers. "I'm starting to wonder if, perhaps, there is more to this duke than he has led you to believe."

"As am I, and I don't know how I feel about it."

Penelope whipped her head back around. "What do you mean by that?"

"He is handsome, wealthy, personable, bad at chess—all things I admire. My one complaint of him is that he has no passion. And now, suddenly—"

"Mercy."

"What?"

"Don't tell me you are jealous of that sad, quiet woman."

Mercy leaned forward until she was only inches away from Penelope's face. "What is so wrong with me? Am I not attractive? He has never once tried to get me alone or take advantage of me."

Penelope pushed her lips tightly together, but her wide, sparking eyes betrayed the fact that she was about to laugh.

Mercy narrowed her eyes. "I'm serious."

Penelope shook her head and allowed her laugh to escape. "You must be the only woman in London who, upon hearing that her admirer has raised false hope in other women, likes him better for it."

"I didn't say I like him better for it."

"You didn't have to. I can see it. Passion and philandering are two very different things, Mercy."

"While you were cavorting with Lord Bryant, you didn't seem to worry about that. And look at him now, completely devoted to his wife."

Penelope stilled. "Do not use Lord Bryant as your compass for what a loyal husband might look like before marriage. He's not the man Society painted him to be."

"It seems that neither is the Duke of Harrington. He wants everyone to think he is the most proper man in London, but that is only a facade."

"Mercy, are you certain you aren't sabotaging your courtship because you're hurt the duke hasn't been arduous with you?"

Penelope didn't understand. She hadn't seen the look on Miss Morgan's face while she was so obviously remembering her *very* pleasant trysts with the duke. "No. I'm not at all certain of that."

"Because if you change your mind and he finds out we've done this—"

"I know." What could she say? Miss Morgan had awakened a beast from somewhere so deep inside Mercy, she hadn't even realized the beast existed. The duke had pulled away from Mercy every single time she'd touched him. And now, in the course of two days, she'd learned of as many women who had gotten much more than scintillating conversations over chessboards with him.

Devil take his thick lashes and smile that made her want to reach out to him, when he had no desire to do the same. She would not settle for a man who saw her only as a way to solidify his social standing, even if he wanted that social standing for noble reasons. She would wait and give her heart to someone who didn't see her has chattel. "I just want to go back to being the person I was a few weeks ago. Someone who doesn't care one whit for the Duke of Harrington."

Penelope pushed her lips together in thought and sighed. "All right, then. Let's start that list. One way or another, we will either get the duke a wife or, at the very least, destroy any connection you have to him."

Mercy jumped from her seat and dashed over to the writing table before she could change her mind. Making a list of possible suitors for a man who was courting her would be a pleasant way to spend the remainder of her morning, and the sooner she got this over with, the sooner her life could return to normal. The next time she saw Harrington, she would be the one in charge of their courtship for a change, and she would get to see how he handled his perfectly organized world becoming invaded by chaos.

CHAPTER 16

Nicholas stood in the entrance hall of the Driarwood home and struggled to keep from pacing. For some reason, the Driarwood butler had asked him to wait here instead of showing him to the drawing room. Was he going to be dismissed?

It had been three days since Nicholas had laid eyes on Lady Mercy. Three very long days in which he debated whether or not he should have been so forthcoming to her about his involvement with Lady Plymton. It certainly looked like he shouldn't have; now her family didn't even want to admit him to the drawing room. He took two steps to the right, then clenched his jaw and kept his feet still. He was not some young, inexperienced man who couldn't control his feet while he waited to be attended to.

All thoughts of pacing left him, though, when Lady Mercy appeared alone at the top of the stairs. Her pale-pink dress was simple elegance, well cut and made from fabric sturdier than her ballgowns but just as flattering. She stopped and placed a hand on the banister, smiling down at him. But it wasn't her dress or even the fact that he hadn't seen her in days that made his breath hitch. Something had changed. In the past three days of not seeing each other, something must have changed.

Her smile was vibrant, covering her face in the joy and satisfaction of a friend or a lover reuniting after long days apart. It was a smile that spoke, and the words it said were *this woman is excited to see you*, as if, perhaps, like him, she had counted the last hours and then minutes until he would be in her home again. He didn't move, not certain he could trust this vision of her, but as she descended the stairs, her smile did not waver, nor did the spark in her eye diminish.

She shouldn't be coming down those stairs smiling at him like that. If anything, he had thought their last conversation would have damaged his chances. That he would have to try even harder to win her over, to convince her that despite his past, he was committed to doing everything correctly and properly with her. But he must have been wrong.

Had sharing about his history helped his cause? Lord and Lady Bryant had visited the morning after the ball, ecstatic about his choice of woman to court. Lord Bryant had wasted no time in giving him terrible flirting advice. It was all incidental touching—he would absolutely not be doing that—and longing glances—something he was quite certain he was incapable of. However, before Lord Bryant left, he'd pulled Nicholas to the side and said the one thing that actually made a bit of sense. "Touching, complimenting, eye contact. Those are great starting points and quite enjoyable. But the truth is, if you want a woman to fall in love with you, you are going to have to share yourself with her. She can't fall in love with a shadow. And when you know you want to spend the rest of your life with her, don't keep her guessing. Tell her."

When he knew he wanted to spend the rest of his life with her? Their eyes met and held while Lady Mercy made her way down the last two steps. They sparked with an energy of a woman with a plan, and based on the way they held his, for the first time, he thought her plans might include him.

Blast. He did want to spend the rest of his life with this woman. He didn't want to deal with three-day periods where he didn't see her. And if he did have to travel somewhere without her, he wanted her to be at his home when he returned. He wouldn't stand waiting near the door for her to come to him, nor would he have to tell her how much he missed her. He would rush to her, grab her by the waist before she even reached the bottom of the stairs, and show her how much he'd missed her. First, he'd let her neck know by dragging a finger softly up it to her jaw. Then he'd let her mouth in on the secret. And then she'd be completely wrapped in his arms, laughing and making certain his face, arms, neck, chest, every part of him, knew she'd missed him as well.

The pace of his heart was nearing dangerous levels when Lady Mercy reached him and held out her hand. It wasn't lifting her in the air or kissing those lips, but it was a better greeting than he'd ever received from her. Every other time they had met, she had given him wary bows or half smiles. Her hand was gloved in a soft crème leather, each finger covered in that smooth supple blanket of fabric. Perhaps she meant for him to shake it, and he should. He really should.

But her cheerful countenance had awoken the part of himself he tried so desperately to keep sleeping. Whether on account of Lord Bryant's advice still fresh in his mind or simply the desire to actually touch the marvelous woman he courted, he grasped her fingers, so soft and trusting in his hand. With his grip light, he brought her knuckles toward his lips. He moved slowly, giving her the chance to pull away or stop him, but she didn't. He placed the briefest of kisses on her fingers, and the room brightened, as if the sun had broken through the clouds outside and was streaming through the windows.

At her swift intake of breath, he dropped her hand and straightened sharply. Lady Mercy pulled her hand to her chest, and her eyes went wide, but it wasn't disgust or anger he saw in them. Only surprise.

He'd surprised her.

She'd surprised him first. He smiled, knowing full well that his smile would not bring the devastation and hope that hers did to him, but perhaps . . . perhaps it could bring her a bit of happiness to know he was excited to see her too. "Lady Mercy, you look lovely this afternoon."

Blast his tongue. Could he think of nothing more eloquent to say? She looked more than lovely, but any other descriptions might have come out more like poetry and less like appropriate courtship language. He needed to find some sort of middle ground when he spoke with her. *Be specific*, Lord Bryant had said, but telling her that her smile had given him hope or that the freckles on her face and collarbone drove him mad seemed an even worse idea than poetry.

"Thank you, Your Grace. My parents are already in the drawing room, as well as a few other guests. I wanted to warn you that we would not be alone."

"Actually, we are alone. Next time, it would be no trouble for me to wait in the drawing room, no matter the company."

Lady Mercy's smile faltered slightly, just at the corners, and if she weren't standing so close to him, he might have missed it. "My parents won't think anything of the two of us standing here with them on the other side of the door, and Mrs. Brooksby is just down the corridor."

"And you don't mind?" If Lady Mercy had a fault, and he wasn't completely certain she did, it would be that she was too trusting. If she knew how much he thought of her when they were apart or, worse, the way he was thinking of her now, she would be more careful. He'd spent years bottling up the emotions he'd allowed to control his life with Lady Plymton, and now that he was turning the keys in those locks, he was afraid whatever he'd imprisoned might escape with such force that he would terrify the woman who stood so innocently before him.

She laughed in a way that made him quite certain she did not see into his mind and arched an eyebrow. "Do you have some evil design on me that you can accomplish silently in the next thirty seconds?"

Her laughter was tranquil and spontaneous, and it echoed in the hall, even after it was gone. Telling her he wanted to spend the rest of his life with her didn't count as an evil plan, did it? "I don't."

She smiled a soft smile and sighed in what he thought might be contentment. They stood there, silent, watching the stairs and occasionally taking glimpses at each other, neither of them feeling a strong enough desire to speak to break the comfortable quiet of just being near each other.

He closed his eyes for the briefest of moments and savored the moment. Somehow, his plan was working. Everything was falling into place. Lady Mercy had become comfortable with him, smiled at him, and even trusted him. His feelings for her were steadily growing, whether they were together or apart.

He had *known* doing things the proper way would work. Despite Patience being blissfully happy in her innocent yet ill-gotten marriage, he knew that wasn't the only way to find happiness. It couldn't be. And yet, he still scarcely believed he could be so fortunate.

Lady Mercy cleared her throat softly, and he turned to her. "I believe you know Lord and Lady Yolten?"

"Yes." Not very well, but he knew them. He had seen a few marriages made between those with titles and money, but he had never seen one happier than Lord and Lady Yolten's. Lady Yolten was an interesting young lady. He was never certain how she would answer or respond to any given situation. She and his sister, Patience, would make for extreme trouble if they ever got to know each other well.

"Lady Yolten is my closest friend. She and a friend of hers are in the drawing room. Shall we join them?"

He nodded. As long as he had the opportunity to spend time with Lady Mercy, he didn't care if all of London descended upon her home. Lady Mercy wrapped her hand around his arm, and almost without thinking, he placed his hand on top of hers and gave her fingers the slightest of squeezes before letting his hand drop back down to his side. Twice. Twice he had held her hand today. And after he had convinced himself he would ignore that piece of advice from Lord Bryant.

"Wonderful." Lady Mercy's voice was light and airy. "Lady Yolten's friend is Miss Morgan."

Nicholas missed a step. Miss Morgan was in the drawing room? Miss Morgan was calculating to a fault, and Lady Yolten was one of the most unique, but also genuine, women in London. He never would have thought the two of them would be close friends.

This day had just become much more complicated.

Lady Mercy glanced at him from the corner of her eye. Was his distress noticeable? He straightened his spine and plastered a smile on his face. He had spent the last two years pretending to be delighted every time he saw Miss Morgan, even flirting with her when necessary to keep her appeased. There were several other people who knew of the indiscretions that had led to Patience's marriage, but he trusted every single other person to keep it a secret.

Every person except Miss Morgan and her family.

"I take it you know Miss Morgan?" Lady Mercy said, with a low strange tone in her voice.

Blast. He hadn't hidden his surprise—not at all. "Yes, we are acquainted," he said stiffly.

"Well then," Lady Mercy said, the strange quality in her voice gone. Perhaps he had imagined it. "This should be a delightful afternoon. She mentioned she knew you."

"She did?" Blast. Had she told Lady Mercy about Patience? How could it be that Miss Morgan was the friend Lady Yolten invited? He wanted to curse. He was fully prepared to follow Lord Bryant's advice and confess his feelings toward Lady Mercy, but instead, now he would be involved in a game of cat and mouse with Miss Morgan.

"What did she say?"

"Oh, not much more than that you knew each other. Why? Is there more to it than that?"

Nicholas smiled, but he couldn't get his mouth to work just right. The corners wouldn't turn up properly. Nor could he answer her—not honestly. He could tell Lady Mercy about what happened to Patience. She might not even think any less of anyone for it. But perhaps the story would be told better if Patience were the one to tell it. Especially if his hopes of the two of them becoming sisters-in-law came to fruition. But even more than that, it'd been mere days since he told Lady Mercy about Lady Plymton, and to have the two most scandalous events of his life shared with Lady Mercy without any breathing room between? He couldn't open his mouth and do it.

CHAPTER 17

Mercy pretended to think about where to move her next chess piece, but in reality, she watched the Duke of Harrington from the corner of her eye. Miss Morgan had given him a pretty little bow when he came in, her cheeks aflame, and Harrington had smiled pleasantly at her in return. If she hadn't heard anything of their past history, she might not have noticed the way he kept taking furtive glances at Miss Morgan every time Mercy's eyes were on the board.

Mercy put a finger on top of her queen. "She has a lovely figure, doesn't she?"

Harrington's head jerked back to the chessboard. "Pardon?"

"My queen, both queens, I suppose. The woodworker must have been a master."

"Oh." The Duke of Harrington blinked as if he was only just understanding what she meant. "Yes, I'm certain you're right."

"And where exactly did you meet Miss Morgan?"

Harrington's eyes found hers. He'd always looked at her with at least a modicum of interest. It was such a small amount, she hadn't noticed it, but now that it was gone, she noticed its absence. His eyes were cold, like what his eyes would have looked like had he gone into battle while in the army. Guarded and impartial, as if nothing in the world mattered to him, for he knew he might lose it at any moment.

"My brother-in-law introduced us."

"Really? How long ago was that?"

"About two years ago."

Mercy nodded. That is what Miss Morgan had said as well. He hadn't outright lied to her at least, and it didn't seem as though Miss Morgan had either. His discomfort with this situation was palpable. "And do you plan to continue your acquaintance with her?"

A deep crease furrowed between Harringtons strong brows. "She is someone I will most likely always have a relationship with. In one form or another."

Mercy's finger dropped from her queen. She hadn't moved her. She had no plan. This was probably the worst chess game she had ever played, and the only reason she hadn't lost already was because Harrington wasn't playing any better. She'd wanted to see Miss Morgan and Harrington together, had hoped that . . . well, what? That Miss Morgan had exaggerated her relationship with him? But it didn't look as though she had, which meant Mercy needed to move on to the second wave of her plan, to get the two of them alone together so Miss Morgan could try to convince Harrington not to enter into a loveless marriage.

A loveless marriage. Mercy's worst nightmare made worse by the fact that when Harrington had kissed her fingertips in the entrance hall she had nearly run into the drawing room to tell Penelope she'd changed her mind about their plan and to sneak Miss Morgan out of the house.

How had Mercy gotten herself into this mess, and why couldn't Miss Morgan have shown up earlier, before Mercy cared one whit about how the duke's hand felt on top of her own? And before her pride had mixed in with her other feelings for him, turning her into a jealous mess every time his eyes drifted to Miss Morgan's side of the room.

"Do you see her as someone who could help you socially, someone who could help you influence others to see your line of thinking where the Irish are concerned?"

A cough-like laugh escaped Harrington's throat. "Definitely not. Her family is . . . well, they aren't exactly altruistically motivated."

"And my family is?"

The Duke of Harrington quirked his head to one side as if she'd asked a ridiculous question. "Yes," he said, with the kind of quiet devotion she was almost convinced could be passionate.

"My parents are rather remarkable that way, aren't they?"

He leaned forward until his head was above the chessboard, his coldness gone. His eyes held a heat that if she didn't know better was the kind that did lead couples into darkened corners and secluded gardens. "And they have raised a daughter to be the same."

Holy heavens. Mercy gripped the sides of her little chess table, forcing her hands to stay in place and not reach out for him or do something irreversible, like grab his face and just make him kiss her already. If he'd spoken in this manner to Miss Morgan, it was no wonder she was willing to come to Mercy for help to win him back.

"I want you to know," Mercy forced her voice to remain steady, "that my family will help you in your causes no matter what happens between the two of us. We care about the Irish too."

The Duke of Harrington's smile was confident. "I know."

"So, if your relationship with Miss Morgan prevents . . . prevents . . ." What? She couldn't assume he was preparing to ask to marry her, even if she was fairly certain he was.

"My relationship with Miss Morgan won't prevent anything. We don't even have a relationship. Not really. We also don't *not* have a relationship. It is a strange story, and one I would like my sister to tell."

"Your sister?" Why would he want his sister to tell her about his affair with Miss Morgan?

"Yes, I will undoubtedly say something wrong, and she will flay me and call me the most unromantic man in England because she thinks all that matters in life is love, and I happen to think if love makes you as ridiculous as it made her—well, I simply don't believe it has to make people ridiculous. I believe it can be controlled and happen in a perfectly respectable way without a mania of emotions influencing the parties involved to make scandalous choices."

Mercy heard the words coming out of his mouth and saw the ways his eyes lit up just as fervently as they had when he had declared her remarkably altruistic, but nothing about his words and eyes added up. Was he fervent about her at all? Or only about his belief that love could be controlled and commanded?

He'd had at least two relationships with women he couldn't actually control himself around, and all Mercy wanted from him was for him to feel as strongly about her as he had about them. No, not *him*. It didn't have to be him. She wanted *someone* to love her without boundaries, and it couldn't be him. Because he didn't. He'd probably chosen to court her because he knew he wouldn't be tempted by her like he had been by Lady Plymton and Miss Morgan. Either that or the part of him that had allowed his heart and his emotions to have a say in his actions was dead.

He'd killed it.

"Respect." She smiled at him in a way that if he knew her at all, he would know she didn't agree with him. "The core of all romance."

The duke nodded, as if what Mercy just said had been said in earnest. "Which is why I was perplexed to see Miss Morgan here and so soon after you found out about Lady Plymton. The timing is unfortunate to say the least. But I need you to know that I am driven now to do everything as correct as possible. It is important to me as my father's son, because of the title I hold, and the people's lives who could quite possibly be at stake if I'm not."

"You shouldn't put that kind of pressure on yourself."

"I don't mind the pressure. It makes me a better person."

But did it make him happy? Mercy was not ready to choose a life like that. One where love was measured by the good it could do for Society and one small mistake from her could cost the lives of some of the most vulnerable people in Ireland.

"Are you certain you want to live that way?"

"Lady Mercy, I truthfully don't feel like I have another choice."

Mercy slid her queen forward and took a rook. It was a sacrifice; the Duke of Harrington would easily take her queen in his next move, and it wasn't even a sacrifice that would give her a later advantage.

She wanted this chess match to be over. The sooner, the better.

The Duke of Harrington's priorities were so far removed from her own, he made her head spin. Even if his decisive courting suddenly made all the sense in the world.

He didn't have a choice to make; it'd been made for him. The duke hadn't chosen her. Society and her place in it had.

If she told him now that their relationship would never work, she would break her parents' hearts, and he would go off and find the next best bride he could. She might not understand the duke, but she did want him to be happy.

She wanted him to know he did have a choice.

And she couldn't think of a better candidate to tell him that than the woman he hadn't been able to keep his eyes off the whole afternoon. She just needed to give the two of them a chance to be alone and work it all out.

CHAPTER 18

Miss Morgan must be a better friend to Lady Mercy than Nicholas had previously thought. For when he met Lady Mercy and her family at the Zoological Garden two days after his house visit, Miss Morgan and Lady Yolten were once again in her family's company. The three young ladies stood together in a group, eyes shining as they watched the llamas eat the hay that was laid out before them. Nicholas should join them, but he kept his distance for the moment, but he couldn't focus on the long hair and beady eyes of the llamas in front of him. His eyes kept drifting to Miss Morgan. Why was she here with Lady Mercy and her parents? Again?

And she was acting so strange. Just as she had been at the Driarwood home, she hadn't tried to speak with him, nor had she tried to manipulate or control the conversation around Patience.

Lady Yolten caught Nicholas's eye and strode toward him. "It is interesting, isn't it?" Lady Yolten had a fast and comfortable way of speaking. "The different animals that can be found around the world. Some are so foreign, it is hard to imagine them existing at all, and yet, here they are, in the Zoological Garden. It's as if they were waiting for us to discover them and admit that perhaps, here in England, we do not know everything that is to be known in the world."

Nicholas chuckled. "Don't let Lord John Russell hear you speaking such blasphemies."

Lady Yolten's eyes glanced skyward. "If I were to meet him, that is the last thing I would tell him. First I would let him know that he needs to clean up the Thames."

"Shall I convey that message to him the next time I see him?"

Lady Yolten blinked in a blatant attempt at innocence. "You would do that for me?"

"Most likely not," Nicholas answered honestly. "But I have spoken with him about it several times for myself."

Lady Yolten gave him a strange look. "You have?"

Nicholas frowned. Was that so hard for Lady Yolten to believe? "Of course. It isn't healthy for anyone."

Lady Yolten's eyes searched his face for a moment, then forced a garbled laugh from her throat, as if she were trying to change the subject. "Mercy is much too enthralled with these llamas. I have heard enough of her stories. Lord and Lady Driarwood have already left us to see the giraffes, and I think we should join them. Who knows when Lady Mercy will finish her descriptions of their stomachs and chewing habits with poor Miss Morgan?"

Nicholas glanced at Lady Mercy. Her hands were in the air, her face alight, as she explained something to Miss Morgan that obviously fascinated her. The corners of his mouth raised, and he wished for nothing more than to join the two women and hear what Lady Mercy found so exciting about the animals' stomachs. But that would also mean standing with Miss Morgan, and Patience hadn't yet had the chance to speak to Lady Mercy about her courtship with Ottersby. He would much rather not have that conversation started by Miss Morgan.

Nicholas turned to Lady Yolten and nodded. Lord and Lady Driarwood were already at least twenty feet down the path toward the giraffes. He extended his arm, and Lady Yolten took it.

They walked together in comfortable silence for several minutes before Lady Yolten spoke. "So you want to help the Irish and clean up the Thames. Any chance you would like to tell me something nefarious about yourself to make me feel better about my lack of aspiration?"

Nicholas scoffed. "I'm hardly a saint. Trust me."

Lady Yolten sighed deeply. "I'm afraid I *am* going to have to trust you on that. As much as I would really rather have proof."

"You want proof of my nefariousness? When I am courting your purported best friend?"

"As Yolty likes to tell me, I don't always make a lot of sense."

"Yes, well, Lord Yolten doesn't seem to mind. He is disgustingly happy with you."

Lady Yolten winked at him. "Being disgustingly happy is our specialty. You should try it sometime."

Nicholas's mouth quirked. Disgustingly happy was exactly what he was planning to be.

Lady Yolten stopped them a few moments later so they could investigate some dark-green shrubbery. "That would be perfect in my garden. Do you know what it is?"

"I'm afraid all my plant knowledge revolves around crops. I haven't the faintest idea."

She spent a few minutes explaining what made that particular plant unique from every other shrub they'd passed before Nicholas finally plucked a stem from it. "We will ask one of the caretakers. They are certain to know the name of this miraculous foliage."

Lady Yolten smiled. "Brilliant." Before long, they rounded a tree-lined corner, and the giraffe house came into view. And so did a running Miss Morgan.

And she was alone.

Nicholas's feet froze to the ground, a sickening tightness darkened the world. He hadn't felt this much foreboding since the day Patience came tear-streaked into his study, unable to put a voice to the devastating news of their father's passing.

His eyes frantically searched the path behind Miss Morgan, but Lady Mercy was nowhere to be seen. Her parents weren't visible either; they must have already entered the viewing area of the giraffe house.

Miss Morgan slowed when she got within earshot. "Did Lady Mercy come this way?" she asked, out of breath.

Nicholas's vision tunneled to the space surrounding Miss Morgan. He should have known. He should have said something immediately when he learned that Miss Morgan would be joining them. If she was near, there would always be trouble. His only mistake had been assuming the trouble would be with him. "She isn't with you?" Each word out of Nicholas's mouth sounded like they had been chiseled from stone. There was no warmth in his voice, only sharpness and unyielding command. "We left the two of you together."

"I know." Miss Morgan looked as though she were about to cry, but he'd seen her summon stronger emotions with less preparation. "But she was going on and on about the llamas, and yes, they are fascinating, but also, I knew you were going to the giraffe house, and I did so want to see the giraffes."

"So, you left her there? Alone?" He was already darting back toward the llama house.

Miss Morgan's face turned to a pout. "I didn't *leave* her there. I started meandering this way in hopes that she would understand my meaning, but when I turned around, she was gone. I thought, perhaps, she had taken the other, longer path to the giraffe house, but it looks as though she isn't here.

Unless . . . Is she with her parents? Could she have beaten you there and joined them?"

"No, we would have seen her if she'd come our way, and we can see you ran the other way around and would have overtaken her unless she'd also run," Lady Yolten said. "And she would have no reason to."

Blast. It didn't matter how it had happened, only that Lady Mercy was alone, without a chaperone or any protection. Inside the Zoological Garden, she should be safe, but if she made her way back out to Regent's Park, anyone could cross her path.

He turned around. He started with a brisk walk, then, with a curse under his breath, he ran. It was only a few minutes before the path turned and the llama house came into view, but just as Miss Morgan had said, Lady Mercy was nowhere to be seen.

"Lady Mercy!" he called out, but only the sounds of the park around him answered back. He dashed to the doorway and looked inside. Three llamas turned their heads and looked curiously back at him, but she wasn't there either. He looked down the path that Miss Morgan had taken and strode toward it. The curve of the trees outlining the walkway made it nearly impossible to see more than ten feet in front of him. He started running again, pulling at his cravat. Sometimes he hated that deuced thing. Who invented such a torture device?

After a few moments of jogging, a woman came into view.

But it was not Lady Mercy.

It was Miss Morgan.

Again. She had made the loop from the giraffe house in the opposite direction.

He pulled at his cravat again. "Did you find her?"

Miss Morgan shook her head. "No, but I wanted to help. I thought, perhaps, if I retraced my steps, we would know at least where she wasn't."

"And there was no sign of her?" It was a stupid question—if there had been, she would have already told him.

"No," Miss Morgan said slower this time, as if she wanted to make certain he understood. "You checked the llama house?"

"Yes. She isn't there." Nicholas closed his eyes. He had lost Lady Mercy, and now he was alone with Miss Morgan. This day could not get any worse. He opened his eyes. Miss Morgan had somehow managed to silently creep forward and was now no more than two feet away from him.

Nicholas started and took a quick step back. "Why are you here?"

Miss Morgan blinked her wide eyes in innocence. "I'm looking for Lady Mercy."

"I mean here, today. Why are you at the gardens?"

"Lady Yolten invited me."

That was only half an answer, and they both knew it. "Because the two of you are such great friends?"

"We are."

Since when? Ottersby would know. He had done anything and everything to try to wed Miss Morgan before Patience came into his life. Getting to know her close friends would have been high on his list of tasks. Did Miss Morgan know secrets about Lady Yolten she was trying to leverage into damaging Lady Mercy?

Miss Morgan's lips made a perfect pout. "Don't you want me here? You don't think I would tell the Driarwoods about Patience, do you?"

Nicholas gritted his teeth. "She is Lady Ottersby."

Miss Morgan laughed, and the sound echoed through the zoo. If Lady Mercy was nearby, she would find them laughing and talking instead of looking for her. He strode down the path in the same direction he'd been going. Perhaps there was a turnoff Miss Morgan had missed.

Miss Morgan quickly caught up to him. "I've always thought that Ottersby is a silly name. I have a hard time using it. Especially with someone I thought was a maid."

Nicholas had nearly grown used to it. It was one thing for him to think it silly, but a completely different matter for Miss Morgan to say so. He didn't slow his pace but turned his head toward her. "It's not really silly."

Another laugh escaped her lips and this one sounded false, as if she were performing in a home production of one of Shakespeare's comedies. "It is almost as if you were upset with the man when you helped him get the title."

He *had* been upset with Ottersby. He had spent the better part of a few months receiving long, detailed apologies and proposals about courting Patience nearly every day. "Your point is?"

"My point is . . ." Miss Morgan softened her tone, and her hand went to his elbow. She tugged on it slightly, as if inviting him to slow down so she could keep up with him, but he ignored the gesture. "I would never tell them. Lady Yolten is a friend of mine. You, I hope, are still a friend of mine. I would never want to hurt you or anyone around you. I'm happy our circles of friends are joining together. Perhaps we will be able to see more of each other."

He grunted in response, and they walked another few feet in silence.

"She doesn't want to marry you, you know."

"What?"

"Lady Mercy. She doesn't want to marry you."

He was not about to discuss his relationship with Lady Mercy with Miss Morgan. "Then it is a good thing I have not proposed to her. I'd appreciate you not becoming involved in my courtship." His jaw clenched tighter, and a pain emerged behind his right ear.

"Oh, I wouldn't dream of becoming involved. I simply thought you should know. I'd had no idea Lord Ottersby no longer wanted to marry me, and the shock when he found another woman—"

"Be careful, Miss Morgan." His voice was nearly a growl. "That *other woman* is my sister."

Miss Morgan made a sound like a puff of air blowing out of a fireplace bellows. "I simply thought you should know. That's all."

He doubted there was anything simple about her thinking. Miss Morgan was a master manipulator. Someone whose word meant little to nothing. A walkway opened to their right. "Did you check down this path?"

"No. I assumed she would go the direction of the giraffe house. But she must be down that path. Where else could she have gone?"

Nicholas was inclined to agree with her, but the narrow track led deep into the trees, the farther the two of them went, the more isolated and secluded they would become. Was it better to split up and find Lady Mercy on his own or search with a female companion? He had half a mind to return to the giraffe house and beg Lord and Lady Driarwood to join them in the search. But if they did that, they might miss Lady Mercy.

No part of him wanted to move away from where Lady Mercy could be, so he pressed forward without suggesting they should find more people to accompany them on their search. They stomped ahead, both looking around corners and behind bushes.

"What if she climbed a tree?" Miss Morgan asked, looking up at the canopied oak trees above them.

"I highly doubt Lady Mercy would have climbed a tree."

"It was only a thought," Miss Morgan said.

Nicholas shook his head, but he wasn't going to argue with her. He continued to look for Lady Mercy in some of the animal exhibits and small alcoves that cropped up along their path.

"Oh, what is—"

Miss Morgan was looking up and pointing at something hiding in the branches of an ancient-looking pine. He narrowed his eyes but couldn't spot anything in the dark canopy of needles.

"Oh!" Miss Morgan exclaimed, and the shock in her voice made him turn. He only got a quick glance at her before she was careening forward, her feet behind her and her arms outstretched.

He put his arms out to catch her, but he was too slow, and her gloved hands raked across his face. Her fingers snagged his mouth and dragged down his chin until they reached his cravat and took hold of it.

Nicholas made a strangled sound, and Miss Morgan tumbled into him.

As soon as Miss Morgan's feet were steady, he pulled her hand off his cravat and pushed away from her. "Pardon," he said almost automatically, then dragged a hand over his lips to inspect for blood. Thankfully her gloves had protected him from her nails, and his hand came away clean. He shook his head, cursing the fact that he hadn't sent her back to get Lord and Lady Driarwood. "Perhaps you should abandon the idea of Lady Mercy being in trees and keep an eye on the path in front of your feet, Miss Morgan."

Her response was a laugh. "Your Grace, I'm dreadfully sorry," she managed to get out between giggles.

"It was an accident."

"But what an accident." She pulled on his elbow, forcing him to stop and turn toward her. "Let me fix your cravat at least. I'm afraid I've rather spoiled it." Miss Morgan reached for his neck.

Nicholas put a hand up and stopped her. "No. In fact, I think we should return to the giraffe house and continue our search from there, with Lady Mercy's parents."

"But we haven't looked down those two paths."

He glanced forward, where, certainly enough, their course opened to two other pathways besides the one heading to the giraffe house. He pinched the bridge of his nose. He hated to leave Miss Morgan alone, but even worse would be to stay with her. He wasn't entirely certain her falling and catching hold of his cravat was a mistake, and the stinging on his face wasn't helping his mood.

"I'll take the one on the right."

"No." Miss Morgan looked at both paths. "I'll take that one. It will lead back to the giraffe house sooner. Why don't you take the one on the left?"

He would take any path in order to be rid of her. He simply nodded and stalked away.

CHAPTER 19

THE LAUGHTER HAD COME FROM the larger path Mercy had left behind, and it had definitely been Miss Morgan's. Harrington hadn't laughed in returned, but his low, unmistakable, if unintelligible, voice had elicited giggles consistently enough for Mercy to understand the two of them were undoubtedly enjoying a pleasant rendezvous.

Perhaps Mercy should take up giggling.

Mercy gritted her teeth, because no, she was not the type of woman to change herself just to attract a man, even if the man was a duke, and besides, at the moment she had more pressing matters to think about than an unfaithful suitor. She crouched lower, but the effort only made the tiny, injured bird in front of her scoot farther into the small, spiked bushes.

Blast it all. Where was a fellow of the Zoological Society when Mercy needed one? She should have returned to the giraffe house by now. She'd told Miss Morgan to take all the time she needed with the duke before returning to the group, and from the happy sounds that had echoed throughout the garden moments ago, the two of them might still be a while. But the plan was for Mercy to be back before the two of them returned. She didn't want to worry her parents.

She removed her bonnet from her head. What were a few more freckles? Mama had long since given up on any of her daughters having porcelain-smooth skin. It simply wasn't in their nature. If she could scoop the bird into her bonnet, she could find a member of the Zoological Society who would know where the little beasty belonged.

Mercy lifted a branch of the bush with her free hand so she could creep forward. The bird made a tiny squawking noise and scrambled away. She grunted. Why couldn't the poor thing see that she was trying to help?

Perhaps slow and steady was not the way to win this particular fight. The bird was injured, so it wouldn't be able to fly away, and it hadn't run quickly up to this point. But if it creeped any deeper into the brambles, she would never reach it.

She took one slow, steady breath, then pounced forward, shoving her bonnet deep into the underbrush. Her back foot slipped in the soft, pine needle–covered dirt, and she pitched forward. Her chest landed on the ground, but her bonnet plopped down right over the bird.

She'd done it.

"Lady Mercy?" The duke's voice was low and surprised, with a hint of something else . . . anger?

Mercy jerked her head around, but she couldn't move her arm or the little guy under her bonnet would escape. "Yes?"

"What the devil are you doing? Are you hurt? Hiding from someone? Is someone distressing you?"

She *had* been hiding from him but was not currently. And while the sounds of him enjoying himself with Miss Morgan had distressed her while listening to them, she was completely past caring now. Or at least, she was determined to act as if she were. "No, I'm all right."

The duke strode to her and bent low. His hair, which was always tamed, now had several tufts of waves sticking out in unnatural ways, as if someone— Miss Morgan no doubt—had been running her fingers through it. His face was red, lips almost swollen, and most incriminating of all, his cravat had come partially undone. The Duke of Harrington she knew would never be caught without a perfectly tied cravat. Something twisted in her stomach. She'd heard from Miss Morgan about the duke's prowess, and she'd even heard evidence of it only a few moments ago, but something about seeing it firsthand made her feel like she'd been doused with lake water.

He'd been courting her for weeks, and not once had his hair been mussed, nor had his cravat been the tiniest bit askew.

"Come out of there." His voice was low and gravelly, still filled with emotion from whatever he and Miss Morgan had been doing. "We need to rejoin the group."

Mercy shook her head. "I can't."

"You can't?"

"No. I've caught something."

The duke's stormy eyes followed the length of her arm down to her bonnet, then he raised an eyebrow. "What, exactly, have you caught?"

"A *wee eejit*." Embarrassment from being sprawled out in such a position in front of the duke, who had so obviously been enjoying some time with

Miss Morgan—made her voice come out like Bridget's. Jittery nerves made her Irish, apparently.

The duke tipped his head to one side and offered her a hand. She wanted nothing more than to take it and stand up, but the rustling inside her bonnet made her shake her head. "I only just managed to catch the poor thing. It's injured, and it needs to be returned to its enclosure."

"The wee eejit?" The dangerously low and rough quality of the duke's brogue sounded much more authentic than her own had been, and something about his ruffled appearance, plus the Irish tone in his voice, made her face heat.

Why had she called the bird an eejit? Why couldn't she speak like a calm, collected woman, who simply happened to be lying prostrate on the ground, holding a bird in her bonnet while staring up at a devilish duke who enjoyed ravishing pretty much any woman but her? She swallowed. She could do better. "It is a bird. Its wing has been injured, and I thought it needed help."

The duke heaved a deep sigh and strode through the bushes, ignoring the way they caught on his trouser legs. He scooped up her bonnet, bird and all. He folded the edges of the bonnet together in one hand to keep the bird inside, then offered her the other.

This time, she gratefully took it.

As soon as his hand clasped over hers, he pulled her up brusquely. The force lifted her into the air, and she fell forward into him.

He didn't let go of her hand, nor did he step away. His chest rose and fell twice, hard and impenetrable. Her breathing quickened, but somehow it matched his.

"I—" He cleared his throat, and his hand tightened around hers. "I was worried about you." He let go of her fingers only to splay his hand against the small of her back and press her to him. "Out of my mind, actually. I cannot lose another person I . . ." He didn't finish his sentence. Instead, he leaned forward and rested his forehead against hers. "Thank the heavens you are all right."

Mercy had been held by men before. Lots of men. Always while dancing, of course, but still, being held by the Duke of Harrington shouldn't be so different, even if his head was pressed against hers. But it was. There was no music, no movement, just the two of them alone in this corner of the world.

She closed her eyes for the briefest of moments and considered imitating Miss Morgan's laugh. What would happen between the two of them if she did? Isn't this exactly what she'd wanted from him? For him to hold her and show her that he didn't just want to court and marry her for what she could do for him politically, but because he cherished her and found her desirable as well?

"Are you hurt?" he asked.

"No, I simply . . ." She simply what? Wanted to remain in his arms longer? She lifted her head away from his and searched his eyes for anything more than concern. But she couldn't read him. She didn't know what that look of tenderness was, not for certain. Perhaps he'd dreaded telling her parents she'd been lost, or perhaps he worried about her being left alone and her reputation being ruined, making her of no value to him and his pursuits.

If that was what made his face go soft and his eyes darken into burning coals, he must *really* want to be respected by the members of Parliament. The way he searched her face for any cause of harm was like a magnet, drawing her closer to him, lifting her chin until she was once again only inches from him. Or was his face dipping down toward hers? She wasn't certain which of them was moving, but the six inches between their mouths reduced to four and then two.

The Duke of Harrington was about to kiss her, and she hadn't even tried to giggle. Her breathing was uneven, and he must have noticed, but if anything, it only seemed to spark a fire in the coal of his eyes. She'd never seen a reaction like this from a man before, but it was exactly what she'd been waiting for. Her eyes slid down his face to his mouth and then made the mistake of dipping lower and catching sight of his cravat, still loose and unraveled from his time with Miss Morgan, and her body went rigid.

The duke froze, the fire in his eyes extinguished immediately, gone, as if it had never been there in the first place. His arm dropped to his side, and he stepped away abruptly. With a hard swallow, he glanced at the path behind them, the mouth that had been so soft and inviting only moments ago was now a deep frown etched into his face like it was made of unyielding granite.

The world went cold.

Mercy tried to paste on a smile, but it probably looked more like a grimace. Much like the grimace on the duke's face. "I'm sorry I worried you. We should return to the others before Penelope sends all of London's constables to find us."

The duke blinked and stepped back again. He was at least four feet from her now. Was she really that repellant to him? He shook his head slightly and managed to break through the stone of his face enough to bring the edges of his lips upward. Whatever look had been in his eyes when he held her tight against him was gone. What she had mistaken as a fire of interest in her must have been something left over from his time with Miss Morgan.

Hopefully Miss Morgan had managed to resurrect whatever needed rekindling with the Duke of Harrington, because Mercy didn't have the stomach to push them together again. She was done trying to sabotage her own courtship. The duke and Miss Morgan needed to commandeer those duties from now on.

They started back down the path, keeping several feet between them as they walked. The duke kept her bonnet lifted and out to the side, careful to not open it up or let the bird out.

Mercy let out a sigh, trying to convince herself it was a natural one. "Mama is going to have a fit when she sees my bonnet."

"I'm sorry." The duke's voice was soft but still raw and low, as if he hadn't used it for too long. "I fear I have damaged it."

Mercy laughed. "I believe I was the one who damaged it. Don't worry, Your Grace. Her concern won't actually be with the bonnet; she will only worry about the fact that I have acted so badly around you."

"Because you removed your bonnet?"

"She will have to pretend that our family cares about our complexions, when in actuality, we don't. There was no chance we won't get Mama's freckles, and her mother was completely insufferable about it, so she was determined not to pester her daughters about their skin. But she may have to pretend in front of you."

"I find those flecks on your skin fascinating. They keep me up at night."

Mercy stopped breathing. Fascinating? She bit her lower lip. Her entire plan was to have the duke find himself alone with Miss Morgan so that he could be overcome with affection for her, and while it seemed as though that plan had worked, Mercy being found by the duke had been an unforeseen oversight. Now *she* was the one alone with him and . . . well, she was not unaffected.

Fascinating. She had never minded her freckles, but she had never been under the delusion that a man would find them fascinating.

Harrington cleared his throat as if the sound would perhaps make her forget the words he'd just said. "And were those Irish phrases part of what your lady's maid has taught you?"

"Oh no." Thank the heavens her voice hadn't come out shaky. "I learned those from Bridget."

"Ah," Harrington said, like he'd just found the last piece of a puzzle. "And who is Bridget?"

"Our new scullery maid."

The duke nodded, and a slight smile tugged at the corner of his lips. "And are all of your servants Irish?"

"No, Mrs. Brooksby isn't. Plus a few others who have been working for us for ages. Does that bother you?"

"That you have a few English servants?"

She snorted. "No, that we have so many who are Irish."

"Lady Mercy, do you think I speak only of helping the Irish without doing what I can to help them in reality? My household workforce is slowly becoming Irish as well. Perhaps between both of our families we can bring Irish workers into fashion, and they won't have as much trouble finding work."

"You really think the two of us could hold that kind of sway on Society."

"I think so. I'm counting on it, actually. I've been a duke for over four years now, and yet, in the House of Lords, I'm still seen as a child. No one wants to take advice from a child."

"I don't think you should underestimate your own power, even if it is taking time to develop."

The duke's lips formed a line, and he nodded, but it looked as though he'd already moved on from their conversation. The giraffe house was about to come into view. He tried his best to smooth his hair and fix his cravat with one hand.

If she had been the one to disturb them, she might have offered to help him. Instead, she reached for her bonnet and its little prisoner so that he could have use of both his hands.

Before they took six more steps, the Duke of Harrington, with his nearly perfect hair and impeccable clothing, had returned.

CHAPTER 20

How did one manage courtship *and* debates in a single day? Not very well, it seemed, at least in Nicholas's case. He'd had Lady Mercy in his arms only a few hours ago. How was he supposed to deal with the inane arguments Lord Rayleigh kept spewing while standing in front of his seat at Parliament?

"The time to take action is now." Nicholas closed his eyes. "Every day we delay aid, families are suffering."

"You say the time is now," Lord Rayleigh countered. "But the time was now two years ago, and for all we know, it will be for the next two years. The Irish won't solve any of their problems if we are constantly sending them aid. We need to allow them time to make the adjustments needed in production and labor. Those families you speak of will be better off in the long run if they become independent."

The two of them had been standing for the past ten minutes without any sort of conclusion. Nicholas could see the rest of the lords growing weary of the conversation. The only thing worse than opposing lords were disinterested ones. At least an opposing lord had a mind Nicholas could try to change. Most of them men surrounding him seemed more interested in finishing this conversation and filling their own bellies than filling the bellies of the starving in Ireland.

Nicholas spun completely around, glancing at as many men in the eye as he could manage. Only a few even looked at him, and only Lord Driarwood managed an encouraging smile. The man had to. Nicholas was courting his daughter. This was futile. He wasn't his father, nor would he ever be. He'd almost kissed Lady Mercy, for heaven's sake. How could he expect these men to listen to him when he could barely manage to govern himself?

He didn't bother with a response. He turned and stalked passed the men sitting to his right until he had a clear path out of the chamber. If he wasn't doing any good, he might as well leave. Let the House of Lords have their dinner. He was done stopping them.

He'd been out of the room for only a few paces when he heard steps behind him. He didn't turn. If Lord Woodbury wanted to cajole him into returning, this time he wasn't going to be able to do it.

"Harrington." The voice behind him was not his old general's. It was too suave, with a bored drawl that no man who'd purposely followed another down a corridor should have.

Nicholas sighed and turned around. "Lord Bryant, to what do I owe the pleasure?"

Lord Bryant smirked, and his crooked smile simply managed to make him look more like an Adonis statue in a garden. Nicholas didn't have the patience to deal with him now. "I wasn't about to stay in that stuffy room after you left it. I only go because Diana thinks I can be a good influence somewhere. But, thus far, I haven't seen an opportunity for it."

"Perhaps if you'd dallied with fewer daughters of the men in there, you might have more luck."

Lord Bryant tipped his head to one side. "Perhaps." He lifted a shoulder. "But still, if given the choice, I'd rather impress those daughters of whom you speak than their fathers. They are much more pleasant to look at." Nicholas couldn't argue with him on that point, especially after walking out of the chamber unable to look at any of the men another minute. "That is my excuse, but what is yours? You gave up on your arguments rather quickly today. Is something wrong?"

Nicholas resumed walking. He didn't want to have to make small talk with any other lords leaving the chamber. Lord Bryant accosting him was bad enough. The man came beside him and matched his stride.

"Trust me. You are about the last man who would understand my concerns."

"Has your cravat gone flat?" Lord Bryant groaned. "Because if that is the case, you are right. I can't help you. I don't care one lick about cravats. But I'm fairly well versed in most any other subject."

"My cravat is perfectly well-behaved, thank you very much."

"But Lady Mercy is not?"

Nicholas coughed, but at least he managed to keep one foot moving in front of the other. Had a member of the Zoological Society been watching Nicholas and Lady Mercy when they were alone? Had Lord Bryant heard something? "What the devil do you mean by that? And be careful in your words, Bryant. I outrank you, and I won't have Lady Mercy's name besmirched."

"Ah, touched a nerve, have I? I wouldn't besmirch Lady Mercy. She is lovely, and even more lovely because of that mischievous glint in her eye. She is trouble of the highest and best nature. I was only wondering if she finally managed to crack that perfect gentleman's demeanor of yours? Heaven knows we are all waiting."

Nicholas scoffed. Him? A perfect gentlemen? That only showed how little Lord Bryant knew of him. "Trust me. I will crack long before she tries to manage me in any way."

"What makes you—" Lord Bryant stopped. He grabbed Nicholas by the elbow, pulling him to a stop as well. In just a few more feet, they would be out of the building and he could put a stop to this undignified conversation. "You've cracked already, haven't you? Well, well, well."

"No, I haven't cracked." He couldn't allow Lord Bryant to get the wrong impression. Lady Mercy's reputation was at stake.

"But you wouldn't mind cracking. Is that what you are saying?"

"No. I mean yes." Nicholas ran a hand through his hair. He would be in his carriage in a moment anyway, so he shouldn't have to see anyone else. He sighed. "What I mean is she might have seen me . . . that is to say . . . she might have deduced from my treatment of her that I am not uninterested in . . . um . . ." When did he become such a bumbling idiot? "In cracking."

Lord Bryant did nothing. Said nothing. He stood in the corridor with his hand on his hip, staring at Nicholas as if he were an unanswered but elementary mathematical problem. After a moment, he dropped his hand. "And?"

"And what?"

Lord Bryant raised his eyes to the ceiling as if Nicholas were an exasperating child. "How did Lady Mercy react?"

"She was shocked."

"No."

"Yes, she was. I'm a thousand steps ahead of her in this courtship. I'd happily make her my wife tomorrow." *Happy* was not at all the right word to describe the way his body reacted to the idea of calling her his wife. For a plan he'd been more than hesitant about when Ottersby had first mentioned it, he was suddenly quite taken with the idea of becoming a married man.

"You could always ask her."

"To marry me?"

"I suppose that would work. It does leave you open for rejection. But I meant ask her if she wants you to ask her to marry her."

"That feels a bit convoluted."

"It sounds like giving the young woman a choice."

Blast. It was a sad day in London when Lord Bryant was the voice of reason when it came to women. But the man had a point.

CHAPTER 21

THE NEXT MORNING, PENELOPE SAT in Mercy's drawing room. She'd arrived earlier than the accustomed visiting hour, so Mama was not quite ready, and Mercy met with her alone. As soon as Mrs. Brooksby set up the tea things and left the room, Penelope spun on Mercy. "Tell me all about the Zoological Garden. You weren't supposed to be the one alone with the duke. What happened?"

"I was only alone with him for a moment."

"To catch your finch. I followed that well enough yesterday, but what happened, exactly?"

"In my defense, I didn't know it was a finch. I thought it might be some rare bird specimen."

"Honestly, Mercy, do you never look at the birds around you?" Penelope's smile was dangerously close to a laugh. How was she supposed to know the little bird was only a finch? She hadn't had a good look at it in the garden, and she had just passed a bird enclosure. Was it her fault that her mind had been stuck on exotic species? "How is the little patient doing?"

Mercy had brought the little bird home and was feeding and caring for it in the back garden. Apparently the Zoological Society didn't care for common finches. "He seems to be doing well. Time will tell, I suppose."

"I'm sure with your supervision he will recover. Now, tell me what happened when the two of you were alone. The duke came back looking a bit disheveled." Penelope had a look in her eye like she was ready to pounce on whatever delicious information Mercy was about to give her.

Rather than answer, Mercy poured tea, her hands much steadier than her heart. "He looked a lot worse than that when I first saw him. He'd mostly put himself back together by the time we returned." There was a moment of silence. Mercy didn't look up to see the expression on Penelope's face. Penelope was a romantic at heart, just as Mercy was. No doubt she saw no better ending to this whole charade than for Mercy and the Duke of Harrington to fall helplessly in love. "I did hear Miss Morgan laughing with him just before he found me, though."

"Oh," Penelope replied, and Mercy didn't have to see her face to know she was disappointed.

They both sipped their tea, and for the first time since she'd met Penelope, the woman remained silent. In between sips, Penelope would perk up like she was about to say something, and then stop. Finally, on her third try, she managed to string together a few words. "It is just that I had thought—"

"I know exactly what you thought, and you were wrong. Or rather, you were correct about what happened, only incorrect about with whom it happened." Why did her tea taste wrong? She stirred in another clump of sugar to counteract the bitterness.

"But—" Penelope shook her head. "Well, that simply ruins everything. I had such interesting news to bring you about your duke."

"He isn't my duke."

Penelope narrowed one eye at her as if to say, *He could be, and we both know it.* But she was wrong. Oh, Mercy could marry him—she had no doubt about that. But he would never fully be hers. She may have even been able to resign herself to the fact that he was not a passionate person, although that would have been painful. But to know he could ardently pursue another woman, and he simply did not show any signs of attraction to her?

It would be purgatory.

"Yolty knows him a little. And, well . . . if I knew something wonderful about the Duke of Harrington, would you want to hear it?"

Mercy clenched her jaw, and then relaxed it. It wasn't Penelope's fault that the man would happily take advantage of a few moments alone with Miss Morgan, but when he had the same opportunity with Mercy, he kept her at arm's length. "Is it that he is dying to wrap me in his arms, and he has no interest in any other woman?"

"No."

"Then, no. I don't suppose I do."

"But—"

"He has always been one of the most wonderful men in London. Everyone has told me that since the moment I caught his eye. But he isn't drawn to me for any other reason than the fact that he feels we are suitable. You and I both know that."

"Are you completely certain that is the only thing he likes about you?"

Mercy sighed heavily. She probably shouldn't mention it, as Penelope was bound to jump to conclusions, but at the same time, Harrington's compliment still burned when she thought of it, and she wanted to share its heat. "He may also like my freckles. But again, hardly a reason to get married."

Penelope bolted straight up. "Well, that's something, isn't it?"

"It is something that holds no bearing at all."

"Oh, Mercy. You don't know the first thing about love. I probably could have given up Yolty if it weren't for the cowlick in the middle of the back of his head. I'd resign myself to a life lived without him, and then I'd see that clump of hair that just wouldn't behave, and I knew I would never actually be able to be happy with anyone else."

"Really? Was that before or after your affair with Lord Bryant?"

"That cowlick was what caused my affair with Lord Bryant."

"Does he have a cowlick?"

"Not even close. His hair always lays perfectly. Someday I'll tell you all about my relationship with Lord Bryant."

"I'd really rather you didn't."

Penelope snorted and then raised both of her eyebrows. "I promise you, you would rather I did. Are you certain I can't talk you into bewitching the man who wants to marry you?"

"Of course I'm certain. It shouldn't be that much work, especially when he seems quite easily bewitched by other women."

Penelope looked as though she might argue, but instead, she sighed. "How is Bridget settling in?"

"Her accent is improving, and she works hard. Best of all, the hollows in her cheeks are starting to fill in."

"She hasn't written to all of her relations to tell them to come work for you?"

"No, but if she does, you know I will help them find positions."

"Oh, I know—most likely in my home. Soon enough, none of my servants will speak proper English either."

"Then we both can pick up Irish."

"That will make us quite popular among the *ton*. It is bad enough that I come from manufacturing stock. What will Yolty do with me?"

"The same as he has always done. Love you for those things."

Penelope smiled and raised her teacup to her mouth. This was a woman completely content in her home life. A life that used to give Mercy hope for her future. Instead of comforting her, though, a niggle of resentment stirred deep inside her gut, making her sickeningly sweet tea taste bitter again.

What was happening to her? Mercy wasn't a spiteful person. She'd always been happy for other people's joy. This whole situation with the duke was poisoning every aspect of her world.

Mrs. Brooksby knocked and announced Lady Ottersby had arrived for a morning visit. Lady Ottersby? The duke's sister?

Penelope put her cup down and sat up straighter. "I've heard lovely things about Lady Ottersby. If nothing else, this duke fiasco has you meeting with some of the best people in London. And I don't mean because of their titles."

Lady Ottersby swept into the room like spring had arrived in the Driarwood home. She immediately rushed to Mercy and kissed her cheek with undisguised affection. Were the two siblings actually related? For certain?

But then, the memory of his mussed hair and ruined cravat flashed through her mind. She needed to stop thinking of him as staid. He was obviously not. He simply wasn't interested in being anything else around Mercy.

"Lady Mercy, it is lovely to see you. I hope you don't mind me coming without notice?"

"Of course not," Mercy answered. Lady Ottersby's auburn hair was styled in curls lifted up and away from her face. The color was not the same as her brother's, but it reminded her of the way his had formed loose waves when unleashed at the Zoological Garden. "It is a pleasure. You will have to excuse my mother; she was up late with preparations for our upcoming ball and is still resting."

Lady Ottersby nodded as if the pleasantries were already over. "Nicholas told me Miss Morgan accompanied you to the gardens yesterday."

"Yes."

"Are you, indeed, great friends with Miss Morgan?"

Mercy didn't know how to answer. She barely knew either of these women. If she were going to continue to support Miss Morgan and the duke's relationship, then she needed to claim at least some intimate friendship with her. However, something about Lady Ottersby's open and honest face made it hard to lie to her.

"I am," Penelope spoke up before Mercy could answer. "She is a dear friend of mine." Apparently Penelope had no such qualms about lying.

"Oh," said Lady Ottersby.

Mercy motioned for Lady Ottersby to sit down. "Why do you ask?" Was she here to warn Mercy that Miss Morgan could be a threat to their courtship? Well, she knew that. In fact, she was counting on it.

Lady Ottersby dropped into her seat as if she had no one watching. "I have some history with Miss Morgan. My husband courted her for two years."

"Two years?" Penelope sputtered. She had only just taken a sip of tea, and she had to swallow it down hard. "That is quite the courtship."

"Yes, well, my husband was not titled at the time. I assure you, had he been, they would have been married in weeks."

"What are you saying?" Penelope asked.

"Only that I am surprised that, if she is such a dear friend, you didn't know about it. Their courtship only ended a little over two years ago."

Penelope tipped her head up. "We have become friends recently."

"How recently? As recently as last month?"

Penelope and Lady Ottersby stared at each other, neither willing to concede that the other was correct.

The two of them were being ridiculous. Lady Ottersby seemed determined to protect her brother, and Penelope to protect Mercy. Mercy shrugged. "It was last week."

Patience spun toward her. "How did she talk you into inviting her on your outing?"

"She didn't talk us in to anything. We asked her to come."

"Why?"

Mercy leaned forward, catching Lady Ottersby's gaze. It might not be pleasant to hear that her brother was a philanderer, but it was time she knew. "Because I believe your brother and Miss Morgan have a much stronger connection that he and I do, and I won't keep pursuing a relationship with him if his heart belongs elsewhere."

Patience pressed her lips together. Her eyes went wide, and then she covered her mouth with her gloved hand. "Nicholas and Miss Morgan?"

"Yes."

"I have seen him flirt with her on occasion, but he has no interest in Miss Morgan or her family."

Penelope leaned forward in her chair. "She is quiet and timid, but some men like that sort of thing. And while I agree that her mother would be an atrocious in-law, a woman should never be judged harshly because of her family."

"Miss Morgan is neither quiet nor timid. Of that I can assure you."

"Your brother seemed quite interested in her at the gardens." That laughter, his voice rumbling back . . . "And at the risk of sounding insolent, he has not shown such attentions to me."

"What do you mean, attentions?" Lady Ottersby asked, her face a mask of confusion. But all Mercy had to do was raise her eyebrows, and Lady Ottersby's face cleared. "I'm sure you must be mistaken. How do I explain my brother? I don't know that I can. I used to know him better. He wasn't always so stoic and serious. But somewhere along the way, all that changed. A part of him died. A good part of him—the brother who would laugh and not take the world so seriously. And with you, Lady Mercy, I see it coming back. He is smiling more. He gets excited about things. Life isn't so much a drudgery. He looks forward to attending balls and spending time with you. I promise you, Nicholas is capable of showering you with attention. He just needs time."

Lady Ottersby was passionate in her speech, enough so that Mercy at least believed that Lady Ottersby believed this version of her brother, but if she didn't know what had changed him, Mercy might know more about the duke than his sister did. "Did this unfortunate change correspond with your father sending him into the army?"

Lady Ottersby eyebrows furrowed. "Yes, it did. He changed drastically while under my father-in-law's command. How did you know?"

"I've gotten to know your brother a little." Perhaps in this one thing even better than his sister did. It wasn't the army that had changed him; it was the forced loss of the woman he loved. The stunning Lady Plymton. "And how long has he known Miss Morgan?"

"Only since the time I became engaged. Two years."

"And are you certain she is not the reason he's been changing?"

"Heavens no. She does, however, possess knowledge of our family that Nicholas would rather keep away from the public. If he ever looks concerned when she is around, it has nothing to do with her as a person."

That was an interesting tidbit. What was the duke hiding? "What kind of—" Mercy started, but another knock interrupted her.

Mrs. Brooksby walked in and handed Mercy another card. Mrs. and Miss Morgan. Well, this was about to get very interesting. Mercy looked up from the card. "Mrs. and Miss Morgan will be joining us."

Penelope's face brightened. She loved anything lively, and this morning was turning out to be very lively indeed. Lady Ottersby, on the other hand, scowled.

"Shall I invite them in?" Mrs. Brooksby asked.

Mercy looked at the two women already seated at the table. There was still room for several more, so why not? Miss Morgan should at the very least have the chance to defend herself. "Yes."

Mrs. Brooksby left to fetch them, and Lady Ottersby grabbed Mercy's hand. "I first met my husband when I ran away from home and pretended to be a maid in his household." Her voice was low and fast, as if she were trying to explain as much as she could before Miss Morgan walked through the door. "He was courting Miss Morgan at the time, and she is one of very few people who know what I did. Nicholas would rather die than have this get out among the *ton*. I personally don't care. But that is what Miss Morgan and her family hold over my brother. That and only that."

Mrs. Brooksby announced Mrs. and Miss Morgan the second after Lady Ottersby finished her rushed speech, and Mercy's open jaw clamped closed while her mind tried to process everything Lady Ottersby had said.

Despite their very different temperaments, both Miss Morgan's and her mother's faces registered shock in a similar fashion. At the sight of Lady Ottersby, their smiles wavered, then their eyes flashed to each other's, then almost simultaneously, their lips curved into friendly grins.

Lady Ottersby's story was so absolutely unprecedented that Mercy still wasn't certain she'd heard her correctly. The stunning woman sitting opposite her working as a maid? It was preposterous. But the looks on her newest guests' faces made Mercy think that perhaps Lady Ottersby knew exactly what these two women were about.

The five of them chatted about the weather, and Miss Morgan thanked Penelope once again for inviting her to the Zoological Garden. She practically fawned over Lady Ottersby. Where was the shy woman who could barely manage a few words the last time she was here?

Mercy finished her tea and set down her cup. "Miss Morgan, I am trying to decide which book to read next. Would you mind joining me at the bookshelf? I'd love your opinion."

Miss Morgan looked at her mother, who gave her an almost imperceptible nod, and then she smiled and stood. The bookcase was on the other side of the room, near the chess table. Pieces from her last game with the Duke of Harrington still stood in their place, waiting for him to return so they could finish. She'd planned her next move two days ago, but he hadn't been here to allow her to use it.

"What type of books to you prefer?" Miss Morgan said in a voice loud enough that it would carry to the rest of their party, still taking tea.

"That depends a lot on my mood." Mercy dragged a finger along the row of books. They both knew they hadn't come here to speak of them. She lowered her voice. It was time to test a theory. "How did you enjoy your time at the gardens?"

Miss Morgan let out a long, drawn-out sigh. "It was positively delightful. I knew that all the duke and I needed was a moment alone for us to rekindle our—" A pretty blush touched her cheeks, not unlike the ones she had at the garden after they had all rejoined each other. Could the woman blush on demand?

"I wasn't certain our plan had worked. The story His Grace told me hadn't sounded very romantic. I wondered if perhaps all our efforts were for naught."

Miss Morgan froze, one finger on the title of a book. "He must still want to keep what happened a secret. If I know him, he probably made up some story of me falling into him, or something nonsensical. He used to do that all the time. When will he finally admit his feelings?"

The laughter she had heard and the low voice that followed . . . Could that have been because Miss Morgan *had* fallen into him? That could also explain his ruffled appearance. The duke had shown almost no interest in Miss Morgan for the rest of the day. When he'd reached Mercy, he had seemed more upset than anything. "But he had a very clever explanation for why his face was swollen. I am inclined to believe him."

"Let me guess. He said I scraped his face with my hand as I fell? He's used that excuse several times before."

Mercy nodded, as if what Miss Morgan said calmed her suspicions. Someone in this room was lying, and at least with Miss Morgan, the truth was easy to sort out. If Miss Morgan and the duke had actually fallen back in together, she would no longer need Mercy's help. "Well then, it seems our work is done. I assume now that you have rekindled your relationship with His Grace, you won't need my help anymore."

Miss Morgan's jaw flexed, but she didn't look up. Instead, she pulled a book from the shelf and flipped through its pages. "Have you broken the courtship?"

"I'll wait for him to broach that subject. I'm certain he will, based on what you've told me."

Miss Morgan snapped the book closed. "But that's the woman's responsibility. You must see that."

Blast. She had a point. "True." Mercy tipped her head to one side. "I suppose I will think about it."

"And while you are thinking about it, could we arrange another meeting with the duke? If he comes to see me at my home, I'm afraid Mama's hopes will soar, and I would rather not put her through that again before we are certain."

Mercy kept her smile in check, but Miss Morgan had just shown her hand. The little conniver. "How could I possibly do that?" Mercy shook her head. "If I am to break off the courtship, I won't have any reason to meet with him again."

Miss Morgan opened her mouth to say something but then closed it. Opened it again and shook her head. "I suppose you're correct."

"Shall we return to tea, then?"

Miss Morgan and her daughter were determined to stay longer than Lady Ottersby, and Lady Ottersby seemed to also want more time to speak with Mercy alone, but after five cups of tea and Mama joining them, Lady Ottersby finally gave up and left. She embraced both Mercy and Penelope, then with a squeeze of Mercy's hand, she was gone.

A few minutes later, the Morgans left as well.

Poor Penelope had stayed through all of it. Mama excused herself, and once the door clicked closed, Mercy turned to Penelope. "We are done putting Miss Morgan in the duke's path. I'm afraid Lady Ottersby was right about her."

"You are certain?"

"Very." She was nothing like the girl she had been the first time they met, and her story about falling on the duke made a lot more sense than the two of them kissing in the gardens. "I think I owe the duke an apology."

"But you can't tell him."

"No, I can't. It would be highly embarrassing."

"So, we are through with our plotting. And I can finally tell you what Yolty said about the duke. It turns out he just hired a team of agriculturists to go to Ireland and work on ways to combat the blight. He wants Parliament to vote for more aid, but he is also taking the matter into his own hands."

Mercy closed her eyes. Of course he was.

Count on the Duke of Harrington to be a saint. As if liking her freckles didn't make him saint enough. Mercy sighed. "I have no doubts about his goodness, at least as far as the welfare of others is concerned. No one in England takes duty as seriously as he does. But it isn't his steadfastness I'm worried about—it is my place in his heart."

"Mercy." Penelope took her hand. "I think he may like you."

"Perhaps. But you heard what Lady Ottersby said about how unhappy he has been the past few years. I happen to know that happiness was lost when his father ended his relationship with Lady Plymton."

"Mercy . . ." Penelope frowned. "You cannot be serious."

Mercy stood. She was serious. "You haven't seen the way he jumps away from me whenever we get close. It is like he is trying to convince himself that he can be happy with me, but it never works. He looks miserable after every interaction. I cannot live my life that way."

Especially not now. When a small part of her wanted this more than she cared to admit. How could she live the rest of her life on the smallest scraps of affection the duke was willing to give? She couldn't. "One more test, Penelope. Miss Morgan was the wrong woman. That is all. We will conduct one more test. I think the most likely location to push the two of them together would be at my family's ball next week. I'll make certain she is on the guest list. We need to make a plan, but this time I need to be far from the duke when he meets her."

Penelope groaned. "Why don't you just ask him about her?"

"Because Lady Plymton won't help his social causes, not like I would. He won't allow his heart to rule his head, and even Miss Morgan knows that about him. If I speak to him, he will just use that head of his to explain everything away. Seeing her again will open his heart."

"And if it doesn't?"

"If it doesn't, then I will have a terrible decision to make."

Penelope raised her eyebrow in a question. "What decision?"

Mercy sighed. "Whether or not I can be happy married to a man who I think I might one day fall in love with, when I know he won't ever feel the same about me."

"But—"

"I know what you are going to say, and please just don't. I've seen you and Lord Yolten together, Richard and Rosalind, Lord and Lady Bryant, my parents. I know what love looks like. And what the duke and I have isn't even close."

Penelope dropped both of her hands to her side in defeat. She heaved a heavy sigh and then dragged one of her hands down the front of her face. "This is such a terrible idea."

"And that is why you are the only person I trust to help me with it."

CHAPTER 22

NICHOLAS HAD JUST FINISHED ORDERING the flowers he was sending to Lady Mercy's family in anticipation of their ball the next day when he heard a knock at the front door. It was probably a woman come to see Mama, but there was a chance that woman could be Lady Mercy, wasn't there? He pushed aside his order form and reached for his cravat. It was still starched and perfectly in place. A few moments later, there was a soft knock at his study.

His lungs filled with air. Lady Mercy had come to visit him, for the first time without him inviting her. He called out for the door to be opened.

McCarthy stepped in and handed him a card.

The deep breath of air he'd inhaled when he thought Lady Mercy was calling froze in his lungs.

The card was from Lady Plymton.

"This woman is here, now?"

"Yes."

"Does she have a companion with her?"

"No, Your Grace, she is alone."

"Did you send her to the drawing room?"

McCarthy didn't answer right away. "I wasn't certain it would be prudent to, as I didn't know if you would want to receive her."

"Well done, McCarthy. I don't want to see her. You may tell her I'm not available."

A small smile tugged at McCarthy's lips. He'd worked his way up to butler over the past few years, but he'd been a part of the household before Nicholas served in the army, and no scandals ever escaped the servants' notice. Apparently he wouldn't mind putting Lady Plymton in her place. "I'll do that."

Nicholas held the edge of his desk and listened for the sound of a door shutting and a carriage pulling away, but neither happened. Instead, a few moments later, there was another knock at his study door.

"Come in." Nicholas sounded gruffer than he meant to be, but having his hopes of a visit from Lady Mercy be dashed by a visit from Lady Plymton had him on edge.

McCarthy stepped in. "The lady requested to wait in your drawing room until you became available. When I told her it could be hours and waiting in the drawing room was not possible, she said she would wait in her carriage instead."

"Is that exactly what she said?"

"I believe what she actually said was that she would be happy to leave her carriage, marked with the Plymton seal, outside for hours while she either waited inside the house or the carriage."

How had Nicholas ever found the woman attractive? He groaned and stood. "Where is she now?"

"Still at the door."

Nicholas marched out of his study and to the entrance hall. The door was open, and certainly enough, there stood Lady Plymton, a smile plastered on her rouged mouth. "Nicholas, what a pleasant surprise. I thought you were busy."

"You will address me as Your Grace."

Her mouth formed an O, and she covered it with her fingers. "I'm sorry, my dear. I thought we were long past formalities."

"No, we are long past any sort of friendship. What do you want?"

"Friendship? Is that what you call our former relationship? I must say, I envy whatever lady friends you have now."

Nicholas stopped five feet in front of the open doorway and clenched his jaw. "What do I need to do in order to make you leave?"

"I only want to speak with you for a moment. Would you rather I do that here, in the open, where everyone passing by on the street can see us?"

"Almost no one passes by here. We aren't exactly in the middle of Town." But still, he couldn't quite bring himself to leave her standing out in the open. He motioned to McCarthy, and his butler opened the door wider for her. She came in, then McCarthy closed the door behind her.

"Stay here, McCarthy. We won't be sitting in the drawing room."

Lady Plymton shrugged. "I don't mind the help hearing what I have to say. But do you feel the same?"

"Unconditionally," Nicholas replied. McCarthy had been part of his father's staff since he was a boy. He trusted him infinitely more than he trusted the woman in front of him. There was no need to hide anything from him.

Lady Plymton took two steps forward, swallowing up the distance between them until she was only an arm's length away. She lowered her gaze to his mouth and parted her lips. "Do you actually think a sweet little creature like Lady Mercy is going to satisfy you? If you let this courtship of yours go on much longer, you are only going to damage her reputation when you wake up and come back to me."

Every muscle in Nicholas's body clenched, but he managed to get a strangled laugh to escape his throat. "You were never mine to come back to."

"But I could be now."

"No, Lady Plymton, you cannot. The damage you caused me and my family can never be undone. I have no interest in any sort of relationship with you, and if you try to approach me in public, I will have no choice but to make that abundantly clear. Somehow I don't think a cut like that would be a good start to your time in London."

Lady Plymton lowered her lashes and bit her lower lip. There was a time when Nicholas might have found the gesture enticing. Now, he only wanted her gone. She arched one eyebrow in his direction and raised her eyes. "You act as if you weren't a participant in our sordid affair."

Nicholas's jaw clenched so hard he could already feel the beginning of a headache coming on. Lady Plymton knew exactly how to hit him where it hurt. He had been nearly obsessed with this woman, and yes, he was young, and yes, she knew exactly what she had been doing by pursuing him when he was so young, but still, the fact that he'd been so willing to be enticed and completely besotted by her still made him feel like a fool. "No, I act as if I was and am deeply ashamed by it. Now, please leave."

"You'd better do as my son asks." Mother's voice sounded from behind him, and Nicholas spun. Mother stood on the last step of the stairway with her hand on the banister, her head held high.

"Your Grace." If Lady Plymton was embarrassed or ashamed at Mother's rebuke, she didn't show it. She only broadened her stained smile. "It is lovely to see you."

Mother strode forward, stopping only when she reached Nicholas's side. "I don't ever recall the two of us being introduced. And if you don't mind, I believe I should like to keep it that way."

Lady Plymton opened her mouth as if she were about to speak but then seemed to think better of it and slid it closed. Still smiling, she gave a bow to

Mother and an even lower bow to Nicholas. "I'll bid you farewell. Feel free to seek me out when you change your mind."

McCarthy had the door opened before she'd even turned and shut it behind her so quickly the back of her heel was almost caught in the door.

A huge weight lifted off Nicholas's shoulders the second Lady Plymton was out of sight. She was the most glaring reminder of the rash and exploitable person he used to be, and he'd spent too long trying to distance himself from that young man to ever be comfortable facing him head-on.

"Thank you, Mother."

"My pleasure." Mother smiled, and any last vestibules of the hard woman she'd been only a moment ago faded. "I rather like being the overbearing parent for once."

"Nothing about that was overbearing. It was appropriate."

"Well, imagine that—me being appropriate. You've finally managed to rub off on me."

"I think our most recent guest is proof that I'm not a shining example of propriety."

Mother took his arm, and McCarthy glided quietly through the door that led to the back of the house. "Nicholas, your father and I hadn't even thought to start preparing you for a woman like that to enter your life when she did."

"He shouldn't have had to teach me anything. Watching how he lived should have been enough."

Mother shook her head. "You were young, and that was a hard time in our family. Your father loved you, and as upset as he was for what was happening in your life, he was even more upset with himself. He'd been so focused on *his* reputation and position in Society that he didn't get around to teaching you to protect yours until it was too late."

Nicholas blinked hard. "I wish I could go back and do everything differently. I wasn't trying to be scandalous with Lady Plymton. I'd honestly thought myself in love and had been too blinded by passion to see the truth that was so apparent to everyone else in London."

"Thinking you are in love with someone isn't a sin."

"But stupidity might be."

Mother laughed. "No, if it were, no one would be entering the gates of heaven. Especially not your mother. I've done things I'm not proud of because of stupidity as well, Nicholas. We all have."

And even though Mother made no mention of her leaving him with Patience so soon after Father died so she could find joy in Paris, he knew that was exactly what she was talking about. "I'm glad you are here. It turns out I'm not quite ready to handle all my problems on my own."

"No one ever has to be. I should've remembered that when I left the two of you to deal with my problems alone." And then a strange thing happened. Mother folded herself into Nicholas's chest and rested her head against his shoulder. It took Nicholas a breath or two longer than it should have for him to remember exactly what he was supposed to do in these types of situations, but eventually his hand made it to her back, and he pulled her into him.

The last time he'd embraced her, he must have been young, for she seemed especially frail now. He swallowed hard, tamping down the emotions that rose up at the thought. "Mother, there is something I have to tell you." She nodded but didn't pull away. He leaned back just enough to see her face while keeping his arm around her. She glanced up at him. "I'm going to speak with Lady Mercy about marriage. If all goes well, her family might announce an engagement at their upcoming ball. But I want you to know you will always have a place with us."

Mother's eyes brightened. "Oh, Nicholas, congratulations."

"Your congratulations are a bit premature." Nicholas wasn't entirely certain Lady Mercy wanted to marry him, but he was more than ready to find out.

Mother ignored him, her shoulders lifting and her face smoothing out, as if she were years younger. "We'll be having a wedding." Celebrations were Mother's specialty. She handled them much better than hardships. So much for his time of peace and quiet. Mother might move into the dower house, but having a novelty like Lady Mercy in their home would most likely mean Mother and Nicholas would be vying for his new wife's attention. But oddly, the thought didn't disturb him. Perhaps Mother's singing wouldn't be quite so unbearable if he had Lady Mercy here to share in his torment.

Mother's eyes clouded and then shifted to the door. "You aren't proposing because of that woman, are you?"

"No, I'm proposing because of Lady Mercy. I can't have anyone thinking I am only leading her on or that my intentions aren't honorable, because they are. I want only what is best for her, and I hope that is me. With Lady Plymton here in London, people are bound to talk. It wasn't as though we were discrete, even though since she was engaged, we should have been. Like I said, I was an idiot. I won't be again."

Mother took a step back and grasped both of his elbows. "Are you in love with Lady Mercy?"

This was a question he should know the answer to, especially if he planned to propose. A niggle of worry reared its head, but Nicholas pushed it down. Marriage was an enormous step. Of course he would be nervous. "I might be." Mother raised an eyebrow. His answer must not have been the right one. "I can't imagine building a life with anyone else. And I'm tired of being apart from her. I want her here. I want to claim her as family." And, more than anything, he didn't want to have to hold himself back the next time she was in his arms.

Mother squeezed his elbows and smiled. "That is more that most couples start with. It will be enough."

CHAPTER 23

NICHOLAS TAPPED HIS FINGERS IDLY on the chess table where he and Lady Mercy had played the past several weeks. Their pieces were still in place, waiting for the two of them to be in the room together so they could finish their game. He was early for the ball, and with all the preparations the family was certain to be busy with, today would not be the day they finished. He should have made an appointment. He was bullocks at courting. He simply wanted to be engaged and have the whole thing settled. He'd nearly kissed Lady Mercy in the Zoological Garden, and the feel of her in his arms had haunted him ever since.

The sooner he was engaged, the better. Lady Mercy would walk through the door with her parents. He would ask to speak to Lord Driarwood, and after he was given permission, he would return here, give Lady Mercy the present he'd brought her and ask her to be his wife.

Wife.

His fingers drummed faster, then stopped.

Wife. He closed his eyes. When Ottersby had suggested the idea of marriage, Nicholas had been quite certain his brother-in-law was delusional. Now no other course in life made any sense to him. Nothing in the past few years had made him more excited than sitting with Mother sorting through all of the family jewelry until he'd found the perfect piece to bring Lady Mercy today.

Mother had raised an eyebrow at his choice but hadn't said anything. She trusted him to know what would best suit Lady Mercy, and Nicholas had no doubt he'd chosen well.

The door crept open slowly, and he jumped to his feet in order to greet Lord and Lady Driarwood. But only Lady Mercy set foot in the room. Her eyes were wary and downcast, her hands together at her waist, with her fingers playing each other like a harp.

He looked behind her, but she was alone.

"Your parents?" he asked.

She took a deep breath and squeezed her eyes nearly shut. "They are seeing to some last-minute preparations for tonight's ball and asked me to come speak with you."

"Alone."

She shrugged. "It would seem so."

Lord and Lady Driarwood had sent Lady Mercy to speak with him? Alone? Did Lord Driarwood think he would propose without speaking to him first? Lady Mercy still hadn't completely entered the room. One foot was on the carpeting of the drawing room while the other still stood in the entrance hall.

"I was hoping to speak with your father tonight."

"Tonight?" Lady Mercy's voice had a high-pitched quality he wasn't used to. She must be uncomfortable with the two of them being alone. He had no answer to that. He could reach behind her and shut the door, but that would make the situation worse, and although her father must know the two of them were alone at the moment, it wasn't quite the same thing as asking for permission to propose marriage. Was it? Were her parents upstairs, hoping that was exactly what he was planning on doing, and because of the stress of the ball, they decided to forgo formalities?

But formalities were formalities for a reason. And the reason for this one was obvious in Lady Mercy's wide eyes and the uncomfortable way she held her hands together at her waist.

"Lady Mercy, please come in. Your father must know what I am about or he wouldn't have sent you here."

She raised an eyebrow but did not bring her foot into the room. "What, exactly, are you about?"

He strode toward her—one of them needed to have confidence—and placed his hand on the doorknob. She swallowed but stepped inside, and he shut the door behind her.

A quiet settled over the room, and he stepped in front of Lady Mercy. "What I am about is—" This wasn't how it was supposed to work. He should confess his love and devotion to her or at least let her know how much he had missed her whenever they spent time apart. Somewhere over the course of the past few weeks, being near Lady Mercy had become a habit, like filling his lungs with air or falling into bed at night. She'd become a part of his life, and proposing marriage to her felt like a formality. He had no idea if she felt the same way, but he was ready to find out. And if he let her know his intentions first, then he could speak to her of love without restraint. "Frankly, I came here to speak to you about marriage."

Her jaw clenched, and her hands stopped fidgeting. "In general? As in, you would like my opinion on the practice on the whole?"

"No," Nicholas answered. Had she really no idea what he meant? The two of them were courting. Where else would a successful courtship lead? "Specifically. As in, two of us."

She blinked up at him in surprise. "Why?"

Why? Nicholas opened his mouth and then snapped it closed again. He hadn't expected her to ask that. He wasn't even certain how to answer it. He took in her face, those freckles across the bridge of her nose . . . Someday he would count them. She was constantly surprising him, and it had been too long since his life had held surprises. "Because I think we suit each other, don't you?"

"Is that all?"

What else could he say? He hadn't realized he needed to prepare an argument for the case of their marriage. She must have known he was planning to propose soon. He hadn't been subtle about his interest.

He couldn't exactly tell her that ever since he had started courting her, ghosts of past relationships had come out in full force. Everywhere he turned, there was Miss Morgan, trying to get him alone. Or Lady Plymton, with her pitying eyes and touches that belonged in less suitable establishments than ballrooms. He was floundering—he had been for quite sometime— and somehow, she'd become his anchor. The one solid point, upon which, if he fixed his mark, he would not become lost. His northern star. "Isn't that reason enough?"

She stepped forward, leaving him at the door. When she reached their little table by the fireplace, she turned and faced him once again. She no longer looked nervous. "I must admit I had entertained hopes of a love match."

Nicholas slid his jaw to one side. She didn't love him, then. Had he rushed her? Was she saying she needed more time to fall in love with him, or did she think that would never be possible? He wanted a love match too, and he thought the two of them were well on their way to one. But he had no idea how to make her fall in love with him in the rare snippets of time they had together. Would she want him to keep trying, or was this to be their last conversation? The thought made him wish he could start over or, no, not start over, not start this conversation at all. "You don't think you can love me?" The question was out of his mouth before he could convince himself otherwise.

A faint smile traced her lips, and she examined the chair in front of her. "I don't know," she said softly. "And it seems like a thing a person should know before agreeing to marriage." Her eyes lifted to his. "Do you love me? Because I don't believe I've seen evidence of it."

Nicholas rubbed the back of his neck. He knew the correct answer to this. If he wanted a woman to marry him, the correct thing to do would be to pull out the necklace he'd brought her and declare his undying love. But what did she mean by the fact that she'd never seen evidence of it? Hadn't courting her been evidence? Seeking her out all the times he did? He wanted her as his wife so excruciatingly, he didn't know what he would do with himself if she rejected him. Was that love? He'd thought it was, but now she had him doubting. What exactly was she looking for?

"Lady Mercy." He leaned forward, resisting the urge to sit down at the chess table. He needed to think. He hadn't done everything properly—he was supposed to get her father's blessing first. But she had come in alone, and that had felt like blessing enough. "The type of relationship I hope to form with my wife will only be possible with prolonged exposure. The kind of exposure that is not truly possible in ballrooms or Zoological Garden, but in time spent together daily—doing the small tasks that husband and wife do together—building a life together. You ask me if I love you? The thought of you haunts me anytime I'm not with you. I measure my days by when I can see you again, and I have a strange fascination with your skin. Am I certain I love you? No, but I'm certain you are the only woman I'm going to love for the rest of my life. I had no plans for a love match, or at least no plans for love to be the mitigating factor of my decision to marry, but somehow now I need it. You've made me need it. But my heart has been foolish before, and I don't think it will let me fall completely in love unless I know you can love me back. What I feel for you is a spark, an ember that somehow burns as hot as any wildfire, and I know it will consume me whole when I give it the chance."

Lady Mercy plopped herself down on her chair and played with her queen, still holding court on the back row. If his speech had moved her, she didn't show it. Why did he blurt all that out? His head and heart were a mess, and no woman wanted to hear that after a marriage proposal. The correct answer was yes. *Yes, I love you,* would have been simple, direct, and probably the only way he could get Mercy to agree to marry him.

Mercy grabbed her queen in one hand and stilled it. "Why haven't you given it a chance?" Her eyes shot up to him. "You have been frank with me.

I will also be frank with you. I haven't seen this spark you speak of." Her eyes went back to her queen. "I'm not even certain I know exactly what love would feel like. I might . . . I might feel something like that burning you speak of, but I have seen love in the eyes of other couples. I've seen the way they are with each other. We don't have that, and I won't settle for less."

Nicholas sat across from her but kept his hands safe in his lap. He had seen love too. Patience and Ottersby were desperate for each other, and Lady Mercy's parents had a mature version of that—mutual respect and joy in each other's company. But he couldn't find a woman the way Ottersby had found his sister. Their courtship had been ripe with scandal. Ottersby must live in fear for the day Society discovered Patience had lived in his home as a maid for a month before they were married. He didn't want something like that hanging over his marriage. Did he want more love than his parents had shared? Yes. His relationship with Lady Mercy had been a perfect blend of his family's two examples of successful marriage. Proper, like his parents, yet fueled by the yearning he saw between Patience and Ottersby. Their relationship was as sensible as it was desirable. At least, that was what he'd thought.

He had no response for her. He thought he had done everything correctly, and nothing about their relationship had felt like he was settling for less. Lady Mercy and what he felt for her was more than he'd ever dared hoped for.

Lady Mercy sighed and leaned against her chair. She shook her head and motioned between the two of them. "What I have seen from you is calculations and strategy. You live your life like you dance: all the steps in the right order but none of the passion. Doesn't that make for a hollow existence? The few times I thought perhaps you desired me, you would always reel away in irritation. Do you expect me to live like that?"

The room stilled into a silence where even the mantle clock stopped its ticking. *That* is what Lady Mercy needed from him? Passion? Passion had *never* been his problem. At least not in the way Lady Mercy was implying. He had more desire than he knew what to do with. He couldn't trust himself. The last time he allowed himself to unleash his fervor for a woman, it had nearly ruined his life and cost him the respect of his father.

For the first time since meeting Lady Mercy in the corridor, the difference in their ages seemed astounding. She hadn't seen what that kind of passion could do to a family and a home when it wasn't controlled. When rules weren't followed. He'd been in her place at one time, and he refused to become her Lady Plymton.

He closed his eyes, unsure how to answer her. "All the examples of wonderful couples you gave me . . . those are the good stories. The ones with happy endings. For every one of those, there are dozens of unfortunate cases of women's reputations being ruined and men becoming known as rakes. We are always being watched by Society, even if you don't realize it. And everyone in the House of Lords is waiting for me to make another mistake."

"Another mistake?" Her voice was soft, and even though his eyes were still closed, he could sense her moving closer to him.

"Like I made with Lady Plymton."

"Are you certain that *was* a mistake?"

His eyes flew open. Lady Mercy was directly in front of him, only six inches away. She had leaned forward while his eyes were closed, and now she studied him, her head tipped to one side as if trying to understand him better.

"Of course it was a mistake."

"There is nothing wrong with falling for a woman you want to marry. I know Lady Plymton ended up married to someone else after your father separated you, but you can't spend your whole life worried that you will get hurt again. Nor can you base all of your decisions on whether or not London is watching your every move."

How had their roles switched so completely? Lady Mercy was calm and collected, and he was the one nervous and fidgeting. All it had taken for Lady Mercy to feel in control was to let him know she didn't want to marry him. Now that she had, she was ready to discuss his problems and fears, as if they were two lifelong friends. What kind of irony was this? "London *is* watching my every move." He leaned in closer. Her freckles were even more hypnotizing, now that he knew he would never get the chance to run his fingers over them or let his lips roam the skin on which they lay. "I won't be seen as a philanderer. I cannot be. If I have been overly proper with you, it is not because I don't—" He stopped. He couldn't say out loud the things he thought about her. How could she not see the wrestle he had every time she walked into a room? How could she need proof? Couldn't she see what was simmering beneath the surface? When that spark he had been so carefully guarding was released from its prison, the two of them would make the city burn.

Lady Mercy pursed her lips together and considered him like she would an unsolvable puzzle. She placed both hands on the chess table and pushed herself up. Nicholas rose as well, his faculties not so far gone that he would stay seated in a lady's presence. On the fireplace mantel sat a vase full of white roses. He had sent them to her only a few days ago. Lady Mercy reached up and broke off the top of one of the flowers. She returned to him and tucked the rose into the breast pocket of his jacket. Her touch was soft and illuminating, like fireflies had landed on his chest. She dropped her right hand slowly, her fingertips grazing his side, then leaned in close and put her mouth to his ear. "You may think me young and naive, but I need proof. I won't agree to marry you without it. You asked me earlier if I loved you, and I'm telling you, I think I could. I think I might already, but I cannot understand how you can claim to almost love me and not want to kiss me and hold me like I want you to."

Nicholas didn't dare breathe. Her scent would awaken something in him that he wasn't certain he would ever be able to tamp down again. Once again, the ticking of the clock on the mantel hushed, and then the ticking returned, growing louder in his ears every second.

He needed to leave.

He needed to thank her for her honesty and revisit the idea of a betrothal after the ball or in another few months, after they'd had more time together. But Lady Mercy hadn't asked for more time. She wanted something else from him. Something he wasn't certain he could give. Not without losing himself.

She reached for the flower again, repositioning it in some infinitesimal way that had to have been nothing more than an excuse to touch him. Her eyes met his, only a breath away from him. "No one," she whispered, her voice slow and deliberately intoxicating, "is watching us now."

Blast this glorious woman in front of him. Nicholas's hand stopped hers from leaving him, covering hers on top of the flower she'd placed there.

His touch brought a smile to her dangerous mouth. "You are a duke, Nicholas. It doesn't matter what anyone thinks of you. You could ruin a hundred women, and still, men would line up to have their daughters marry you. What are you so afraid of?"

Nicholas. His name was like honey on her lips. He couldn't be distracted by it. She was playing a perilous game of chess, and every part of him screamed to let her win. He clenched his jaw. He would not allow himself to lose. "I have *no* desire to ruin a hundred women."

"That's not what I asked. I asked what you are afraid of."

What was he afraid of? He released her hand and took a step back. Breathing was painful when she was so near. He placed his hands on his temples and rubbed in circles. He hadn't spoken to anyone about this except General Woodsworth. He clenched his teeth together and dropped his hands, locking eyes with her. "I don't want to be a disappointment. Not again."

Lady Mercy had started to inch forward, closing the gap he had just made between them, but at his words, she stopped. Her head leaned back. "Who in the world was ever disappointed by you?"

He smiled, but it was a grim sort of smile. He could feel the desperation of it on his face. "My father."

CHAPTER 24

MERCY BLINKED. THAT WAS NOT at all what she had been expecting. His father had passed away years ago. "Your father?"

The Duke of Harrington's face darkened. "Yes, my father."

He didn't say anything else, but those three words were hardly an explanation. She folded her arms in front of her chest and waited.

He stumbled away from her and returned to the chess table, pulled out his chair, and sat down. He had never, *never* sat in her presence unless she had been seated first, and the action made her step back. But he didn't even seem to notice. It was as if the mention of his father had prompted a whole layer of stiffness to fall away from him, and he was left sullen and . . . young. She tipped her head to one side. His hair had fallen onto his forehead, which rested on one hand. He looked like a schoolboy who had just been reprimanded by a teacher.

Mercy walked to his side and sat as well. For a moment, they were both silent. She waited for him to explain himself further, but he seemed content to simply slump forward and say nothing. With a sigh, she took hold of her queen. She slid the piece slowly forward until it sat directly beside his king on the opposite end of the board.

"Check."

He looked up, his eyes shrouded in mist, then back at the board. "That was an incredibly foolish move."

"As I told you, I'm not good at chess."

He shook his head slightly but didn't smile. Then, instead of taking her queen, he moved his king diagonally and away, just out of check. She laughed softly, and he met her gaze. "Neither am I."

"I would think, in the army, they would have taught you enough about strategy to make a better move than that. My queen was ripe for the taking."

"I didn't join in order to learn strategy."

"Ah, yes. Lady Plymton." She moved her queen forward one space. "Check."

The king moved diagonally backward. "Lady Plymton," he agreed, his voice flat.

She moved her queen. "Check."

He sat there, looking at the board, his king facing her queen as if more things were at stake than their twelfth chess match.

Mercy had to ask. "Did you love her?"

He laughed and dragged a hand through his hair. He would need to fix it before the ball began. Perhaps this time he would let her help him. "I did think I was in love, I suppose. But she was *not* in love with me."

"How do you know that?" His eyes went heavenward and then she remembered. The woman had been engaged. "She was engaged . . ."

"Yes."

"And you knew? The whole time, you knew?"

"Yes."

"But then . . . why?"

He moved his king to the left again. There were only a few more squares to the left of his king now. Soon their strategy would play out, and Mercy would either win or move her queen back to her side of the board, giving up the cat-and-mouse game.

His fingers dropped away from the king. "Do you think it is an accident that I follow every rule of propriety? I learned the hard way that there are reasons things are done the way they are. I learned that you don't get involved with an engaged woman—not because Society will scorn you, but because if she is engaged to someone else, her heart will probably never fully be yours. But not only that, I learned how many people you can hurt when you ignore Society's rules." He looked up at her, and the greens and browns in his eyes had become a forest under the onslaught of a thunderstorm. "My father never looked at me the same after that. My mother didn't either, although I think she understood me better than my father did. I'm fairly certain my father had never made a mistake in his life."

She moved her queen right next to his king once again. He was in check, but she didn't bother announcing it. "That can't be true."

"You didn't know him. He single-handedly returned honor to our line. His father had been a philanderer and, at times, a cheat. My great-grandfather had been the same. There is something soul-destroying about having power with no consequences. For generations, the men and women in my family took to heart the idea that they were above reproach, but my father put an end to all of that. He lived each day completely aware of the power and influence he had, but he used that power to help others, never for personal gain. He was faithful to his wife and was an upstanding man before marriage. When he saw me following in my grandfather's footsteps, it nearly broke him. He hadn't lived his whole life following every rule of propriety only to have his son destroy everything he had worked for."

"Are you absolutely certain she didn't love you?" Mercy needed to know. She and Penelope had planned for the two of them to meet alone somewhere at the ball. If there was any chance he still longed for the woman who had scorned him in his youth, then she wanted to help him. Wanted him to have a passionate, loving relationship with a woman *he* chose. Not one he felt like Society would choose for him. "I see the way you look at her, and it's not the way you look at me. Perhaps what you feel for me is not as strong as—"

The Duke of Harrington's king rushed forward with force and knocked her queen off the board and onto the floor. He held his king in a death grip, fingers straining. "I was seventeen years old, Mercy. *Seventeen.* She didn't love me. She saw me for what I was. A child with a title, ripe for the taking. All she needed to do was scorn her fiancé and entrap me to the point where my father, who was just the type of man who would make me be honorable to a woman who had no thoughts of being honorable with me, would feel obligated to force us to wed. When my father bought my commission and outwitted her, she pulled the wool over her fiancé's eyes and married him anyway." He shrugged. "He had a title too, after all."

Mercy held his burning gaze as long as she could, then bent down to pick up her queen. *Seventeen.* The thought of that sleek, harsh beauty she'd seen at the Bensons' ball, pursuing an impressionable seventeen-year-old turned her stomach. She took a moment while her head was down to take a deep breath and close her eyes hard against the tears that threatened to form there.

She'd never seen the man in front of her as anything but powerful. She'd never seen him lose control, but before he'd had any power at all, a woman had invaded his life and manipulated and controlled him. If she'd had any doubt that she might love this man, it evaporated, replaced by a sudden need to gut Lady Plymton.

She took one more steadying breath, then sat up, placed her queen on the table, and took the duke's hand in her own. Rage must have still been seething inside him, for he didn't flinch or pull away at her touch. Instead, he dropped his king and rested his free hand on the table. His eyes met hers, steady and unmovable. "If I don't look at you the way I look at her, it is because I don't hate you for ruining my relationship with my father, disappointing my mother, and nearly bringing a viper into the life of my innocent sister. The last few years of my father's life, I tried to prove myself to him, but I'm not certain he ever trusted me again."

Mercy wanted to fold him into her arms. She'd been a fool. How had she never thought to ask him about how long ago his relationship with Lady Plymton had been?

She squeezed his hand. "So you are still trying to prove yourself to him."

"And to everyone else." He blinked slowly. "His shoes are impossible to fill."

She did not let go of his hand, but with her free hand, she pushed his hair back into place. As she pulled back her hand, he grasped it, held her gaze steady with his own, and pulled her palm with aching slowness to his lips. The contact of his mouth on the delicate skin just above her wrist was like fire. His eyes didn't leave hers, and he slid his mouth to the tip of her thumb, kissing that as well. "If I have not shown you the passion that you deserve, I am sorry. I'm lost at how to go about this in a way that both my father and Society would approve of. But it is not because I don't long for you in the way a man should long for his wife. On the contrary, you, Lady Mercy, terrify me. You make me feel like I have learned nothing from that seventeen-year-old boy who had his world ripped out from underneath him by acting on his feelings. If I have been more careful with you than anyone in my acquaintance, it is because I *have* to be."

Mercy's hand was burning. She had toyed with him moments ago, putting that flower in his jacket, wondering if she could illicit the kind of response she had spent a long night imagining Miss Morgan had had in the Zoological Garden. Her attempt was pathetic compared to what the Duke of Harrington was doing to her now. She'd asked for passion. She'd thought he would perhaps answer her request by kissing her on her mouth. She'd had no idea he could prove his desire for her with only her hand and a gaze that promised so much more . . . over a chessboard. The dullest game known to man.

"You *don't* have to be careful with me." Her voice was shaky. Why wasn't she prepared for this? She'd never felt naive until this moment. How did the slightest motion of his bottom lip dragging from her palm to her index finger make it hard to speak?'

"Oh, I plan to be very"—he kissed her index finger—"very"—he turned her hand and grazed the knuckles of her next two fingers with his lips— "careful with you."

When she next inhaled, it was a gasp.

He winked and placed her hand gently back on the table. For all his blasted confidence, his hand shook ever so slightly when he released her. But he straightened his spine and pulled his face back into the mask of propriety he typically wore. That careful facade of a passionless man stood where a man who burned with desire had just been. He gave her a short bow and walked toward the door. "Tell your parents I was sorry to miss them. But know that I don't mean it. I suppose I will wait until we have time to get to know each other a little better before I broach the subject of engagement again." He stopped and turned back to look at her. What must she look like? Stunned, craning around on the chair to see him, most likely with her mouth agape. Her breath was still coming in short little gasps as if she were a fish that had been tossed out of its bowl. A slow smile tugged at his lips. "That is, unless you have changed your mind already."

Changed her mind? Because he kissed her fingers? She snapped her jaw shut and stood, throwing her shoulders back with pride. She would not let him leave the room with his last view being her gaping at him. "Why? Do you think you have done something worthy of changing my mind?"

He raised an eyebrow. "I haven't?"

"Not hardly." She strode toward him, eye on his perfectly tied cravat. She wanted to pull it away and let it fall so she could see that other duke. The one who kissed her hand and made her breath catch. She wanted to make his breath catch this time. "Perhaps we *do* have a spark. But before I agree to anything else, I need to see it burn. Just a bit."

His eyes went to the chess table they were just sitting at, and she knew what he was thinking. Hadn't that counted? Perhaps she should leave it at that. But the great Duke of Harrington had let his guard down, and she wasn't certain how long it would be until she got to see that duke again. She already missed him.

She leaned forward, and to his credit, for once, he didn't step back. "Let's consider, for a moment, that perhaps you are not quite as dispassionate as I assumed. That doesn't mean I don't have any other concerns. In fact, I have a few."

"A few?" His eyes, which had flinched slightly at the word *dispassionate*, furrowed. "Exactly how many is a few?"

"I don't know yet. I'm still coming up with them."

A corner of his mouth lifted, and he eyed the door. "That hardly seems fair. And if you have concerns, I should be allowed some in return." His first concern was extremely apparent. Evidently, he was only comfortable with the door closed when he was on his best behavior.

Mercy smiled. "Crack it open if you're worried."

His shoulders relaxed, and he turned and opened the door a few inches. When he faced her again, it was with more confidence. "Now, tell me your concerns."

This blessed man. How had his propriety seemed so abhorrent to her? It was adorable. "First of all, this whole *Your Grace* business. It wears on me. How can I truly fall in love with a man if I must call him 'Your Grace' all the time?"

His eyes lit up, and he smiled. He hadn't seemed to mind at all when she'd called him Nicholas earlier. "That is easy enough to remedy. Don't call me that. Not anymore."

"But if I call you Harrington—or even worse, Nicholas—what will people think?"

"Oh, people be d—" He stopped. "I see what you are doing."

She widened her eyes innocently. "What?"

"You are trying to entrap me."

"Into marriage? You practically asked me to marry you just a moment ago."

"Into admitting that there are some areas of Society that are hard to navigate, that perhaps could even be ignored at times."

"So . . . what should I call you? If I call you—"

He stepped forward and grasped her fingertips in his own. "Call me Nicholas. If it will help you to see me as someone you could, perhaps, spend your life with, please continue to call me Nicholas."

"Nicholas." She rolled his name around on her tongue, and the way his eyes darkened was a far cry from proper.

He swallowed hard. "But if you call me Nicholas at the ball tonight, you must know that there will be consequences."

"Oh." She leaned forward, widening her eyes and making her mouth form an O, as if she were afraid. "Consequences."

"This isn't a game, Mercy."

She hadn't given him permission to use her Christian name, but in the past half hour something splendid had awoken in him. He had finally understood what *she* needed between them. For the past few weeks, every interaction, except perhaps those she had engineered to put him together with Miss Morgan, had been spent courting the way *he* had thought courting should be done. But now . . . now he was different. Between that awakening and finally understanding what had happened to make him act the way he did, this visit had changed everything. She slid closer to him, her eye on his cravat. The last remaining artifact of the starched man he'd been when she'd walked into the room. "It could be, though. It could be a very enthralling game. Much better than chess." She touched the knot at the center of his throat. "If you let it."

Nicholas eyed the open door, and she felt as if she could see his calculations: What would it look like if her parents came in? What would Society think of this change between them? How would he recover socially if she never agreed to marry him after the two of them were caught alone together?

Before she gave him any more chances to think, she pulled at the knot in his cravat.

Nothing happened.

Nicholas's back had gone ramrod straight again, but he didn't step away or tell her to stop. She pulled again. The silk under her fingers crumpled, but the knot did not come undone. Mercy stepped forward, then with both hands at his neck, she examined the blasted thing closer.

"There is a pin," Nicholas said, his voice quiet. "Thankfully."

"Why thankfully? Don't you get tired of that being tied around your neck?"

"I suppose I do. Which is why I take it off when I am home. Not, however, when I am about to attend a ball. Why do you want it off?"

"I'd like to see your neck." The moment the words came out of her mouth, she could hear how ridiculous she was being. What was she thinking? *Telling* him she wanted to see his neck? Who thinks of such a thing?

But Nicholas simply tipped his head as if she had said the most rational thing in the world, pulled out the pin, and unfastened the knot.

His collar was still high, but the middle of his throat, and a small *v* of skin below it was bare. He neck was strong and corded, a testament to the rigid man standing before her. His Adam's apple was still, hovering in the middle of his throat. *Swallow*, she wanted to demand, but one absolutely preposterous request was, perhaps, all she should allow herself. "You must think I am a complete hoyden."

"Because you wanted to see my neck?"

She nodded.

"I happen to be quite captivated by your neck, so no, I do not think you are a complete hoyden. I do think I should return my cravat once you are done examining me, though. Unless you truly are ready to be engaged, and even then, I believe we are stretching the boundaries of propriety."

"I'm not done."

He would have to swallow, eventually.

His mouth quirked, and he nodded, and in that moment, Mercy knew she was going to marry this man. He was not at all what she thought she wanted, but somehow, he was more—more in every way.

Rosalind could have her Richard who wore his emotions on his sleeve. Mercy would revel in a man who only allowed himself to light on fire when he caught her alone. She motioned to the long, white silken strip falling down his chest on either side of his neck. "May I hold that for a moment?"

He raised an eyebrow. "You aren't going to throw it in the fire, are you?"

"No." She laughed. "Why would I do that?"

"I have no idea. But I wanted to eliminate the possibility. I do have to make myself presentable at some point this evening."

"I will not burn your cravat."

Nicholas raised a hand and pulled on the one side of the cravat, and it slid easily from his neck. He caught the free end of it before it fell to the floor, then held it out to her with both hands. Mercy bit her lip. If she took this next step, there would be no going back. Her eyes met Nicholas's. His were still dark, but curious. He was waiting for her to do . . . something.

Whether she was completely ready or not, she had no desire to disappoint the man she had only just rejected. What a difference a few minutes made. Her parents could walk through that door at any moment, and if they found them here in this state, Mercy would have to lie and tell them she had accepted his marriage proposal. But if she could perform one simple task before they returned, she could ask him to propose one more time, without feeling like she'd given into him with just a few measly kisses on her hand.

Well, not measly, but still. It was the principal of the thing. She couldn't begin a long-term relationship by immediately caving to all of Nicholas's wishes. It was a bad precedent to set.

Had her sister felt such confidence and power when she had been in the same position? Had her mother? How could all the women in one family be so fortunate?

Mercy smiled, put one hand out, and grasped the cravat where it hung lowest, right between his two hands, and pulled it toward her.

CHAPTER 25

NICHOLAS HADN'T A CLUE WHAT Mercy wanted with his cravat. But there wasn't much he wouldn't give her if she asked for it. She stood in front of him, holding it and smiling as if she had something positively wicked planned. The door was open, her parents were at home, and servants wandered nearby. At any moment, they could be disturbed, at which point he would have to ask Mercy to marry him again.

The thought should give him pause. The last time he had asked her, she'd let him know in no uncertain terms that she was not interested.

But that wicked gleam in her eye seemed to suggest she might have changed her mind.

"There is one more thing I would like to try," Mercy said. "But I worry that with your sensibilities, it could be too much."

"My sensibilities?" How prudish did she think he was? He opened his mouth to protest, but then stopped. *Prudish* was actually a fair description of him. At least now. And certainly while they stood alone in the parlor together. If he protested the title, she may ask him to prove that he wasn't. "What would like to try?"

"I won't kiss you. Not exactly. I know that you would much rather wait until an engagement for such things."

He couldn't help a quick glance at her parted lips. What in the world did she mean by that? "You *won't exactly* kiss me?"

"Correct."

"Because you shouldn't kiss me at all. You know that."

"You kissed my hand a moment ago."

"Are you telling me you won't, exactly, kiss my hand?"

"No." Mercy stepped closer to him, his cravat spread out in front of her. "I'm telling you I won't, exactly, kiss your mouth."

"Of course you won't. Correct me if I am wrong, but my understanding was that you rejected my proposal a moment ago."

"Correct *me* if *I'm* wrong, but I told you I wanted to see if our spark could burn a little before I accepted your offer." She smiled haughtily and held his cravat up to his face. "It just so happens that I have come up with the perfect compromise."

She covered his mouth with his cravat then leaned forward wrapping her arms behind him and tying the cravat it in a knot at the back of his head. "You see," she said after she stepped back away from him. "I won't exactly kiss you, but I may kiss that cravat of yours."

He furrowed his brows and tried mightily to not dwell on the brief seconds she'd been pressed against his chest as she tied his cravat. Mercy was playing with fire, and she knew it. Did she think having a thin piece of silk covering his mouth discounted a kiss? He reached up and pulled it below his chin. "If you kiss me with this cravat on my mouth, it is absolutely still a kiss."

"Really?" Her eyes went wide, but he could tell she was doing it on purpose. Acting innocent again. She knew. She knew the affect such a thing would have on him. She had to. "Well then, I'll just remove it, and you can absolutely kiss me without it."

"We have no understanding."

She ignored him, stood up on her toes and placed her arms on his shoulders. She pressed against his chest again, and her fingers went to the knot that had fallen to the base of his head.

She fumbled with the knot in one way and then another. She took a deep breath and then pursed her lips together in what was obviously mock concentration.

"Having a little trouble with that knot?" His voice came out low and pained.

Her eyes met his, and she nodded solemnly. "I am."

He closed his eyes, and the world went black except where Mercy's body touched his; those points burned like brilliant spots of lights, visible even through his eyelids. He should rip off the cravat and storm out of the room. He should return to speak with Mercy and her parents after the ball, engage her hand in marriage, and only spend time with her in short increments, with chaperones standing nearby.

He should do a lot of things, but instead he simply stood there, waiting to see what Mercy would do next.

She. Did. Nothing. Her fingers were still on the knot at the back of his neck, but they weren't even pretending to untie it anymore.

"What are you doing?" he finally asked. His voice sounded like he had been swallowing rocks.

"You said I couldn't kiss you, so . . ."

"So you are waiting for me to kiss you?"

He opened his eyes to find her gazing up at him. Trusting, not at all calculating, just simply hoping he would kiss her. "Don't you want to?"

Didn't he want to? What kind of question was that? Banked coals, ones he was certain he'd snuffed out long ago, roared into life. Proprietary be hanged. He was a gentleman and not the kind of man to leave a woman waiting. "Fix that blasted knot," he practically growled at her.

"You mean untie it? I've done something strange back there, and I can't quite—"

"Tie it back up. I'll play your games today. And then, when you are ready, I hope you will join me in being serious."

Her fingers slid from the back of his neck to his face. She replaced the cravat over his mouth, the coolness of her touch grazing his lips, and then, before he knew it, she was tightening the cravat with a quick tug.

She gazed up at him, innocence and curiosity mingled in such a tantalizing package. How had he ever thought he could resist her? He was doomed from the first word she'd spoken to him in the corridor. And by the gods, it was time he accepted his fate.

Then her mouth split into a grin, and a short strangled laugh escaped her lips.

"What?" he managed to bark thought the linen.

"It is just that you look positively . . . frightened, as if I have taken you prisoner. I can't look you in the eye, not seriously." She tipped her head to one side. "But I think I know how to fix that." Mercy's hands dropped from the sides of his face to his shoulders. She tugged on him, bringing him lower. "All I have to do is close my eyes." Before he had any more time to accustom himself to the idea, her eyes had fluttered closed and her lips were on his.

Or rather, they were on the thin fabric that covered his. Which meant basically the same thing.

He closed his eyes and folded his arms around her.

He couldn't see her freckles. He couldn't see the delicate slope of her shoulders or the sparks of fire in her eyes that had so consumed him. Mercy became her breath, heating the fabric between them, the scent of rosewater, and the feather touch of her fingers atop his jacket. Her lips grazed his through the silk of his cravat. Behind his closed eyes, the world grew smaller, collapsing in on itself, until it was just the two of them in the darkness behind his eyelids.

She didn't move closer—she barely moved. It felt as if she were waiting. Waiting for him, pleading for him, to show her how much he needed her touch. But if he kissed her now, there would be no going back, cravat notwithstanding.

Not for him.

If he kissed her fully and she walked away, he wouldn't only lose her—he would lose himself. He should say something, at least. Anything. Explain himself better. It was no common thing for him to go about kissing women. As a duke, he knew he could be given liberties by Society, but after losing his father's respect, those kinds of liberties had never tempted him.

Not until now.

But if he could do this right . . . Mercy had practically agreed to marry him if he could get this one thing right. A kiss. One very good kiss. He would have the chance to spend the rest of his life with this woman.

Nicholas's fingers were first to move, each knuckle tightening until his hands became claws, taking purchase on the bodice of her dress. He pulled her more firmly into him, letting their bodies collied in a way that sent every one of his nerves reeling. Mercy's breathing hitched, her chest rising, pressing into his own.

His mouth was the last to catch up to what his fingers, hands, and arms had been doing. He lifted a hand to the back of her head and crushed his lips onto hers. Every suppressed desire, every chance he'd had to hold Mercy, and politely refused, every emotion he had held in check for years, exploded to the surface. Mercy's kiss had been tentative, a question he hadn't answered. His kiss was a declaration, a claim, a promise, and there was nothing tentative about it.

The cloth between them was inconsequential, so thin he could still feel the curve of her mouth as it molded to him. He knew the moment her breath came back, for it mingled hot with his own. His fingers laced through her hair and then closed into a fist, capturing her and keeping her exactly where he wanted her—in his arms with his mouth on hers.

One of Mercy's hands slid up his chest, her delicate fingers leaving a trail of fire in their wake. When her hand reached his neck, he thought she would wrap her hand behind his neck, but instead she brought her fingertips to his throat.

He swallowed, and her hand followed the movement, then wrapped around his neck and pulled him down, lifting her chin and kissing him back in matched desperation. Why had they waited so long to do this?

He slid his lips to her cheek, cursing the fabric over his mouth for the first time because it robbed him of the touch of those wonderous flecks on her skin.

"Mercy." Her name was a choked prayer, one he had muttered over and over in his lifetime, but he'd never meant it in the way he meant it now.

Mercy.

Heaven have mercy on him, but he wanted this woman in his life. He didn't care if she helped his public opinion or if she would be a buffer between him and Mother. He wanted her as his wife so he could kiss her like this whenever they were alone. Based on the way she sank into him, his chances had increased dramatically in the past few minutes.

He reached up to the cravat, grasped the smooth silk with his fingers, and tore it down from his mouth. Mercy's eyes widened, but this time he wouldn't mistake her motions as fear or disappointment. He'd surprised her, but based on the glint that flashed in her green eyes, she had no objections to what he'd just done.

Her mouth was begging to be kissed now that he was free from the constraints of the silk, but first thing was first. He bent low and trailed kisses along her cheekbone, taking his time, finding a particular grouping of flecks on her skin and covering them, then dragging his lips higher, stopping often, reveling in the fact that he finally had the chance to claim her freckles as his own.

When his mouth reached her ear, he whispered her name again. She responded by pulling her arms tighter around his neck and lifting herself upward.

He pulled away just enough so that he could dip back down again and crush her lips with his own, skin on skin, with no silk to impede him. He'd thought the cravat hadn't mattered; he'd thought he could feel the intricate details of her mouth with it between them, but he'd been wrong. Very wrong. Her lips tasted of honey and lavender, and their softness made his silk cravat feel like sandstone in comparison.

Mercy took a step forward into him, and her movement left him nowhere for him to go but back. His thigh hit the corner of the door, and it swung shut with a loud thud. They were alone, kissing, and the door was closed tight behind them.

Her mouth curved into a smile beneath his. With a chuckle, she shifted, her warm breath trailing up the side of his face, until she brought her lips to his ear. "Not so proper now, are we?"

He pursed his lips together. He would have none of that. He *was* proper. Or, at least, as proper as he could be with his cravat hanging from his neck and Mercy wrapped in his arms. He made certain his left hand still held her firmly against him—he could not bear to part with her. Not yet—and reached for the doorknob with his right. He pushed the two of them away from the door slightly and opened it a few inches.

"I'm always proper." His lips were just above hers, ready to kiss her again.

Mercy laughed softly, and he could feel the rumble of her joy in his chest. How had he ever lived without this? Then she lifted one of her hands off the back of his neck to shove the door closed. This time when it shut, she grinned. "My parents sent me here *alone*. They aren't fools; they were hoping this would happen."

He tipped his head to one side. "Devil woman."

She shrugged.

He reached for the door and opened it again, then stepped away from her as if offended. Mercy came into full view. Her lips were swollen and her eyes bright. He certainly hoped she was right about her parents' wishes, because it would be very hard to hide what the two of them had been doing.

The thought didn't horrify him.

He placed his palm on her cheek and brushed his thumb across the skin on her cheekbones. "Have I told you"—he dropped a kiss onto one of her most prominent freckles—"how much I love your skin?" She pursed her lips together and nodded. He leaned forward and kissed the very corner of her lips, the spot where her upper and lower lips met, the spot where her smiles always started. Mercy's breath caught, and her eyes met his. "Putting that cravat over my mouth was the most thoughtful thing anyone has ever done for me. Thank you." He paused and rubbed his thumb along her bottom lip. Had he really only just been kissing her? The thought brought too much air into his lungs. "Thank you for seeing exactly who I am and giving me what I need."

Mercy's eyes blinked slowly, like she was still coming out of a haze and his words weren't helping. If this was what it was going to be like for the two of them, all of his plans were going to backfire. He was never going to get any work done in Parliament. "I'd like to claim I kissed you without it because I wanted to give you what you wanted, but I'm afraid I wasn't thinking quite that clearly. All I knew was I needed to kiss you like I needed air. But now that I have breathed that air, can I pretend that I did it to please you? Because I want this kind of care for each other to be a part of who we are from now on."

"Deal," she said with a smile. "And, for starters, I think I need you to kiss me again."

He laughed and pulled her close again, dipping his face toward hers, and her eyes fluttered closed. For the briefest moment, he dropped a kiss on the other corner of her mouth, honoring again the edge of her lips. Then he lifted only breath away from her and dropped his lips reverently but fully on hers.

Her lips were sweet and loving, and no part of him felt ashamed. Not of her, not of him, and most definitely not for taking this moment to fight for her and what she wanted from him. Mercy tasted like redemption and forgiveness and the bravery that came with moving forward instead of looking back.

Because the two of them together had to be his future, and he wouldn't taint it with thoughts of unworthiness.

She kissed him back, and her kiss was a promise, one that had him a breath away from kicking the door closed and repeating the last few minutes all over again. With an unsteady sigh, he pulled away. He knew he must be smiling like an idiot, and he didn't care. He didn't need to hide any part of him from Mercy. "I think perhaps you should go speak to your parents."

"I certainly should. No doubt they will be curious as to what we have been . . ." Mercy arched an eyebrow. "Talking about."

Her hand went to the doorknob, and he stopped her by covering it with his own. She spun around, her kiss-roughened lips curving into an impish grin, and her eyes went straight to his mouth. Oh no, he'd made his point. He was done kissing her, at least for now.

He squeezed her hand underneath his. "Wait. Before you go, I have something for you." He lifted his hand to his breast pocket and pulled out the thin silver chain. It was a family heirloom, but not one anyone had worn for generations. "I brought you this."

"But, Nicholas." Mercy's hand went to her heart, as if she were thoroughly scandalized. "We aren't even engaged."

"A point I would like to remedy as soon as possible. Wear that tonight. It won't impede your dancing."

Mercy reached for the chain and slid it between her finger and thumb. "It is lovely. But if I wear a present of yours, people may assume we are engaged."

"If what we just did doesn't make you assume the same, I'm afraid I have sorely misread you."

"I suppose I don't have to tell anyone where I got it."

"Mercy." Nicholas dipped his head low and dropped one more soft of kiss on her lips. "I want you to wear it and tell everyone where you got it."

She lowered her head and looked up at him as if she were shy and not the kind of woman who had demanded he take off his cravat so she could look at his neck and then proceeded to use that cravat to make a game out of his sensibilities.

"If I do, then I suppose you will have the answer to the question you never even bothered to ask me." She smiled, pulled the door wide open, and stepped out of the room. "Put that cravat back on." She motioned toward it with her head then winked at him. "You look much too tempting without it."

CHAPTER 26

W HEN MERCY LOOKED BACK AFTER leaving the drawing room, she had
expected to see Nicholas untying the knots on his cravat and putting himself to rights, but instead he was still standing in the doorway, watching her
as she walked away.

She clenched his necklace tightly in her left fist, blew him a kiss, and
practically skipped up the stairs. The world would see her silver chain as not
even coming close to comparing to Mama's emeralds. But Mama couldn't
have felt more pleasure in her stones than Mercy did in the gift Nicholas
had given her. He could have given her emeralds that she would never wear.
Instead, he'd chosen something simple for her. Something she could put on
tonight and never take off. She couldn't wait to show it to Kate and have her
help her put it on, but first she needed to speak with Mama and Papa.

She knocked on Mama's door a moment later, and Mama beckoned for
her to come in. The moment Mercy stepped in the room, her parents leaned
forward expectantly. Mercy smiled. They would be very happy about the
news. For two people who had always claimed to have no particular interests
in ranks and positions, they certainly put a lot of hope in Mercy marrying
a duke.

She was about to make them very, very happy.

But perhaps she could have a little fun first. Something about her encounter
with Nicholas had left her insides bubbling like champagne. She hadn't felt
this giddy since she was a young girl receiving her first pair of dancing slippers.
"Are the two of you ready? Guests should be arriving any moment."

Mama's eyes narrowed. "You have no news for us?"

"What do you mean?"

"The duke . . ." Papa stepped forward. "Has he . . ."

Mercy blinked, eyes wide. "Has he what?"

"Devil take it, Mercy. You know better than to toy with us," Papa said, his eyes narrowed and his voice like a growl. The room went cold. Papa never cursed, at least not in front of Mercy or Mama. "You need to make him propose, and you need to accept. The sooner, the better."

"Joseph—" Mama started, but Papa waved her aside. First swearing, and now dismissing Mama like that? What was going on?

Mercy's stomach tightened and felt heavy, like she had eaten a whole loaf of hard, dry bread. She slowly slipped Nicholas's necklace into the small pocket on the inside of her belt. This conversation needed to come first. "Why?"

"We want you to be happ—" This time Mercy cut off Mama. Papa's mood was spreading.

"I know you want me to be happy. My whole life you have made that abundantly clear. But why must I convince the Duke of Harrington to marry me *sooner than later*, Papa?"

Mama went to Papa's side and took a hold of his elbow. She shook her head at him. "Don't."

"No, I've held back long enough. She needs to know."

"Know what?" Mercy asked.

Papa pulled his arm out of Mama's grasp. "It is imperative that we see you settled as soon as possible. If not with the duke, then with someone else. Although it seems to me that he is the obvious choice. He is a good man, and he is quite taken with you."

How had her father been able to see what had taken Mercy so very long to uncover? Nicholas did care for her. She simply hadn't see it through all his propriety. But now was not the time to question that particular revelation. "What's wrong?"

Mama stepped forward and took Mercy's hand. "Nothing. Nothing is wrong. At least nothing that concerns you."

"But it will concern her." Papa sat on Mama's bed and put his head in his hands. "Your sister—"

"Rosalind? What has happened? Is she all right?"

Mama tugged Mercy toward the doorway. "She is. Now, come downstairs."

"No." Mercy tore her hand out of Mama's grip. "Not until I understand what is going on."

"We have to tell her," Papa said. "Whether she marries the duke or not, we have to tell her. Warn her." Papa turned to me. "We were wrong. Your mother and I. We indulged both you and Rosalind, and we are all paying for it now."

"We can talk of this later. Is the duke still here?" Mama's voice quivered.

Papa lifted his head, and grief poured from his eyes. "It is too late. She's in Mercy's room, Edith. We can't continue to shelter her."

"Who is in my room?" Mercy asked, her heart racing. "Rosalind? She's home? Are she and Richard here for the ball?"

"No, Rosalind will not be attending the ball," Papa said.

"Whatever do you mean? What's happened to Rosalind?"

Mama pulled a handkerchief from her sleeve and covered her nose with a sniff. "Nothing has happened—"

But Mercy didn't wait for Mama to finish. She dashed out of the door and down the corridor and then threw open her bedroom door. Rosalind lay on the bed, her head turned toward the window.

Rosaland head whipped around, and she rose with a burst. "Mercy!" she cried. Then she strode to the door and threw her arms around Mercy. Rosalind looked healthy; her arms were strong, and she dashed out of the bed without any sort of complaint.

Mercy pulled back, put both on her hands on Rosalind's shoulders and inspected her. Nothing looked wrong. "When did you arrive? I've been dying to talk to you this past month."

"And I you. Mama and Papa tell me you are being courted by the Duke of Harrington. How in the world did that happen?"

"I wrote to you about it," Mercy responded.

"Yes, but I want to hear it from you. See your face as you speak of him. Make certain you aren't making a mistake."

"A mistake by marrying him, or by not?" she asked Rosalind.

"I'll know when I hear you speak of him." She took both of Mercy's hands and led her back to the bed. They both sat. "Tell me all about it."

Rosalind's face was glowing, she looked as happy as ever. What in the world had Mama and Papa been worried about, and why wouldn't she be attending the ball? "Well, I must admit our courtship has been very different from yours and Richard's—"

Rosalind grimaced and made a strange sound in the back of her throat. "Ugh . . . Richard. He's such an oaf."

Whatever comfort she'd had at the sight of Rosalind vanished. "What?"

"Mama and Papa haven't told you? I've left Richard. And I won't be in London long, but I had to see you before I left. Even if Papa won't let me show my face or speak to anyone until you are properly married off."

Mercy couldn't respond. Rosalind was making no sense. In no version of her world did Rosalind and Richard not belong together.

"Oh." Rosalind patted Mercy's shoulder. "I've worried you. Don't fret. If you don't want to marry this duke, I can wait a while longer. Not too much longer, mind you. Richard is bound to start talking at some point, and I'm positively dying to get on the boat to Austria."

"Austria?" That wasn't even in the country, and already Rosalind's letters had been arriving less and less frequently. How would she survive with her sister so far away? "Rosalind, why are you going to Austria? It is so far away from us, and from Richard—"

"I need you to stop speaking of Richard." Rosalind's face had a hard edge she'd never seen before. But then it softened in to the dreamy-eyed sister she'd always loved. "I've fallen in love with someone else, and Mercy, it is as if the whole world was dull and now I see the brightest of colors. And not just colors, the sounds, oh, the beautiful sounds that follow me now." Rosalind grabbed Mercy by the shoulders. "If the duke doesn't make you feel as though you would burn the world for him, don't marry him. Especially not on my account."

Mercy was going to be sick. How could the world be full of light one minute and then fog the next? "Who is it?" Were the only words Mercy could muster.

Rosalind's smile widened. "That is the best part. You know him. Or rather, you know of him. If you could meet one composer, just one, in your whole lifetime, who would you pick?"

A composer? What in the world was Rosalind talking about? Mercy had never been as proficient at the pianoforte as Rosalind. But she did know which composer Rosalind would pick. "Dobler?"

Rosalind clapped her hands and then hugged herself. "Yes! Dobler, Martin Dobler."

"But . . . Dobler is married, isn't he?"

Rosalind waved a hand in the air. "He was, or rather he has been, a few times. But we don't care about that."

Mercy opened her mouth to ask another question, but the look in Rosalind's eyes told her she would not appreciate Mercy questioning her about the man's age. He had to be at least as old as Papa. Mercy stood. Her legs shook beneath her, but she had to leave. She couldn't sit with Rosalind while she had that look in her eye. "I need a minute. I need to speak with Mama and Papa, I need to . . ." She didn't know how to finish that sentence. There wasn't anything she could do to fix or even understand this situation, but she needed to try.

Rosalind pulled her face into a pout. "Oh, all right, but hurry back. I haven't seen you for ages."

Mercy ran back down the corridor. She must have misunderstood Rosalind. Or perhaps the whole business was some sort of sordid trick Rosalind was playing on her. Richard was *everything* to Rosalind. She wouldn't throw that away simply because some other man could string notes together.

Mercy threw open the door to Mama's room. Both of her parents were still there. "Papa, you must stop her. She loved Richard. I know she did."

Papa shook his head. "I tried. Mercy, you must believe me. I tried. I brought her here to try to speak sense to her and get her away from Dobler, but she screamed for the first half hour of our journey and assured me that she would scream all day while in our home and escape the first opportunity she had. She nearly jumped from the carriage multiple times. I did everything I could, save from drugging her or putting her into an institution. And it isn't like Dobler has no power. If I had put her in a home, he would have used his influence to get her out." Papa's head fell to his hands again. "I couldn't lock up my child. And she promised us she could be discrete until you were wed, as long as it did not take you too long."

Mercy's head would not stop shaking. She couldn't believe it. Not any of it. None of this could be true.

Mama made a strangled noise in her throat. "This is all our fault. Your father and I have been so happy in marriage. We wanted the same for our children. We always encouraged you to use your hearts, but we should have encouraged you to use your heads as well."

"No, Mama." Mercy shook her head harder. "That's not true."

But flashes of her time alone with Nicholas only a moment ago made her breath catch. She had received the attentions of an upstanding young gentleman. A man any woman in London would be happy to marry, and not only for his position in Society, but for his looks and character as well. And she had nearly let him go because she hadn't felt properly pursued. What if a man like Dobler had entered her life first? Charming and smooth, with stolen kisses expected, not warded against.

She'd been ripe for the taking. It wouldn't have taken much persuading for a man to convince her she was hopelessly in love with him.

The fact that Nicholas had been such a gentleman with her, when she had encouraged him to be otherwise . . . She started pacing back and forth. Her feet would not be still. It was as if everything she'd ever believed in was crashing down around her.

And Nicholas. What must he think of her?

She shook her head. No. It was all right. They were engaged. Or practically engaged. Other than some breathtaking kisses, they hadn't done anything truly wrong. Luckily one of them had made certain of that.

Papa brushed a stray tendril of hair off her face. "I didn't want to tell you, but I don't know how much longer Rosalind will be able to keep her double life a secret. Richard has already left the country, she is alone, and I have heard that Dobler has taken up residence near her. It would be best if you were safely married before her scandal becomes public knowledge. Scandal won't bother your mother and I. Our hearts are broken by your sister's choices, and we cannot fathom her new path leading to the type of happiness we had always hoped for her. But it isn't too late for you. Harrington will protect you. His name can absorb a multitude of sins without facing the consequences that any other husband might face."

"What?" Mercy's legs stopped their frantic movements.

Mama smoothed down her hair. "The duke is perfect for you. Don't you see? No one will dare spurn you. There will be talk. There is always talk. But as a duke, he can be surrounded by scandal without it really affecting him."

Mercy's hands started shaking, and moisture started pooling in her eyes. Scandal would most definitely affect Nicholas. Just not in the way Mama thought. He'd spent the past three years building an impeccable reputation. He counted on it, and even though he'd shown her how thoroughly attracted he was to her, it was her name and title that had first put her in his path.

He wanted to marry in order to solidify his upstanding reputation.

Mercy would destroy it.

He would be forced to do the one thing he hated more than anything in the world—use his title as a shelter for indiscretions.

"I'm not engaged to the Duke of Harrington."

"Not yet," Mama said. "But I think he may ask you tonight."

"No, Mama." She shook her head. "I don't think he will."

Papa frowned. "What do you mean, you don't think he will?" Papa met her eyes, and she did her best to remain emotionless. His eyes widened. "He's already asked you, hasn't he?" Papa stood and pointed to the door. "Go downstairs and tell him you've changed your mind."

"No, Papa, he didn't ask me. We spoke and—" Her voice broke. She couldn't tell them that although he hadn't asked her to marry him, he had told her he was planning to ask her father for permission to do so. "He isn't in love with me. He told me he wasn't in love with me."

"He came here early in order to tell you he wasn't in love with you?"

"No, that isn't *why* he stopped in. But he said it, nonetheless." He'd also made it very clear he was nearly in love with her. All he needed was for her to love him back. But her parents couldn't ever know that.

"Stopped in? Has he left already?"

Mercy couldn't tell them he was still downstairs. They would speak to him, and the first thing Nicholas would do would be to ask for her hand in marriage. For some reason, she couldn't bring herself to verbally lie to Papa, but she did give him a short nod. A nod could mean anything. Perhaps she had nodded as a simple goodbye. Mercy jumped from the bed and put a hand to her forehead. "I need to prepare for the ball." She needed out of the room. She needed the silence and quiet of her own room to process what she had learned. Rosalind running off with another man? Richard letting her slip from his grasp? How had any of it happened?

Apparently love couldn't be measured by lingering touches and pounding hearts. Her own sister had proven that.

What was she going to do about Nicholas? He was going to feel obligated to marry her because they'd kissed. She wouldn't be the reason his family line became tainted again.

She rushed down the corridor to her room. She couldn't go back to the drawing room. He would take one look at her face and know something was wrong. And she didn't trust herself to not give in and marry him, scandal and all. Rosalind must've gone to her old room, because Mercy's was blessedly empty.

Nicholas would find his way into the ballroom eventually, and with enough people around for her not to be tempted to cry or fall into his arms, she would inform him of her decision not to marry him.

Or, even better, she could write him a letter. Then she wouldn't have to speak to him face-to-face. After he read it, she could simply refuse his calls until after the scandal with Rosalind broke out, at which time he would stop calling on her and find a more suitable woman to court.

And if he wanted to call on her after the scandal broke?

No. She wouldn't allow herself the luxury of hope. He'd been clear about what he needed in a wife, and she no longer fit his requirements. She carefully pulled Nicholas's necklace from her pocket, walked over to her jewelry box, lifted the lid, and lowered the chain slowly, watching the delicate silver pool into a circle at the back of a compartment. After looking at it for far too long, she pulled a piece of paper out of her writing desk. Writing to him was hardly proper, seeing as they weren't engaged, but after what had transpired in the drawing room, a note was the least of her concerns.

CHAPTER 27

NICHOLAS WAS STILL IN THE drawing room twenty minutes after Mercy left him when the first guest arrived. The first few minutes Nicholas waited for Mercy and her parents to return had been filled with a jittery hope. He'd clumsily retied his cravat with shaking fingers, cursed himself for being a fool, pulled it off, and after a long, slow breath, finally got it right on the second try. His mind had bounded to the future—his future. He'd thought Mercy and her parents would return at any moment, and if all went well, they could announce their engagement at supper.

It wasn't until Mercy had been gone for a full ten minutes that his first doubts began creeping in. If neither Mercy nor her father came to speak with him before the ball, what would that mean? Mercy's broad smile had been answer enough only a few minutes earlier, but as the mantle clock ticked incessantly, a sneaking uncertainty started clouding his thinking. She hadn't agreed to marry him. She had only told him she might.

An oversight he would remedy the moment he saw her.

But now, with the first guests' voices trailing into the drawing room from the entry hall, he was no longer certain of anything.

Why was he still here? Mercy or one of her parents would fetch him, wouldn't they? They wouldn't have a duke skulk about the house and enter the ballroom on his own, without being announced.

More and more guests arrived, and Nicholas paced. A steady stream of people was arriving, and he didn't want to leave the room while anyone was in the entrance hall. He pulled a book from a side table and sat in an armchair. It was a history of Ireland, and a ribbon marked a page with a drawing of the rolling hills of Wicklow County. Mercy had mentioned that being the home county of her family's new scullery maid. Who had been reading this? Mercy? Or the maid? He ran his fingers down the drawing.

Perhaps both of them. Mercy would want to show the young girl something of her homeland, and she would mark the page for her so she could come see it whenever she was feeling homesick. He ran a finger over the largest hill, and a smile crept over his face.

He continued to riffle through the book, looking for any mentions of locations some of his friends had come from. It wasn't long until the raps at the door became less frequent. He stood. If the ball was well underway, then it was time he made an appearance.

The moment his fingers touched the doorknob, some of his worries softened. Mercy had shut the door solidly behind him not forty-five minutes ago, in order for him to kiss her more thoroughly. How much could have changed in forty-five minutes? Preparing for a ball would be a huge undertaking, and the family could have easily gotten swept up in urgent matters of puddings and musical choices.

He cracked open the door. A footman standing near the front door immediately caught sight of him. He was not the one who had let him in, nor did Nicholas recognize him from his other visits. Nicholas straightened his back, crossed the hall, and handed him his card. Whatever surprise had registered on the footman's face when he stepped out of the room was schooled as he read his name. He gave Nicholas a bow and led him to the ballroom, handing his card to the master of ceremonies. Nicholas was announced just as well as if he *had* come in through the front door.

Mercy's parents' heads whipped around at the sound of his name. He wasn't certain exactly what expression he had expected to see in their eyes, but their quick glances between each other and schooled expressions made a knot form at the base of his neck. They did not look happy to see him.

And he didn't see Mercy anywhere.

He swallowed and marched forward, as if this were a typical evening ball. The ballroom was a small one, lined with grand paintings of biblical scenes. He hadn't been in the room before, but he suspected it was typically used as a large gathering hall or walking room and the furniture had been removed for the event.

Patience and Ottersby immediately excused themselves from the conversation they were having and wove their way through the crowd to meet with him.

"What's wrong?" Patience asked as soon as she reached him.

Nicholas furrowed his brows. "What do you mean?" Nothing was wrong. In fact, this could possibly be one of the happiest evenings of his life. He opened his mouth to say as much but stopped.

He couldn't share any information about his time with Mercy until he had a clear understanding from both her and her parents.

Patience took his arm. "You look as though a ghost is going to come sneaking about the corner at any moment."

"Have you seen Lady Mercy?"

Ottersby nodded. "I've arranged to dance a set with her later."

Patience pulled on Nicholas's sleeve. "She looked as though she was expecting a ghost as well. What has happened between the two of you?"

He had kissed her soundly in the drawing room, and her touch had healed things that had been broken since he was seventeen. That was what had happened. "What do you mean, she looks like she is expecting a ghost?"

Patience frowned and glanced around them for prying eyes. No one was especially close, but they couldn't exactly get away from everyone either. "I don't know exactly. She was pale and skittish, glancing around as if something frightening was around the corner. If I didn't know better, I would think she was some sad maiden dragged from a dungeon and pressed into playing mistress of the ball. Her parents were cordial, but even they seemed less enthusiastic than the last time we met."

"Where is she?" He needed to see her himself. Mercy didn't need to be pressed into balls. Balls were where she came alive.

"I believe she is dancing with Lord Dowdle at the moment," Ottersby said. "But I agree with Patience. Something is wrong. Did you do something to upset the family?"

The light in the ballroom faded, and the niggling worry that had gnawed at the back of his mind since Mercy hadn't returned to the drawing tore through him. He shook his head slightly and blinked. Had he done something to upset the family? He put a hand to the back of his neck and inhaled deeply. He'd thought . . . Well, Mercy had led him to believe she'd wanted that kiss . . .

But that wasn't the problem, was it? She was young, almost as young as he'd been when Lady Plymton had entered his life. He, of all people, should have protected her innocence at all costs. He searched the ballroom once again. Where was she? Just as he was about to give up and ask Patience where she had seen Mercy last, the crowd of dancers parted, and there she was.

Lord Dowdle had his hand on her back, and she smiled up at him, but he could see in the stiffness of her shoulders and the redness around her eyes that something had upset her. Patience had explained Mercy's appearance perfectly. Like she had been dragged out of a dungeon.

Those few minutes of bliss had him dreaming of a future with Mercy, but less than an hour later, Mercy looked as if she were ill. He glanced at her neck. It was bare. No emeralds, no pearls, and even from here, he could tell, no silver chain.

He had his answer.

Nicholas had made enough plans in his life to know when one wasn't going to work out. There would be no engagement announced at supper. Not at this ball, and to Mercy? Perhaps never. The room darkened further, as if each chandelier had been replaced by a single candle. What had he done? For weeks, he'd managed to court Lacy Mercy in a controlled, public manner. But in the end, he had succumbed to his same, disgraceful self. He had kissed her. Kissed her thoroughly. And his intent in that kiss was very different from the kisses he had shared with Lady Plymton. His kisses at seventeen had been young and inexperienced. They were experimental, curious, and had more to do with the fact that he wanted to kiss someone, anyone, than the fact that he wanted to kiss a particular person.

His time in the army had taught him restraint and loss. One of the keys to having restraint was not to surround yourself with temptation. He had known the risks going into this courtship, and he had still chosen a woman who enticed him, instead of one he could have more easily resisted. He had made all of the mistakes, and look where it had brought him.

When Mercy told the story of her life, Nicholas would be her villain. She would no longer be the trusting and optimistic woman who'd enchanted him at every turn. Nicholas had wounded her, and he should have known better.

Patience put an arm on his shoulder. "Nicholas, what's wrong? What happened?"

"I need to speak to her."

"And you shall." Ottersby stepped slightly in front of the two of them, effectively blocking Nicholas's view of the ballroom. His shoulders broadened, as if to protect Nicholas from the sight of what was happening behind them. "The night is still young. But for this set, let's find a quiet place to regroup."

Understanding eked its way into Nicholas's brain. Ottersby was not blocking his view of the ballroom. He was blocking the ballroom from viewing Nicholas. What must he look like? Not like a man who had been dragged away from a dungeon, for no part of him felt as though he'd escaped something. No. He was headed in the opposite direction—toward the dungeon—and he had no possibility of ever being freed.

Ottersby was right. It was time to retreat.

"Most likely," Nicholas said, "servants will be the only ones in the entrance hall."

Ottersby nodded and took him by the elbow, steering him out of the ballroom. The path to the entrance hall was simple and familiar. He knew this house almost as well as some of his less-used estates. Still, he managed to stumble, and Ottersby tightened his grip.

There was no one in the hall, other than the hired servant he had seen earlier. The young man caught their eye and quickly looked away. The only thing he knew about Nicholas was that he was a duke. He wouldn't bother them.

The entrance hall was bare of any furniture, so Ottersby led him to a window that looked out on the street and propped him on the thick sill. "Sit for a moment."

Nicholas nodded and dropped to the narrow piece of wood. He sank his head back against the cool glass of the window, then closed his eyes and inhaled.

"You look unwell," Patience said, her voice a floating cloud of concern somewhere above his head. "Perhaps we should go."

Nicholas cracked open one eye. "Give me a moment to think."

Leaving would, perhaps, be the best answer. He could return to speak with Mercy and her parents tomorrow, without all the eyes of London on them. He had acted wrongly, but he was willing to do whatever her family asked to right that wrong. Marriage seemed the best choice, but if Mercy were willing to marry him, wouldn't she have sought him out and worn the necklace? She wouldn't have that look of dejection on her face.

Had the brashness of the moment overtaken her, and now she felt as though she no longer had a choice in the matter? She'd asked him not to propose to her. Was he so confident in himself that after a rejection, he thought she would *want* to be kissed?

But she had . . . hadn't she?

Nicholas shook his head. "I don't want to leave. Not yet."

"Would you like to dance my set with her?" Ottersby offered.

"No. I will ask her. If she doesn't want to dance with me, I won't force her."

Patience had already asked several times what had happened between them, and he could see that she wanted to ask again.

The music slowed, and if he wanted a chance to speak with Mercy before her next dance, he needed to return to the ballroom. He stood and took a deep breath, forcing his shoulders back, as General Woodsworth had taught

ESTHER HATCH196

him. He had been trained for battle. Surely he could speak to a woman. "I'll ask her now."

Each step that brought him closer to Mercy hardened something inside him. He didn't need to get married. He'd wanted to—it had seemed like a good plan—but plans must remain flexible. If Mercy didn't want him, she didn't want him. He would move on with his life and, in a few years, find a woman who would be grateful for all he had to offer. A wife might have helped him gain favor in the House of Lords, but had he really thought being married would suddenly make him influential enough to make a difference?

It had been a terrible plan, and he had executed it poorly.

He shook off Ottersby's offer to hold his elbow again as something hot and angry took root in his chest. If he were going to choose a woman to court, he should have chosen one that had some interest in him.

The ballrooms were literally filled with them.

The moment he set foot in the room, his eyes found Mercy, but he was too late to speak to her. She was already on the arm of another man. Mr. Beauford, the best dancer in London, by her own admission. He turned to the first lovely face that brightened at his presence. Lady Marion. The woman had intrigued him once. Nothing about her interested him now, but he'd made eye contact, and she was without a dance partner. He'd have to dance with her.

Lady Marion's eyes brightened even further when he asked her to dance. This was the type of woman he should have pursued. It could have been so easy. Instead, he'd had to chase after a woman who didn't want him, simply because she had interesting freckles and he'd seen her cry outside Donald's funeral.

Lady Marion asked him a question, but he didn't hear it. He leaned closer to her and asked her to repeat herself.

"Will you be spending time at Brushbend this Season? Or staying in London?"

Would he? He wasn't certain. London was the place to be in order to find a bride, but if he had given up on that venture, he might as well return to Hampshire and see to the affairs of the estate. "That remains to be seen."

"I've heard how lovely it is. It would be an amazing sight to see."

"Perhaps I should host a house party later in the year."

Lady Marion's mouth split into a grin. "That is the most wonderful of ideas. I imagine it's breathtaking in the spring."

Brushbend was. In fact, he had been hoping to take Mercy. He gritted his teeth, banning the image of her smile from his mind. Lady Marion smiled easily. The smiles and teasing he had received only this afternoon from Mercy had been hard fought.

And useless. The lack of adornment around her neck was the final nail in his coffin.

"I will speak to my sister about the idea. It has been a long time since we had guests at Brushbend. I suppose a house party is long overdue."

The dance finished, and he escorted Lady Marion back to her mother. Mercy's family was on the other side of the ballroom. If he wanted a chance to speak with Mercy before the music started again, he would have to rush there. Lady Marion mentioned the idea of a house party to her mother, and he nodded politely before excusing himself and turning toward the closest door.

It had been a noble idea, to speak to Mercy, but he couldn't, not here, with hundreds of eyes watching. He needed air.

He marched through the crowd, unaware of the people he passed. It wasn't until his shoulder slammed into the side of a woman that he blinked and took in his surroundings.

"Your Grace!" the woman said. He blinked again. He knew her. Her hands went to his shoulders, and she looked him in the eye. "Are you all right?"

Lady Yolten.

In the short time he had known Lady Yolten, she had never seemed one to be overly concerned about propriety, and even less so now, as she kept her hands on him, then patted his side as if to make certain nothing was wrong.

He stepped aside. "I am perfectly all right." He gave her a short nod and proceeded toward the door. If he could get out of door and turn right, there was an exit to the back garden. It was a cold night, but cold night air was exactly what he needed. He managed to make it the rest of the way out of the house without another incident.

Once outside, he strode to the back of the garden, shielded himself behind a large knotted oak, and pressed his forehead against the rough bark. He closed his eyes and took several slow, deep breaths. Beads of sweat formed on his brow. He reached into the pocket of his jacket for his handkerchief, and his knuckles brushed up against something thin and stiff there as well.

He pulled it out.

It was a note. How had a note ended up in his pocket?

There was no seal—only a piece of paper folded in half. He opened it. It was not addressed to him, nor was it signed. The type of note that would incriminate no one if found.

> *I must speak to you. I cannot leave things the way we left them. I have not given up hope for a future together. Meet me in the library at ten o'clock.*

What the devil? Had Mercy given him this note? When would she have had the chance? In the drawing room, her hands had roamed his person freely. She could have slipped the note inside his pocket, but what would have been the point? They'd been speaking then. No, she must have written this note after she'd left him. But how had it gotten into his jacket pocket?

Lady Yolten.

As informal as she was, she had never laid her hands on him as intimately as she had moments ago. He had chalked that up to how terrible he must have looked, but he was wrong. She was a close friend of Mercy and would not be the type to faint at the prospect of delivering a clandestine correspondence. No wonder her hands had lingered on him longer than he thought necessary. It wasn't because she had been worried about him. She had simply wanted to deliver this message.

He pulled out his pocket watch. It was half past nine.

I have not given up hope for a future together.

He dug his fingers into the bark of the dark oak in front of him. From despair to hope. How quickly could one body handle the change of such emotions? He needed to be cautious. He'd practically invited Lady Marion to his estate, for heaven's sake.

But that was not the same as an engagement. Or even a courtship. He was still free to pursue Mercy if she wanted him.

Why the library? And why another meeting alone? The last one had proven to be a disaster. He'd taken advantage of Mercy's innocence when he should have protected her instead. If she wanted a repeat of what happened in the drawing room, it wouldn't happen without an official engagement first. The smart thing to do would be to deliver a card after the ball asking to call in the morning. It was the only logical answer.

But as much as he tried to talk himself out of meeting with Mercy, he knew he would be in that library at ten. Years of training himself to think with his head and not with his heart had come to nothing where Mercy was concerned.

He had to find out what was wrong.

CHAPTER 28

MERCY THANKED MR. PALMER FOR a lovely dance, and he led her to Mama. She'd never danced with Mr. Palmer before, and she doubted she would have the opportunity again. She had hardly been an encouraging dance partner.

She hadn't seen Nicholas since his dance with Lady Marion.

Mama smiled at Mr. Palmer and at Mercy, but her smile toward Mercy was forced. She still hadn't forgiven her for not being able to coerce Nicholas into proposing to her.

Another half hour and she should be all right. She'd only thought herself in love with him for a few short minutes. Before speaking with Rosalind, she may have thought falling in love was out of her control, that if she didn't take this chance with Nicholas, she would never have another shot at love. But Nicholas had been right all along; love shouldn't make a person forget everyone else around them or make them do things they knew to be wrong. Love should be calculating, and it should make sense.

And she was certain living without Nicholas would make sense someday. Years from now.

In the meantime, she would not bring disgrace to his family.

"Mercy," a low voice hissed to her left, and she spun. Penelope was smiling and motioning toward the door with her eyebrows.

"Excuse me, Mama. I'm going to visit with Penelope."

Mama glanced at Penelope, her eyes pausing at her elaborate headdress of feathers and pearls. Based on her quick frown, it seemed that even Mama had a limit to how much jewelry was acceptable, and Penelope had managed to exceed it.

Still, Mama smiled. Penelope was one of Mercy's highest-ranking friends, and while that hadn't mattered in the past, suddenly every relation that might be willing to weather this storm with them mattered now. "Of course."

Penelope took Mercy's hand and practically dragged her to the corridor. Once alone, she took both of Mercy's hands in her own. "I've done it. I've got everything arranged for tonight. We simply need to decide how far we want to take this business with His Grace and Lady Plymton."

Mercy shook her head and tried to piece together what Penelope was saying. "What do you mean, His Grace and Lady Plymton?"

"The next step in our plan. I delivered a letter to him while you were dancing. He's to meet her in the library."

"He's *what?*"

"I've arranged it all with Lady Plymton. She was more than happy to comply."

Heavens, *their plan.* They'd planned to push Nicholas into the arms of other women, and their next target had been Lady Plymton. "Oh, no. Penelope, you didn't."

Penelope's face fell. For a woman who never looked sad, she could certainly pout well. "What do you mean, I didn't? I did. And it wasn't easy. I had to get my hands all over your duke."

"He isn't *my* duke."

"He is going to be Lady Plymton's duke before long. She seems to be the influential type. One that can convince a man to do . . . well . . . anything."

Mercy took a deep breath. Nicholas could take care of himself, and even if Mercy had disappointed him, he still would never agree to meet Lady Plymton. "He won't meet her. I misunderstood his relationship with her, so your note should be of no consequence."

"Oh, she didn't have me sign her name. She didn't want anything to be traced back to either one of them. For all he knows, it could be anyone waiting for him in the library. Even you."

Mercy closed her eyes. He wouldn't, would he? Not after she'd pushed him past where he was comfortable in the drawing room and then ignored him. When she'd shown up without the necklace, he must have known their courtship was over. Even if he thought it was Mercy waiting in the library, he wouldn't meet her alone. Not again.

A man and two women strode into the corridor. The women's heads were pressed together, and they didn't even notice Penelope and Mercy. She only made out a few words as they passed, but one of those words was unmistakably "library."

Mercy froze. "What time were they supposed to meet?"

Penelope shrugged "They should've met a few minutes ago. Should we see what is happening? This could be the beginning of a great love story. Lady Plymton was extreme—"

Mercy pushed herself off the wall and grabbed Penelope by the shoulders. "Go block the library door."

"What?"

"Lady Plymton was not the love of Nicholas's life. She is a viper, and I think the group that just passed us is going to the library. Go tackle those people if you have to, but do not let anyone make it into the library before you do. Do you understand?"

Penelope eyes mapped Mercy's face. She hadn't missed the fact that somehow the Duke of Harrington had become Nicholas. But she didn't ask any questions. Instead, she spun her head to look down the corridor, and nodded seriously. "I'll do it." Penelope picked up her silk skirt and ran.

If there were ever a time for Nicholas to be late for a meeting, this was it. Or to miss a meeting, that would be even better. If Lady Plymton was willing to manipulate a seventeen-year-old boy, there was no telling what she would be willing to do in order to secure Nicholas and his title now.

Mercy dashed down the corridor in the opposite direction of Penelope. She turned into one of the morning rooms that had a door leading outside and into the back garden. She couldn't break Nicholas's heart and involve him in a public scandal all in one day. She tore open the door and ignored the blast of cold air. The library had windows opening to the outside. They would be locked, but she could knock and distract Nicholas and Lady Plymton from . . . whatever it was they would be doing. Talking, hopefully. But even talking alone in a room could lead to someone calling for a marriage proposal, especially if Lady Plymton asked some of her friends to do exactly that.

Her slippers were soaked through almost immediately from the damp grass. She would have no possible explanation to give Mama, but she would deal with that after she saved Nicholas from the two things he despised most in this world: Lady Plymton and dishonor on the title of Harrington.

She reached the window, her breath ragged and gasping. The library was dimly lit, with only a few candles, and thank the heavens, the door to the well-lit corridor was still closed. Penelope must have found a way to stop the group of people from entering.

Mercy would find a way to thank her later.

She banged her fist against the glass. "Nicholas!" she shouted, not caring who heard her. She pounded again. "Nicholas!" This time, she hissed the name. Because she had no right to call him that, and Nicholas wouldn't want a scandal with Mercy either. She grabbed the window frame and shook it, knowing it was locked, but to her surprise, it creaked open. She stuck her head inside. "Your Grace?" She repented of shouting out his Christian name where anyone could hear her. "Are you in here?"

"He left," a voice, low, feminine, and jaded, replied in the darkness.

Mercy's head whipped to her left. There, practically reclining on a sofa, sat Lady Plymton. In the dim light, her eyes were catlike and vicious. How had Mercy ever thought it would be a good idea for Nicholas to be alone with this woman? Miss Morgan might be conniving, but Lady Plymton was a predator who'd gone without prey for much too long.

Mercy narrowed her eyes. "Where did he go?"

Lady Plymton flicked some imaginary dust from the sofa. "Why? Have you finally wizened up?" Her pretty mouth curled into something dangerous. "Do you know how many women would give their toes to be in your position? And what do you do? Try to throw the man in anyone else's direction? How idiotic can you be?"

A bump sounded near the door that led to the corridor, and muffled voices rose in some kind of shock or surprise. Whatever Penelope was doing was starting to cause a commotion. Mercy pulled up her skirt and climbed over the two-foot masonry work and into the library.

"They're too late," Lady Plymton said flatly.

"Who are?"

"My friends. They were supposed to find me here with . . ." She paused and looked meaningfully at the window where Mercy had been only moments before. "Nicholas."

Mercy gritted her teeth. The sound of his name coming from this woman's lips made her want to tear them off.

Instead, she took a deep breath and turned away from Lady Plymton, then tore open the door. "What is—" She broke off mid-sentence. Penelope had been sitting on the floor with her back and shoulders against the door. She fell into the room with a small yelp, only just catching herself with her hands before her head hit the ground.

Five people stood behind Penelope. They ignored her and Mercy, a few of them stepping over and around Penelope to get inside the library. They narrowed their eyes in the dim light, looking for something.

Looking for some*one*. But Nicholas was gone, and finding Lady Plymton and Mercy together in the library was hardly the scandal they'd hoped to witness.

One more figure, taller and marching like a soldier, joined the last few people still in the corridor. "The woman is ill. Everyone, please back away." The deep tones of Nicholas's baritone voice broke something inside Mercy. Their eyes met, and his were unrecognizable. Gone were the subtle hues and softness of the forest. The trees had caught fire, burned to black and blazing with such scalding heat she had to shrink away from them.

But Nicholas didn't wince or step away from her. He took action. He pushed one of the men aside and grabbed his shoulder. "Go fetch Lord Yolten. This is his wife."

The man, struck by that same scorching heat in Nicholas's eyes, nodded and dashed off. Nicholas scooped up Penelope, one arm under her neck and the other beneath her knees, and strode into the library. He reached the sofa where Lady Plymton sat. "Move," he said in a commanding tone that could only have been learned during his time in the army.

Lady Plymton wrinkled her nose but stood.

Nicholas laid Penelope on the sofa and strode back to the door. "Give this woman her privacy. I do not want anyone but her husband to enter this room. Do you understand?" Lady Plympton's friends nodded in unison, those that had pushed their way into the library shuffled back out of it, and then Nicholas shut the door.

Mercy ran to Penelope's side. Was she truly injured? Had the people on the other side of the door wanted in so badly they'd done something to her? Mercy grabbed both her hands, and one of Penelope's eyes cracked open. She glanced quickly at Nicholas, lifted both of her eyebrows, gave him a quick whooshing breath of appreciation, and closed her eyes again.

Mercy slid her jaw to one side. Penelope was most definitely unharmed.

But it looked like she might need a week of convalescence to recover from being carried by Nicholas. Apparently being married to the love of her life hadn't left her without an appreciation for men with broad shoulders and an overactive sense of duty and honor.

Nicholas paced in front of the door. "The three of you will explain exactly what is going on here."

"I don't need to explain anything," Lady Plymton said. "I was simply hoping to reconnect with you tonight, and instead, you had to go dashing out the window."

That was why the window was unlocked and how he had returned to the library from the outside. He hadn't needed her help, after all. Nicholas could have avoided scandal on his own. Of course he could have. He'd probably been dodging scheming women for most of his adult life.

"If that were the case, how did that note make it into my pocket? I hadn't been anywhere near you before it arrived." He turned to Mercy. She swallowed and tried to make herself look smaller. "How did you know to come to the library?" His commanding air dropped the smallest of fractions. His eyes raked over her. "Was it your note? Were you coming here to meet me?"

Mercy lowered her head. "No."

He stiffened. "But you knew about it."

She couldn't look at him. Couldn't watch the moment he learned what type of woman he had been courting. "Yes."

"And you didn't try to warn me?"

She didn't answer. As soon as she had learned about it, she had done exactly that. But it *was* her fault the note had made it into his pocket in the first place.

"You didn't just know about it, did you? Did you put that note in my pocket while we were in the drawing room?"

Mercy's eyes flashed up to his. He was going to despise her after the events of this ball, but even she had a limit to what she could live with him thinking of her. "No. Of course not."

He narrowed one eye. "So it was Lady Yolten, but she would have no reason to want me alone with Lady Plymton. Which means the two of you planned this together, and Lady Plymton was only too happy to comply."

Mercy couldn't answer him, but she couldn't hold his gaze any longer either, and apparently when she dropped her eyes, that was answer enough.

"Why would you do this?" His voice was hard but hoarse.

Mercy opened her mouth, but there was nothing she could say to excuse herself, not one thing she could say.

Lady Plymton scoffed. "The fool didn't want to marry you."

Nicholas shot Lady Plymton another one of his looks of fire, and she dropped her eyes as well.

Mercy crossed her hands over her stomach. She could tell him that all of this had been arranged before she'd truly known about Lady Plymton, before she'd asked him to take off his cravat and kiss her. But what good would it do? It wouldn't change their circumstances. She'd been too scared to let him know they couldn't marry. Well, now she wouldn't have to. Penelope and Lady Plymton had accomplished that unpleasant task for her. Now that Nicholas had witnessed her artifice and deception firsthand, he wouldn't want anything to do with her.

She couldn't look at the hurt and anger written all over Nicholas's face. "I'm sorry." Her voice came out as a whisper.

Nicholas returned to his pacing, one hand at the back of his neck as if he was deep in thought, or trying to stop himself from punching a wall. "What about the time Miss Morgan and I got separated from everyone else at the Zoological Garden? Did you plan that as well?"

Mercy swallowed. The absolute shame of what she had done weighed on her, making it hard to breath or talk. It was as if she had suddenly been caught under a landslide and a mountain of rubble pressed down on her chest. But she would not lie. "Yes."

He stopped pacing and walked toward her. She dared a glance at him. It was a mistake. His face was twisted in revulsion. "Of course you did," he said. "Was I so repellant to you that you had to force me onto other women? You could have simply told me."

Mercy rubbed her forehead. "No, I couldn't have." She shook her head. "You saw my parents. They were so happy."

"And you didn't have the courage to tell them you had no interest in a man who only sent flowers and asked you to dance and nothing more?"

"That isn't fair." Penelope sat up, perfectly unharmed. "True, what we did was wrong, but a woman can't possibly know right away whether she is in love with a man. She didn't want to reject you outright."

Nicholas turned on her. "No, she didn't. She only wanted to put me into situations that would damage not only my reputation, but that of other women as well."

"I don't care about my reputation," Lady Plymton said with a shrug. "I'd happily risk it for another chance with you."

"Lady Plymton, you will never have another chance with me. Please keep your distance whenever we have the misfortune of being in a room together. I do not look back at our time together with pleasure—only shame and regret." He turned to Mercy. "That is how rejection should be handled. Clean, clear, and without misunderstanding. Why—" He shook his head again. "And I'd thought . . ."

What? What had he thought? As much as she knew it would kill her, she wanted to know. But she was the one in the wrong, and no amount of begging for forgiveness would change her circumstances. He didn't finish his sentence. Instead, he leaned toward her. Waiting. As if, despite everything, he would, perhaps, give her one more chance to explain herself and make recompense for her wrongs.

But she could not. She mouthed the words, *I'm sorry,* once again. His jaw clenched, and he straightened. His hand went to his cravat and tore at it. First the knot in front came undone, and then the rest of it fell away at his clawing fingers. He ripped it from his neck and dropped it at her feet.

"I'll leave this with you as a memento of our time together. I'll never wear it again," he said with his lips curved into an awful sneer, before striding out of the room.

Nicholas, the Duke of Harrington, the most proper man she had ever known, stormed past the men and women waiting in the corridor with his neck bare and the offending length of silk left, mocking her, in a pile at her feet.

Nicholas almost made it out of the Driarwood home without incident. Even Patience and Ottersby didn't dare stop him as strode past the ballroom. It was only as he stood alone in the entry hall pacing while he waited for the servant to call his carriage and fetch his coat and hat that someone dared approach him.

And it was Lord Rayleigh, blast the deuced man. He must have a death wish. Wasn't interrupting his speech and arguing with him in Parliament enough?

Lord Rayleigh pulled a monocle out of his breast pocket and surveyed Nicholas's open neck. "Have you spent so much time with the Irish that you are adopting their style of dress? Your father would be so disappointed."

Nicholas sighed. His father couldn't have cared less about his cravat. But he would be disappointed to know that Nicholas had allowed this man to disrespect the title of Harrington time and time again. Nicholas looked down toward his neck as if he wasn't extremely aware of his open collar. "You don't think I should be dressed like this?"

Lord Rayleigh grunted. "Of course not. You are a duke, for heaven's sake. Think of your reputation."

"Then I suppose there is nothing to do but for you to give me yours."

"What?"

"I'm fairly certain you heard me. I said give me your cravat."

Lord Rayleigh took a step back as if he had only just realized he was in the company of a madman. He should have realized it sooner; it wasn't as if

Nicholas were trying to hide it. Lord Rayleigh shook his head. "I'm not going to give you my cravat."

"Yes, you are. You know who I am. You know my title and rank. After all, you've reminded me of those things twice. Are you really going to deny me, a duke, this one request?"

"I—" Lord Rayleigh looked left and right. The only other person in the hall was the same servant, looking for all the world as if he couldn't hear their conversation, but the corners of his lips turned up just enough for Nicholas to know he was enjoying it.

"If you make me ask for your cravat again, you will no longer be admitted to Whites, any business dealings our estates share will be halted, and every other Sunday, I'll personally make certain an order of flowers is delivered to your home with your mistress's name on them."

"Your father—"

"If you try to use my father's reputation against me again, the flowers will be arriving twice a week."

Lord Rayleigh swallowed, mumbled something under his breath, then undid his cravat and handed it to him. Nicholas held it up with two fingers. The edges of the linen were yellowed, and the material limp. There was no circumstance under which Nicholas would be putting it around his neck.

"The next time I speak in Parliament, you won't be interrupting me unless it is to voice support for my ideas. Do you understand?" But Lord Rayleigh simply looked at his cravat with confusion and nodded. "Answer me, you low-living piece of filth, or I will speak to the Queen about your insolence."

Lord Rayleigh furrowed his eyebrows but nodded. "I understand."

"Good. I don't care what your views are. You are welcome to go to the devil because of your lack of sympathy to the suffering and dying, but I will not have you impeding my work any longer. I *am* my father's son, and the title of Harrington is mine now. It is time you started treating me with the same deference you treated him."

Lord Rayleigh nodded again, but it seemed to pain him.

"Good. Now then." Nicholas pasted on the broadest and most becoming smile he could muster. "Give my regards to your wife. I'll have my mother send her an invitation for a morning visit, if you think she would enjoy it."

The furrows in Lord Rayleigh forehead smoothed out. Nicholas knew Lady Rayleigh's wife only in passing, but she was definitely the type who would love to drink tea with a duchess. "She would."

"Tell her to look forward to it." Nicholas threw Lord Rayleigh's cravat back at him. "And tell your valet to use more starch."

CHAPTER 29

SPRING IN BRUSHBEND WAS A sight to behold. Nicholas had spent far too much time in London since Father died, and the massive gardens here had remained well kept but unexplored. Patience stood beside him on a path overlooking the lake.

"A house party was a good idea, Nicholas." Patience smiled. She seemed at rest here; it was hard not to be. "It has been too long since I've boated in the lake or felt the cool damp air in the grotto. We should come more often. You were a different person while growing up. I've always thought it was because of your time in the army, but maybe London has been the problem all along."

"Patience." The tone in his voice must have shown his emotion. Patience tipped her head to one side and put a hand on his arm. He'd been so ashamed of what had happened between him and Lady Plymton that he'd never told Patience. "It wasn't the army. It was what happened before the army. You were young then, so Mother and Father protected you, but I was sent there for a reason."

"Father wanted you to become more serious, like him."

Nicholas shook his head. "No. I'd made a mistake, a foolish one, and I needed to gain some perspective on life in order to see that. Father saved me from myself by buying me a commission."

Patience's fingers tightened on his arm. "I don't understand what you mean."

So he told her. Everything. All about Lady Plymton, her fiancé, his heart-break, and the realization about how naive he'd been. Four months ago, he would have done anything to keep this secret from her, but he was tired of always trying to portray himself as upstanding, and of all the people in the world, Patience should be able to see him as the imperfect man he was and still love him despite it. "I thought I was protecting you by not telling you this at the time. But I see now I was only trying to protect myself. I built walls around us, and when you made mistakes, I allowed you to think we were different. But we aren't. We've both been fools for love."

Over the course of his story, Patience's expressive face had shown rage, sorrow, frustration, and understanding. She reached for his other arm and clamped both of her hands tightly on him. "Don't disparage yourself. You were young, and I'm sorry I didn't know. I was so angry at you."

"You'd lost the carefree brother you grew up with. I don't blame you for that, not one bit."

"And I never blamed you either. I knew you had to grow up quickly after Papa died. I missed you though. I think we were both lost. But I never saw you as a fool, and I don't think what you had with Lady Plymton could be classified as love."

This was the terrible part, the truth that burned and raged inside him, more painfully than his secrets about Lady Plymton. "I wasn't talking about Lady Plymton."

Patience stilled, but she didn't say anything. She didn't have to. They both knew exactly what he meant.

"I know I've been more serious, and honestly, I miss the boy I was when we lived here too. But he had to grow up and face the world as it is, not a romanticized version of it."

Patience pulled him closer and wrapped her arms around him. He took a deep breath and allowed himself to sink into her embrace. He felt more whole in this moment than he had in three years. When Patience finally released him, she put both of her hands on his shoulders. "The world is still beautiful, Nicholas, even if it disappoints us sometimes."

Later, when he was alone again, he would have to fight to trust her on that, but for the moment, with the late sun shining over the lake and his carefully crafted walls demolished, he believed it.

Patience pulled him back toward the house. "The guests should be gathering in the music room, and I'm not certain that is the type of social gathering we should leave Mama to host on her own."

Nicholas chuckled. Definitely not. They strode arm in arm down the path. "Thank you for handling all the invitations and coordinating travel. It is good to have the house opened up for guests again. I've been alone so long, I'm even looking forward to Mother's singing."

"Perhaps you shouldn't thank me just yet." Patience's voice held an odd quality, one he was all too familiar with. She'd done something.

"What do you mean?"

"I was considering surprising you. However, after our talk, I've reconsidered the idea."

"Patience . . ."

"Have I ever told you I love it when you use my name that way? It sounds almost as if you are speaking to yourself. And I think today I would advise exactly that—patience, with me."

"What did you do?"

"I've invited Lord and Lady Driarwood. They should be arriving today."

A chill swept up from the lake, and Nicholas stopped. "Only Lord and Lady Driarwood?"

"I believe Lady Mercy will be coming as well." She placed a quick kiss on Nicholas's cheek and then dashed forward. Once she was a safe distance away from him, she turned her head. "I'm sorry!"

It took Nicholas a lot longer than it should have to reach the music room. He hadn't heard any carriages arrive while he and Patience were walking, but still his eyes surveyed the room before he stepped in. It was still the same group that had been here since the day before. Patience, Ottersby, General Woodsworth, Lord and Lady Bryant, Lord Bryant's brother-in-law, Mr. Nate Barton, and his wife and child were in attendance, as well as Lady Marion and her parents—the catalysts for the house party.

Lady Marion stood from the seat next to her parents and joined him at the back of the room. "Do you sing, Your Grace?"

With a musical mother, obsessed with singing? More than he cared to admit. He glanced around the room one more time. Mercy definitely wasn't here. "I do."

"I have 'What Are the Wild Waves Saying' prepared on the piano. Do you know the words? We could sing it together." She looked almost terrified of him, as if he would run her off if he disagreed.

Nicholas had left London without a farewell to her or anyone else but his family. He owed her a song, at least. Plus, it would give him a direct line of sight to the door. "Of course I would. In fact, that would be an excellent way to start the evening."

Lady Marion smiled at him, and he held out his arm and led her to the pianoforte. She sat, placed her slender fingers on the piano keys, and glanced back up at him with a nod before she expertly plucked out the tune.

Nicholas started the first verse, and Lady Marion finished the second half. They sang the chorus together, and Lady Marion's sweet voice was such a stark contrast to Mother's that he was surprised at how well the notes melded together.

There were no surprises in Lady Marion's singing or playing. Everything was done exactly according to plan. Where was the enjoyment in that?

While Lady Marion finished her part, Nicholas strode to the front row of chairs and grabbed Mother's hand. She gave no protest as he pulled her in front of the pianoforte. In fact, she turned and faced her small audience with a flourish, finished the last bar of Lady Marion's part with her, and then rambunctiously launched into the chorus. Nicholas chuckled and belted out his part as well.

Lady Marion's fingers floundered for the first time as she tried to adjust to Mother's unsteady rhythm, and Nicholas gave her a lopsided grin. It was hard to keep up with Mother, but life had always been more exciting when he tried. He turned to catch Patience's eye, only to see her welcoming someone into the room.

His note faltered. Standing at the back of the room were Lord and Lady Driarwood. They walked in with their heads down, whispering softly to Patience. Nicholas rejoined Mother, schooling his face and voice into paying no heed to what was happening at the back of the room.

Were they alone?

Lord and Lady Driarwood stepped to the side, and behind them, in a deep-red gown, Mercy walked into the music room of Brushbend. Her head was lowered, and she did not meet his eye. Her neck was bare. No emeralds, and certainly no simple silver chain. Of course there wasn't. If she was ever going to wear that gift, it would have been two months ago.

What the devil had Patience been thinking?

He steeled his nerves and retreated to a place of safety in the back of his mind. He simply needed to get though one more chorus, and then he could drag his sister out of the back door and—what? Scold her? How exactly did one discipline a grown, married woman?

He would strip Ottersby of his title. He had managed to convince the Queen and Parliament into giving it to him in the first place. Surely he would find a way to rescind it. He did his best to keep his eyes from following Mercy as she sat down on the second row of seats with her parents.

What would have possessed her to accept Patience's invitation? Had her parents convinced her she'd made a terrible mistake letting a duke slip through her fingers? He forced a smile as he finished the last word of the song.

Nicholas kissed Mother's cheek and gave a prodigious smile to Lady Marion. He thanked her and made a show of taking her arm, leading her back to her seat and sitting down next to her. Mercy had been as careful as he had to not meet his eye, but now that he was seated, facing away from her, it was as if he could feel her eyes on the back of his head.

Mother announced that she would sing another song and asked if anyone would accompany her. Mrs. Barton volunteered and played so beautifully that Mother sang another song after that. Nicholas's neck ached from the force of keeping his head forward and resisting the urge to look back. Lord Woodbury then pulled Ottersby up and made him sing "Cheer, Boys, Cheer!", and if Mercy hadn't been there, Nicholas would have joined them. He could never hear the military tune without thinking of Donald.

Mr. Barton came to the pianoforte and offered to play for his wife while she sang. Mr. Barton didn't play very well. He stumbled over a few notes, and the piece was very simple, but once Mrs. Barton lifted her voice to join him, his playing was completely overshadowed by his wife's voice.

For the first time since Nicholas had sat down, he allowed himself to turn his head and look back at Patience. He raised his eyebrows at her. Had she known she had invited a woman whose voice might make angles weep?

He closed his eyes and allowed himself to simply rest and let the music wash over him. The house party would only last three days. He could be in Mercy's presence for three days. It would be over before he knew it, and he could start working on stripping Ottersby of his title next week.

The last strain of Mrs. Barton's voice faded away, and the room went silent.

The musicale was over. No one, save perhaps Mother, would dare to follow that performance, which meant he would have to stand up and greet the last of his guests.

First he stood and congratulated Mrs. Barton. She blushed becomingly, her large blue eyes beaming at her husband. "Nate deserves the credit. He has been working tirelessly on the pianoforte for the past year."

Mr. Barton laughed and planted a kiss on top of his wife's head. "True. I am certain no one even noticed your singing, thanks to my excellent playing."

Nicholas managed to exchange a few more pleasantries with the pair before turning around. Mercy was gone. She and her family must have bid Patience good night and retired for the evening.

He strode to his sister, grabbed her arm, and propelled her out of the room and into the adjoining corridor.

"How could you have invited her, Patience?" he hissed. "How dare you?"

Patience's face fell. "Not you too, Nicholas. I know she hurt you, but I thought you might be willing to forget your resentment to help their family."

He dropped her arm as if she had burned him. "What do you mean, help them? Why would they need my help?"

Patience blinked and narrowed her eyes. "You haven't heard?"

"Heard what?" His heart stumbled. The look on Patience's face was desolate. Was Mercy sick? He had only gotten the one glimpse of her when she walked in the room, but she *was* mightily changed. "Is someone unwell?"

Patience shook her head. "No. As far as I know, everyone in the family is healthy. But they've been shunned from all good society. No one of quality will have anything to do with them."

Nicholas rubbed a hand on his forehead. Shunned? Why would Lord and Lady Driarwood be shunned? "What do you mean? Lord Driarwood is well respected."

Patience put a hand on his arm. "You really haven't heard?"

"No. I haven't been listening to gossip from London. I've been here."

"Sulking."

"Not sulking. Ignoring Society." He brushed aside Patience's sardonic assessment of his character. What could have happened to Mercy's family? Had Mercy run into trouble? Memories of Mercy leaning toward him, pulling off his cravat, flashed before his eyes. She had been so forward and trusting. "She hasn't had trouble with a man, has she?" His hand fisted, the thought making him ill, and then another thought made his stomach churn. What if *he* was the problem? Did Lady Plymton or Miss Morgan say something about the two of them? They had ended their courtship abruptly, without any explanation, and if any wind of what had transpired between them in the drawing room had reached gossiping ears . . .

"Not Lady Mercy. Her sister."

Nicholas blinked. He knew almost nothing of Mercy's sister, except that she was married to Donald's brother and Mercy adored her. "What happened to her sister?"

Patience took a deep breath, as if what she was about to say gave her no pleasure. "It seems she has run off with a composer. And not a significant-enough composer for Society to forgive her for leaving her husband behind. The whole family is disgraced."

Nicholas ran a hand down his face. What a mess, and Nicholas hadn't heard anything about it. He should have reached out to Donald's family. Blasted woman. How could she do that to her husband? And to her family?

Patience eyed the corridor, making certain no one was within earshot. "It's been quite the ordeal for everyone. The Driarwoods have spent most of the last month secluded, partially by choice, but also by lack of invitation. I know they've hurt you, but I saw a chance to ease them back into a good social circle, and I took it."

Nicholas gritted his teeth together. "And you couldn't have invited them to *your* home?"

"I have. But there was only so much I could do. You're a duke, Nicholas. This visit could be a turning point for them."

It would have been easier to be mad at Patience, but he couldn't fault her reasoning. He took a steadying breath. "I appreciate you trying to help them. It is kind of you." The words were hard to produce. He'd looked forward to an opportunity to rejoin Society on a small scale during this house party, but his reintroduction would have to wait. There was no possible way for him to participate in festivities with Mercy so near. He was ready to be around people again, but he was not ready to be around Mercy. "I won't do something ridiculous like make them leave."

"Thank you, Nicholas." Patience beamed up at him. "I'm quite fond of Lady Mercy. It is a pity for her your courtship didn't turn into an engagement. If she'd known what was coming, she would have held on to you for protection's sake."

Nicholas smirked. His sister didn't know Mercy as well as she thought. There was nothing that would make Mercy marry for anything but love. "No, she wouldn't have. If anything, the practicality of that arrangement would have sickened her. And if she'd loved me, she never would have hidden behind—" Nicholas froze. Patience furrowed her eyebrows at him, but he ignored her. Snippets of his courtship with Mercy played through his mind. Their first meeting when she was trying to find out what her father was speaking about. Her parents' excitement about their courtship. He'd assumed that had been because of his title, but what if it had been more than that? What if they'd known what was coming and had planned the whole thing hoping to save Mercy from disgrace? And if so, when had Mercy learned of their plan? She'd been so blasted naive; he doubted she could have been a part of it. "How long ago did you say this happened?"

"The scandal?"

How many nights had he relived their time in the drawing room, certain she had felt for him what he had felt for her? But then she'd changed so drastically after speaking with her parents. He'd gone mad searching for a reason, any reason she'd rejected him, besides not wanting him. "Yes."

"A month ago. Which is why I thought you would've heard by now."

A full month after she had spurned him at the ball, then. The tiny sliver of hope he'd had vanished like a puff a smoke.

"Where is her sister now?"

"In Austria."

"With the composer?"

"Yes. Her sister lived with them for a month without her husband, and then the composer came to London and whisked her away."

"Her sister lived with them before the scandal?"

"Yes. Nicholas, it isn't a very hard story to follow."

"Was her sister at the ball?" He should have been more specific. There were hundreds of balls in London every year, but Patience would know which one he was speaking of. The ball that had changed everything. The one that had him leaving Town faster than Mother had left for Paris after Father had died.

"I left when you did. She may have come late, I suppose. Why? Do you think her sister had something to do with the fact that Mercy rejected you?"

Nicholas rubbed his forehead. "I have no idea."

"Why would her sister coming to London make her feel like she needed to reject you?"

"I don't know. Perhaps I'm a man dying in the desert who has just been given a glimpse of a mirage. But also, I told her that avoiding scandal has been my number one goal since Father died. I told her the most important thing to me was protecting the family name."

"Oh, Nicholas." Patience put a hand on his elbow. "You told her that without also telling her you have a mother that ran off to Paris instead of properly mourning Papa and a sister who has added nothing but shame to the family name and you still love us? Ideals are well and good, but none of us have lived up to them."

"In hindsight, I see that, perhaps, I should have mentioned that as well."

"Perhaps you still can."

Nicholas closed his eyes. He wanted to believe this mirage. He could taste the cool, clear water of believing Mercy had rejected him not because she didn't love him but because she did. But the reality was that he was dragging himself through the desert for sand.

Mercy hadn't simply rejected him. She'd manipulated him into meeting with Lady Plymton. If her reason for rejecting him were to save him from disgrace, then the last thing she would have done was arrange for him to meet Lady Plymton in the library. "No, I don't think I can. I've thought of a thousand reasons why Mercy might have rejected me, and when I follow the logic of them to the end I always come up with the same answer. She didn't *want* to marry me. And if I think too hard about it, I think she may have even wanted to hurt me. So it's best for everyone if I don't think about it and move on with the rest of my life. If there were any logical reason Mercy would've had to end our courtship, while still wanting to marry me, trust me, I would have found it."

"But if she'd known about her sister's scandal—"

"No, Patience. When you mentioned it, I thought perhaps for a moment, but no. The scandal doesn't actually explain anything, and I'm not even certain I'd want it to. She'd spent a large part of our courtship trying to arrange meetings with other women for me. A healthy relationship could never develop from one built on deception."

"Nicholas . . ." Patience's voice had an odd ringing quality to it.

"What?"

"You do know my relationship with Anthony developed while I was deceiving him, don't you?"

Nicholas gritted his teeth. Patience throwing her happy marriage into his face was far from helpful. "The two of you are different, and Ottersby spent months pining over you after you left. I'm not pining over Mercy. I have no interest in her, not anymore."

Patience raised an eyebrow at him.

He took a deep breath and schooled his features. "I don't."

"You've called her by her Christian name twice in this conversation, Nicholas. You, the man who won't leave his house without his stockings starched."

Blast. He had. "I don't starch my stockings." His valet did. "And I have no desire to rekindle a relationship with *Lady* Mercy."

Patience sighed and nodded. He could almost see her filing away this conversation and moving forward. Which hopefully meant she hadn't noticed his lie. His body screamed at him to pull Mercy right back into the moment of their stolen kisses in her drawing room. He simply had to clamp down the thoughts that ran through his head every time he saw her. The news of her family's scandal almost gave him a reason to hope. But unless he had an explanation of how she could have given him that letter from Lady Plymton *after* he'd told her about his fear of bringing shame to his family's name, his hope was as delusional as drinking sand.

CHAPTER 30

MERCY COULD COUNT ON ONE finger the number of humiliating experiences that were worse than setting foot in the music room last night. The only thing worse had been meeting Nicholas's eyes in the library after he'd discovered she'd been trying to foist him off on other women.

Thankfully, she hadn't seen Nicholas since. He hadn't been at breakfast, nor had he shown up in the drawing room later. Lady Ottersby had made an excuse for him, but the truth of the matter was, Nicholas must not want to see her any more than she wanted to see him.

Mercy turned the page of her book. She'd sequestered herself in a corner of the parlor so that if he did decide to show up, at least he would be capable of ignoring her in her current location. But most of the party had been here an hour already, and she'd finally stopped jumping at every movement thinking it might be him. Thirty more minutes and she could excuse herself to go rest in her room. If she simply would have told her parents the truth about what had happened with Nicholas, they never would have brought her here.

But her parents already had one daughter they were extremely disappointed in. She couldn't bring herself to add herself to that list.

The door opened, and just like every other time someone moved or left, Mercy's eyes darted to the door. But this time, it *was* him. Nicholas.

She hadn't dared to look at him the night before, at least not until he'd been sitting in front of her, and even though she knew she should put her head back in her book, she couldn't pull her eyes away from him. His hair was slightly longer than it had been in London, as if he hadn't bothered to keep it perfectly tamed while in the country. But his clothing was still impeccable, the cut of his coat accenting the breadth of his shoulders and his trim waist. The sight of him brought on the familiar ache of loss. His eyes caught her looking at him, and she quickly turned away.

She couldn't remember where she'd been in the book. She couldn't even concentrate well enough to make out a single word. She'd spent the last two months thinking about Nicholas and the long list of her sins against him. She'd never felt the need to impress anyone before. If people enjoyed her company, wonderful. If they didn't, she didn't worry about it. Nicholas was the only person in the world she coveted acceptance from, and he happened to be the one person in the world who had every reason to despise her.

Needless to say, she hadn't been sleeping well at night.

A shadow fell over the book she wasn't reading, and her eyes slid from her book to the sharp line of a perfectly ironed pair of trousers. She swallowed and looked up.

Nicholas wasn't smiling, but he wasn't frowning either. He gave her an almost imperceptible bow. "Lady Mercy, I'm looking for a partner for chess. Would you be interested?"

Perhaps no one was looking at the two of them; it was impossible to say since Mercy couldn't look away from the pair of eyes she'd missed for two months, but it felt as though everyone in the room must be. "Are you certain you would like to play with me? I'm not very skilled."

"I am aware of your skills, and yes, I would like to play with you, but only if you are willing. If you aren't, I will find someone else."

Mercy snapped her book closed. "I'm willing."

She had seen the chess table when she'd first entered the drawing room and had purposely avoided it. She followed Nicholas, and he pulled her chair out for her. The chess pieces were already on the table, laid out and ready for them to start.

Nicholas sat and motioned for her to make the first move. Without putting more thought into it than just survival of the next half hour, she slid one of her pawns forward.

Nicholas lifted his hand to one of his pieces. "How are you enjoying your stay at Brushbend?" he asked and then made his move.

Thus far, her stay had been tortuous. His home was beautiful, his family a delight, and he was so far out of her reach she might as well be in Austria. "It's been lovely." His mouth quirked as if he knew she was lying. She shouldn't be lying to Nicholas. He didn't deserve that. "What I mean to say is, my family appreciates your hospitality very much."

She shook her head, grateful the table was situated far enough from the other guests for them to be out of earshot. How was she going to survive this? She moved another pawn.

Nicholas studied the chessboard as if they had moved more than three pieces and he knew what he was doing. After more than a minute of deliberation, he moved another pawn, then looked up at her. "I didn't sleep very well last night."

"If that was at all my fault, I'm sorry. I begged my parents to let me stay in London or visit Rosalind in Austria. I haven't told them everything that happened between us, so they didn't know how unpleasant it would be for you to have me here. They are innocent in causing you pain."

Nicholas's face was unreadable. "Your apology for descending upon my home is accepted. Now I need to ask you a few questions, and I need you to answer truthfully. Can you do that?"

Mercy bit her lip. "I don't know."

Nicholas tipped his head to one side. "Well, that is honest, at least." He motioned with his chin to her side of the chessboard. She'd forgotten they were playing. She moved her knight. "If it helps, nothing you say will change the way I feel about you. It's been two months since we've seen each other, and that is longer than the time we spent courting. The past is in the past; I'm simply trying to understand it."

His intention there was clear. No matter what she said, or what explanations she gave, he wouldn't be renewing his interest in her. Whatever feelings he'd had were gone, and they wouldn't be returning. She would never again kiss the man who sat across from her, with or without a cravat involved. She closed her eyes for a moment, willing herself to let the past slide away, as he must have. "In that case, yes. I will try my best, and if I cannot tell the truth, at least I will not lie."

"Thank you." Nicholas moved his rook forward four spaces. "Was your sister at your home the night of the ball?"

Mercy had started reaching for a pawn, but her hand froze. She'd been prepared to answer questions about Lady Plymton and Miss Morgan. She hadn't thought Rosalind would be a part of their conversation. "I would rather not answer that question."

Nicholas nodded and didn't press her further—he must not have been too desperate for an answer. She slid a pawn forward one space.

"Lady Yolten gave me the note from Lady Plymton. Did you know she was going to do that?"

"We'd spoken of it, yes."

"When?"

"Before the ball."

"I'm afraid I'm going to have to ask you to be more specific."

She shouldn't tell him. It was better for everyone if he simply thought the worst of her. But she'd lain awake too many nights wanting to explain this exact point. She looked him in the eye and willed him not to read anything more into her answer than the fact that she hadn't wanted to hurt him. "It was two days before the ball, and with all the excitement of the evening, I'd forgotten our plan. I've wanted to apologize daily for the past two months for putting you in that position. If I'd known more about your past, I never would have done it."

Nicholas nodded, then put a hand to his chin and looked so intently at the board one would think he was memorizing it. "Are you in love with me?" he asked.

Mercy ducked her head down and glanced furtively at the other people in the room. "What? You can't ask me that."

He looked up, calm as if he'd only just asked her about the condition of the weather. "I wasn't aware we had put parameters around these questions other than that you wouldn't lie to me."

"Well, I won't answer that question. It is impertinent, even for a duke."

"All right, I'll rephrase the question. Do you regret not getting engaged to me?"

This she could answer and answer truthfully. In the past month her family had been shunned, her sister disgraced, and Mercy had never once wanted to put Nicholas through that. Not after everything he'd already endured at the hand of Lady Plymton.

She'd followed what was happening in the House of Lords thanks to her father, and even though Nicholas remained out of London unless there was an extremely important vote, Nicholas was starting to gain a reputation there. A good one. Already the budget for relief efforts had been increased by a third, and she knew he'd finally hit his stride with the members of Parliament.

If she'd married him and then Rosalind's actions had become known, he would not garner the same respect he had now. "No, I don't. I wish you all the best in the world. You deserve it. And if you feel any regret over—" She paused. How much had those stolen moments with her in the drawing room cost him? Hopefully not as much as they'd cost her. "Anything, I absolve you of it. You only followed my lead. I've seen what you've been accomplishing these past few months in Parliament, and I'm glad to see you moving forward and not back."

A muscle clenched in Nicholas's jaw, and he moved his bishop to the middle of the chessboard almost without looking at it. "I speak of love, and you speak of Parliament. How the tables have turned."

"That was always what our courtship was about, wasn't it?"

He caught her eye, and for a moment, she was lost in what might have been. He shook his head slowly. "No, it was not."

Mercy waited for a follow-up question, but none came. Mercy slid a bishop a few spaces forward and to the right. As soon as her finger came off the piece, Nicholas took one of her knights with his rook. Blast, she needed to start paying attention. His rook was in prime position to make it to her back row on his next move. She moved her bishop so it would prevent him from going there.

Then he took her bishop with his queen.

Move after move, it was like Nicholas was one step ahead of her. Every time she thought she knew what he was thinking, it ended up being a trap. What was going on? He'd never played with her so decisively before.

She gave up thinking about her moves and simply started moving her pieces faster. She moved a pawn forward, and Nicholas slid his queen to the back of the board. He took one solid look at all the pieces and then caught her eye. "Checkmate."

She glanced down at the board. They'd only just started playing. He couldn't be right. But he was. Her king was trapped. He'd won. Her voice was shaky when she looked up. "What just happened?"

"I've been practicing for the past two months with my valet. He is quite good. And I told myself if I ever got the chance to match you in wits again, this time, I'd win."

His smile held no malice, and his victory was anything but boastful. It was more the look of a man that had just shared a secret with her. The spark in his eye made Mercy think perhaps the two of them could be, well, not friends exactly, but acquaintances at least. That was better than enemies at any rate. She returned his grin. "Well, you've executed that plan marvelously. I didn't stand a chance. Congratulations."

He stood from the table and turned away, but before he got more than two steps, he turned back to her. "Don't congratulate me yet, I'm not done matching wits with you. I will see you this evening at dinner, Lady Mercy." Then he strode out of the room.

CHAPTER 31

WHEN LADY BRYANT SUGGESTED A walk in the garden before dinner, Mercy jumped at the chance to spend an hour or so out of the house and in conversation with someone who was more or less uninformed as to what had happened between her and Nicholas.

She needed a distraction from Nicholas's declaration about matching wits. What had he meant? He'd seemed friendly during chess, but was that all a ruse? Was he trying to lull her into a false sense of security and then find some way to make her pay for her treatment of him? She didn't know, but getting away from the house and away from him was an opportunity she wasn't going to pass up.

After fetching their coats, a footman pointed them in the direction of large double doors that opened to a massive stone balcony overlooking the acres of land spilling out behind Brushbend. She'd seen the garden through the window, but that view hadn't done it justice. At the center of the garden was a massive lake. A boathouse stood on the side closest to them, but dotted around the lake were follies and gardens and hills to explore.

Lady Bryant tightened her grip on her arm and turned to her, eyes sparkling. "Which side of the lake should we see first?"

Lady Bryant's excitement was contagious. To the left, Mercy could just make out an octagonal structure, most likely a folly, and to the right, there seemed to be some kind of ruins—broken walls and structures with flowers and plants growing around them.

"The right side," Mercy answered. "The ruins look fascinating."

Lady Bryant nodded with excitement. "I agree."

The two of them crossed to the end of the balcony and climbed down the stone steps. A path opened before them, and they followed it.

The ruins had seemed close by when they stood on the balcony, but as they traversed the path, they came across small gardens of flowers and benches, as well as a bridge that crossed over one tendril part of the lake. Each little mystery had to be explored.

Lady Bryant leaned over the bridge railing. "Can you imagine growing up in a place like this?"

Mercy looked back at the palace behind her. It was much grander than her family's country estate, and she could see from the changes in bricks that at least two additions had been constructed since it was originally built. Probably by one of Nicholas's irresponsible ancestors. Even still, the home paled in comparison to the garden. She would have happily spent hours exploring a garden like this as a child. Had Nicholas known how fortunate he was? No wonder Lady Plymton was so easily able to charm him. He'd had a fairy-tale existence until she'd come along.

After crossing the bridge, the path dipped low, and they took their steps carefully until it flattened out again, just to the side of the lake. They both stopped to take in the sinking sun as it glistened on top of the water.

The crunching of feet on the path behind them made them both turn.

"Ollie!" Lady Ottersby called out before they could even see her. First her feet came into view and then the rest of her as she walked carefully down the hill Mercy and Lady Bryant had just descended.

She was alone. Thankfully.

"Oh," Lady Ottersby said when she saw the two of them. "Have you seen Ollie?"

"You mean that horse you call a pet?" Lady Bryant asked.

"The same." Lady Ottersby smiled and turned to Mercy. "He is actually a Great Dane, not a horse. Did he come this way?"

"Not that I know of, sorry," Mercy answered.

Lady Ottersby's face scrunched into a pout. "Blast."

Mercy pressed her lips together to keep from laughing. Hearing such a word from Nicholas's sister's mouth was unexpected, to say the least.

"We could help you find him," Lady Bryant offered. "Where does he like to go?"

"A few places, and I'm afraid one of them is the falconry on the opposite side of the lake. I need to find him before he reaches it and terrifies the inmates."

Lady Bryant squeezed Mercy's hand. "Lady Mercy and I are up for a run, aren't we?"

Mercy glanced at the two women. After weeks of only Penelope and Lady Ottersby's company at quiet afternoon visits, a spot of brightness rose in her chest. They looked ready for anything. "Of course I am."

"Wonderful," Lady Ottersby said. "I will head directly to the falconry. He also loves the tulip garden and grotto. We will reach those first. Could you each look through one? Ollie is large but harmless. If you find him, take him by the collar and meet me back at the house. First is the tulip garden, which extends to the right, and past that, the grotto dips underground. It's a man-made cave, of sorts. Thank you so much."

Lady Ottersby dashed down the path. Lady Bryant grinned at her and dashed forward as well. Mercy lifted her skirts and followed. Just as Lady Ottersby had said, they reached the tulip garden first. "I'll look here. You head to the grotto," Lady Bryant told her.

Mercy nodded and pushed forward. She could still see Lady Ottersby ahead of her, and at a fork in the path, Lady Ottersby stopped for a moment and pointed Mercy toward the right and then continued on.

Mercy reached the path moments later. Just as Lady Ottersby had said, the path dipped low and to the right. Almost immediately, there was a cave-like entrance with stone walls. Who thought of such things to put in a garden?

She entered the cave, which quickly took a turn, blanketing her in darkness. The air was damp and several degrees cooler than the path she'd been on. Ten feet after the turn, the low tunnel-like cave opened up into a cavern, complete with a small waterfall on one side.

And next to the waterfall stood Nicholas.

She slid to a stop. With his back to her, he stood watching the water as it cascaded from a hole in the roof. The soft roar of the waterfall had muted her footsteps, and he didn't turn. The spray from the water and splash of sunlight coming from above him made Nicholas look like a woodland king. Or, rather, it would have, if woodland kings wore expertly tailored coats.

She allowed herself a moment to study him, to memorize the way he stood, with his hand on one hip and his head lifted to the light. If she'd been a better student of oils, she would have painted him, but her skills wouldn't be able to put this moment to justice, so a memory would be all she would ever get.

That was all she would ever have of Nicholas.

She closed her eyes and took a deep, humid breath. Ollie wasn't here, and the tunnel didn't continue past the cavern. If she turned around very quietly, perhaps he wouldn't even know she'd been near him.

She stepped backward slowly, not taking her eyes off Nicholas. Her skirt grazed the edge of the wall, loosening a rock and sending it skittering toward the waterfall.

Nicholas turned.

She steeled herself for the look of disappointment and repulsion at the sight of her; one chess match wouldn't be enough to wipe away the harm she'd done, even if it had given her hope that someday they could at least be cordial to each other.

But instead of a scorn, his face lifted in a smile.

She almost fell backward at the sight of it.

"Lady Mercy, this is a pleasant surprise." His voice was low and barely audible over the sound of the waterfall behind him.

"I'm looking for Ollie. Have you seen him? I didn't know you were here." Words came cascading out of her mouth faster than the water that fell through the grotto's roof.

Nicholas stepped toward her. How could he smile at her like that? "No, I haven't seen Ollie. But you've stumbled onto one of my favorite places in all of the world."

Mercy pressed her back against the cool stone of the cavern wall. He kept coming closer, and she shouldn't be here, tainting his favorite place with her presence. "I'll go then. Your sister needs my help."

"No, Mercy, she doesn't."

"She does. She is looking for her dog."

"Ollie is back at the house, safe and sound." Nicholas looked at his hands. "A lot like how you were safe and sound when I ended up looking for you, alone, with Miss Morgan in the Zoological Garden."

Heavens above, he was going to kill her. That was the explanation for his smile; it must be. No one would find her body here. It was dark, and she caught her breath. The look in his eye was anything but murderous.

"What do you mean?"

"I thought perhaps it was time to give you a taste of your own medicine. You tried to get me alone with someone you thought I might have feelings for, and now I am doing the same."

Nicholas was only a few feet from her now. He could reach forward and touch her if he wanted. But he wouldn't want to, would he? He must hate her for what she had done, and he'd promised that no matter her answers over the chessboard, his feelings wouldn't change for her.

"What do you mean by that?" She didn't have feelings for Nicholas. Not ones that mattered, anyway. Perhaps at one point they had, but they would do her no good now. "Are you going to torment me?"

"No. At least, I hope not. I have another question for you, and once again, I *need* the truth. It is slightly different from the one I asked you earlier, but the distinction is important." His hand lifted, and he touched the bracelet at her wrist. His fingers were hot in the cool grotto air. "If it weren't for the fact that your sister has disappointed your family and tainted your reputation, would we be engaged today?"

Mercy closed her eyes. She couldn't look at him. It was too painful, and her wrist burned from his touch. "I don't know."

"What do you mean, you don't know? Is that your way of saying you would rather not answer?"

Mercy took a deep breath. He had asked for honesty. It was the least she could give him after what she had put him through. "No, Your Grace. I mean that I truly don't know."

He lifted her bracelet between his thumb and forefinger, spinning its delicate chains between them. Then he wrapped his hand around her wrist. He'd said he hadn't brought her here to torment her, but he was doing exactly that. He leaned forward. "I need you to explain to me why."

Mercy's back was pressed against the cold stone of the grotto, but even in the cool air, her body felt like it was on fire. Nicholas didn't love her. The look in his eyes was something else. It had to be. "If I answer you, do you give me the same promise—that your feelings for me will not change because of what I say?"

Nicholas grinned. "That I can guarantee."

Which meant she could tell him. He wouldn't propose again, and he wouldn't link himself to her and her scandalized family. He'd had two months to forget her, and he practically told her he had done so. "The truth is, we might have been engaged, but—"

"But?" He stepped closer, his face only inches away from hers. He didn't look like a man who'd forgotten her. He looked . . . like a man ready to drag her away from prying eyes and kiss her senseless.

She closed her eyes so her imagination wouldn't run away with her. "But I may not have wanted to wait two months to be married to you. So perhaps we wouldn't have been engaged, not any—"

Suddenly Nicholas's hands were on her waist. She opened her eyes to find his smile gone and the warmth in his eyes replaced by something hard. He pulled her to him, and she let out a small yelp. He hated her. He had to. But then his mouth came to her ear. "Are you telling me that if it weren't for your sister, you might already have become my wife?" The word *wife* came like a growl. He *was* angry, but perhaps not for the reasons she'd believed. For all the words that had been spilling out of her, uncontrolled, now she had none. Tears welled in her eyes. The past two months had been unbearable. Watching Rosalind spurn the love of her youth, learning which few friends of Mercy's were truly her friends, and the ache of knowing how much she had hurt Nicholas—a man who deserved only the best, while she had treated him abominably—nothing about the past two months had been endurable.

She put a hand to his chest and leaned away from him. "I didn't want to bring shame to the Harrington title. I still don't."

"The Harrington title has had its fair share of shame, Mercy. You wouldn't have fit into the family if you were completely above reproach."

Mercy's chin quivered. "I was such a fool, Nicholas."

"Yes, you were. But we have all been fools at one point or another."

She released Nicholas's chest and instead covered her face in her hands. "I never would've tried to foist you on other women had I known you could kiss me the way you did in my drawing room. I was looking for fireworks and fairy tales when, in reality, your steadfastness and honor are the things my dreams should have been made of."

Nicholas pulled her to him. "I wouldn't have been surprised to see a woman go to such lengths in order to marry me, but to have worked so hard to get rid of me? I must admit it was a blow to my pride."

Mercy let her hands fall away from her face. With Nicholas's arms around her, they had nowhere to go but on his shoulders. The softness in his eyes and the warmth of his hands at her waist seemed to imply he wouldn't mind. But did he really understand what he was signing himself up for? He hadn't been in London. He hadn't seen how her family had been treated. She was prepared to spend the rest of her life atoning for what she'd done if Nicholas would let her. But not if he would resent her for damaging his family and not if it meant ruining his chances of sending aid to Ireland. "Nicholas, I'm going to ask you a question, and I need you to tell me the truth."

He tightened his grip at her waist. "Always," he answered.

"Is there any way you can forgive me for what I've done?" Nicholas opened his mouth to answer, but she rushed on. "And if you can, do you think I will hurt your chances of helping the Irish?"

Nicholas narrowed an eye. "That is two questions."

"Add it to my list of transgressions."

"I will." Nicholas's hands slid from her waist to her hips, and he pulled her an inch closer. "Yes, I can forgive you. And while I'm astounded by the lengths you went to get rid of me, I must also acknowledge that I never allowed you to see me as I truly was. I was so busy trying to *be* perfect, I never let you see my true self behind the facade. My family isn't always proper. Patience lived in disguise as a maid in Ottersby's home, for heaven's sake. But I don't begrudge them that. It is what brought them together. I was certain the way I ached for you was a fault, and I hid it. I promise you, I'll never hide it again, even if I may need to control it at times, when we are in public."

He spoke as if they were destined to be together, but he hadn't answered her second question. "And the Irish?"

"I've learned to flaunt my rank a bit since you broke my heart. It turns out that was a much faster way of getting results than actually trying to earn people's respect. At least with some of the less desirable members of Parliament, anyway. I disappointed my father a long time ago, and that regret has affected every decision I've made since. I thought by obeying every rule and only interacting within the proper constraints of Society, I would be able to control the world around me and never feel that kind of devastation again. But it didn't work. Instead, I lost you, and that, dear Mercy, became my greatest regret."

Mercy slid her hand to the back of Nicholas's neck, a movement she couldn't have imagined happening only a few moments ago. Could she truly be this fortunate? All she knew was that no story would ever live up to this one. They would have to temper it for their children; otherwise, they would become as foolishly romantic as she had been. "You haven't lost me. Not if you still want me."

Nicholas pressed his forehead to hers. "I've never wanted anything more in my life." He tipped his chin until his mouth was nearly touching her own. "Except maybe to kiss you, right now. Are you willing to agree to marry me first so I can feel better about it? Or would you rather forgo that formality and have me prove to you that Society can hang for all I care?" His voice was rough and low.

"Society can hang, *and* I'll marry y—"

His mouth was on hers before she finished getting the words out. She closed her eyes and took in the scent of him, the taste of his mouth on hers. He pressed forward, one hand coming to the back of her head. Her back slammed into the rough rock wall of the grotto. The air around them warmed until the chill in the air had turned to heat. The proof he'd offered in the drawing room of his desire for her paled in comparison to the fire he showed her now.

"I had so many plans for you I thought I'd have to give up on." Nicholas's face was still millimeters from hers.

"Really?" Mercy answered breathlessly.

"Yes. First, to kiss every single freckle across the bridge of your nose." His eyes focused on a spot on the left side of her face, and he placed an almost reverent kiss there. "These freckles will be kissed while we are engaged." He slid one finger down her neck and then across her collarbone. She shivered, but it had nothing to do with the cold. "And these ones I will save for when we are married."

"Please tell me that will be soon. Otherwise, I may be forced to call your bluff on that one."

In answer, he kissed the other side of her nose, then slid his lips back down to her mouth. She wrapped her arms around his neck and pulled him tighter. She breathed in his scent, cedarwood and starch. It mingled with the smell of earth and spring water from the grotto. When he finally pulled away, he traced his thumb over her cheek.

"Mercy, I'll marry you whenever you want. I'm yours. If this was some crazy game of chess you've been playing, you've won."

"And you thought I was terrible at chess." Mercy pushed off the wall and then spun around and pressed Nicholas against the wall instead. Then she leaned in and brought her lips to his ear. "It looks as though I've won after all." She grabbed his cravat and placed a kiss on his cheek. "Checkmate."

EPILOGUE

DANCING WITH ONE'S HUSBAND WASN'T necessarily proper. But that never stopped the Duke and Duchess of Harrington. Rumor had it, the duke had only been able to convince his wife to marry him if he learned how to dance properly.

He'd agreed.

Not long after their engagement, the whole of London had learned to give them a wide berth in the ballroom. Otherwise, the duke, who was prone to closing his eyes, might steer the two of them into other attendees.

For when the Duke and Duchess of Harrington danced together, they were lost to anyone but each other. Watching them was enough to make the young people in the room believe in fairy-tale matches and love conquering all.

The duchess, however, strongly discouraged such talk.

"True love," she would say, "isn't about fairy tales or magical encounters. It is about seeing someone for who they truly are and wanting to be with that person always, no matter what."

"And kissing," her husband would add, at which point she would narrow her eyes, rap his knuckles with her fan, and storm out of the room.

The duke would inevitably follow and prove both of them correct.

ACKNOWLEDGMENTS

FIRST, I'D LIKE TO THANK spell-check and my editors for always helping me spell words like *acknowledgments*. Kim Dubois, thank you for making this book less embarrassing when it arrives at Ashley's door, and, Ashley Gebert, thank you for finishing out this series with me. I have always felt your love and support of my writing, and it means the world to me. Our final edits came at a crazy time with surgeries and babies, but we got it done, and I'm excited for the world to finally get Nicholas's story.

Next, my friends, fellow authors, and book community that helped me by reading early versions of this book, encouraging me, and making this book not only happen but happen better. Thank you, Christian Hatch, Lisa Kendrick, Anneka Walker, Joanna Barker, McCall Shoff, Mandy Biesinger, and Nicole Kimzey, Annabelle Liechty, and Geny Aleman.

Covenant Communcations accepted my first book submitted to publishers, and that decision started me on a journey that changed my life. I'm grateful for everyone there who has ever worked on any one of my books. It truly takes a team to make a book possible. Thank you to Tara Leong and the design team for a beautiful cover, Shara Meredith and the marketing team for helping people find this book, and Kami Hancock for putting the final touches on this book to make it as perfect as we could make it.

And, last but not least, I have to thank the people that keep me sane in this crazy world of books, wounded heroes, and kisses that need to be perfect: My tennis family, there are a lot of you and the list grows every year. My family, who are loving and supportive of me, and my neighbors and friends, who encourage and act impressed by me every once in a while—it is appreciated.

And, as always, I thank God for another miracle.

ABOUT THE AUTHOR

ESTHER HATCH GREW UP ON a cherry orchard in rural Utah. After high school, she alternated living in Russia to teach children English and attending Brigham Young University in order to get a degree in archaeology. She began writing when one of her favorite authors invited her to join a critique group. The only catch was she had to be a writer. Not one to be left out of an opportunity to socialize and try something new, she started on her first novel that week.

Learn more about Esther at estherhatch.com and follow her on social media.

Facebook: Author Esther Hatch

Instagram: @AuthorEstherHatch